Broken Spark

Broken Spark

Thomas D. Potter

ISBN: 978-0-557-07485-3

Contents

CHAPTER ONE
***
CASABLANCA

It was early March in Casablanca. Amal Haki and Khalid Zerktouni sat opposite each other at a white, table-clothed table at the Fandango Restaurant on the Corniche. Their eyes were wide as they furtively looked around at the sophisticated European and Moroccan guests in the restaurant. They were both dressed in white cotton galabiyas and hats of cotton Kuftis. Neither of them had ever been to an establishment with such an obvious display of wealth and internationalism. And, they would not be here now if it weren't for their friend and mentor, Taufig Hosain.

Taufig was Pakistani. He had a gentle disposition, but he was a dedicated Muslim, even to the point of fanaticism. Taufig knew that his duty was to recruit and train two young Moroccan men who would be devoted to Islam and hate the West to such a degree that they would volunteer to be suicide bombers. He also knew that the codename for his particular operation was 'Broken Spark'. What he didn't know was that the goals of Broken Spark were much broader, much more sinister, than he could ever have imagined. He had come to Morocco about three months previously and found a hovel in the slum of Al Massira.

Amal had first met Taufig at evening prayers at the Hassan II Mosque. Taufig had unrolled his prayer rug next to Amal, and after evening prayers were concluded had struck up a conversation with him. Taufig had asked leading questions about Amal's life in Al Massira. The questions were gentle and non-threatening. He asked whether Amal had a job, and whether there was enough work to keep him busy throughout the week, and whether the wages were sufficient to feed his family. Amal had replied that he had no family except for his mother and two sisters, but that the backbreaking construction work hadn't provided enough income to keep them. His sisters had to do piecework in a local garment factory which exported shirts to England in order to buttress the family income sufficiently to ensure that there was food on the table.

Amal and Taufig spent as much time as they could together. Taufig seemed to have a great deal of free time, and never seemed to be short of money. Amal wondered about this but did not have the courage to ask. After a month or so, they were fast friends, or at least it seemed that way to Amal. Their conversations spanned a wide variety of subjects, but they always came back to the central topic of how Western and Jewish financial powers were keeping the Islamic peoples under their thumb. They talked about the glorious times when Islamic culture and power ruled the known world, and how the Western colonialists had destroyed Muslim states through superior technology. The only time Taufig became angry was when he described India, calling India a 'mongrel state' and a 'running dog' under Western financial control. One evening, after Amal and Taufig had spent practically the whole day together, Taufig asked Amal if he had any friends who had similar views and experiences and would like to join them for dinner.

Amal immediately thought of Khalid Zerktouni. They had grown up together in the Al Massira shantytown. Khalid's father had died shortly after Khalid was born, when dozens of soldiers and police had invaded the Ben M'sik slum on June 20, 1981, to put down angry demonstrators who were demanding bread. The army and police forces used real bullets, which resulted in thousands of atrocities. Victims, including Khalid's father, were buried in mass graves. Khalid's mother, Khalid and his brother were relocated to Al Massira. On May 16, 2003, Khalid's brother, full of anger, was one of the suicide bombers who emerged from the Al Massira area to attack the Casablanca financial district. Khalid was quiet, keeping his emotions to himself, but Amal knew that fire raged in his heart.

Amal and Khalid had received very little formal education, but they were schooled in hatred for the French colonialists, and what virtually all of the residents of the slum considered the traitorous Moroccan monarchy. All their current ills, backbreaking labor at meager wages, inadequate sanitation and housing in the slum, high costs of food, and the cycle of poverty which they were unable to escape, they blamed on their belief, shared by most in the slum, that the monarchy had sold out to the capitalists in the West and to the Jews.

For the next several months, the three young men were almost inseparable. Taufig was a physicist and had studied in the United States, facts which he revealed over time, in bits and pieces, so as not to overwhelm the young Moroccans. It appeared to them that Taufig was a man of great learning.

For the first month, they talked only of the teachings of the Prophet, of the Sunna and the hadith. Despite being Muslims by birth, neither Amal nor Khalid had received significant education in Islam. Taufig's Socratic method was intense because of the amount of time the three young men spent together, but without seeming to the two young Moroccans to be excessive. Gradually, he began to teach them about the broader world, with a highly ideological view of that world. Primarily, he focused on his perception of the world financial markets and how they were manipulated to suppress Muslim peoples. Taufig's own understanding of financial markets was limited and skewed to his personal view of the reasons why Arab and other Muslim countries were unable to achieve the levels of economic success that prevailed in non-Muslim countries, including India, China, Israel, Western Europe and the United States. He was particularly intense in his obsessive views of India and Israel, the first for obvious reasons because of its success compared to Pakistan, and the second because of his intense, though ill-formed, belief in the innate conflict between Islam and Israel.

By the end of the third month, both Amal and Khalid held an unshakable belief in a world conspiracy led by the West, whose purpose was to prevent Islamic countries from realizing their full potential. Taufig had focused on Khalid's anger over the loss of his brother and had converted it into a feeling of pride and identification with the presumed reasons why his brother had become a suicide bomber. Both young men had developed a powerful psychological hatred of the West and its plutocrats, and they repeatedly asked Taufig what they could do to redress the balance.

Taufig counseled patience but promised that an opportunity would soon be available for them if they were willing to make the required sacrifice. He did not use the term 'suicide bomber', but he made it clear that they should be prepared, if necessary, to lay down their lives in order to carry out the mission he envisioned for them. They enthusiastically affirmed that they were.

"Let us go to dinner, then, to a restaurant in the heart of the capitalists' playground—the Corniche. And so the two young Moroccans found themselves in Fandango, a restaurant whose décor and clients were a world beyond their wildest imaginations, and the epitome of the decadent West. It is said by some that if Humphrey Bogart were operating in Casablanca today, the Fandango might be 'Rick's' place.

To keep his young acolytes focused, Taufig regaled them with the history of the glories of Islam. Islam's triumph over the West in the seventh and eighth centuries was a phenomenon that the world had never seen. From Damascus, the Islamic armies spread with lightning speed westward along the North African coast and eastward through Afghanistan into northern India, which is now Pakistan. The Roman Empire was gone, but there were still armies of the Visigoths in Spain and the Vandals in North Africa to contend with. One of the greatest of the generals from the Umayyad dynasty was General Musa Ibn Nasair, who invaded contemporary Spain and established the dynasty throughout Spain and dominated North Africa in what is now Morocco. The two young men felt overwhelming pride in their Muslim forebear, and angry that they had not known of him until their Pakistani friend told them about him.

After dinner, Taufig returned to his simple accommodation in Al Massira. He went to a bare nightstand by his bed and opened the drawer which contained a false bottom. He lifted out the bottom, removed a prepaid cell phone and dialed a number which he had committed to memory. Upon connection, he spoke rapidly and without greeting in Urdu. "They are ready."

"Good! You may return to the capital of our friendly country and meet with the other members of your cell in the place we discussed. Before you go, however, make arrangements with your friends so that I can contact them directly. I might have need of their services sooner than we planned."

"But I trained them to be suicide bombers," Taufig interrupted. "They are fully committed to that purpose. I thought they would serve under the direction of our leader, Shahid."

"There is much you do not know about Broken Spark, nor should you. Suffice it to say its goals are much greater than random suicide bombings. Make the arrangements! Do you understand?"

"I understand," Taufig replied, but he was dismayed. He felt betrayed and alone. He had spent months training his young acolytes. He felt they were foot soldiers for the glory of Islam, and they were loyal only to Islam and to him. They were not available to carry out the dirty work of someone far away. But now, that someone was stealing them for a purpose unknown to him.

From that point on, he would do two things: he would find out everything he could about Broken Spark, and he would confide in his new friend al-Tabari, a Muslim scholar who had approached him just days before. He could not keep his loneliness and disappointment bottled up without telling someone, and a Muslim scholar seemed the perfect ally for him. Little did Taufig know that his decision to talk to al-Tabari would set off a chain reaction that would lead halfway around the world to a small village in Arizona, and to my cell phone.

CHAPTER TWO

***

TUBAC, ARIZONA

She wasn't supposed to die! Layla and I had been together less than six months, but the bond we had forged during those six months was more spiritual than physical. It had started with her entry into the United States through the very mountains I was now looking at, and had lasted until her brutal death by her own hand in Las Vegas in late December, when she had refused to detonate the suitcase nuclear device in Caesars Palace. How was it possible that I would never again see her gentle smile, hear her soft voice, or feel her tender touch? I would never sense her intensity, her humanity, or marvel at her intelligence again.

I tried to focus on the beauty of the mountains surrounding my home in Tubac. This morning the Tumacacori Mountains to the southwest had just the slightest spray of snow capping their tops. Tumacacori Mountain itself has a peak of sorts, and it too is lightly covered. The butte on the right of Tumacacori Mountain has no name but does have the thickest growth of live oak trees of all the mountains in the range, and the snow mixes with the green of the trees in a winter pastel worthy of Norman Rockwell. A cascade of snow had fallen down into the canyons and crevices of the mountains below the tops, lightly dusting the sparse stand of live oaks struggling for life in the up-thrusted sedimentary rock of the mountains.

To the southwest, I could see the whole range of the Tumacacoris. To the east, I could see the Santa Rita Mountains, which are even more dramatic, though further away. Snow covered both Mt. Hopkins, where the Smithsonian Observatory sits in quiet remove from the deepening darkness below, and Mt. Wrightson, the higher of the two, down to approximately 4,000 feet from their 9,000-foot height. The snow wouldn't last long. In February, the ground was still relatively warm and the snow would disappear in a few days, but for now, it was dazzling. As the sun descended in the west, the color exploded in the east. The color spectrum ranged from rose to purple to indigo on the mountains, the snow cover making a perfect palette. The phrase 'Purple Mountain Majesty' truly had meaning as the mountains turned purple in the evening light, and then indigo as the sun lost its force. My thoughts returned to Layla. She only knew Tubac in the summer. She didn't have the opportunity to see the beauty of the light and color cast by the weak winter sun. The tableau stimulates a reflective frame of mind in me, sensitized to beauty and loss.

I returned to gaze at the Tumacacoris and they stared back at me in passive silence as if to say 'I see you, I recognize you, but you are insignificant. We have been here forever. We were here before you and we will be here after you.'

I felt the chill of a light southwesterly breeze. It was refreshing as I reflected on the heat of Ramallah and Istanbul only weeks before. I looked again at the Tumacacoris over their reflection in the swimming pool. Mozart played softly through the outdoor speakers. The rugged mountains stood in sharp contrast to the cultivated environment of my home. Their cliffs reflected the shadows and light as if they themselves were angry at the primeval forces that had propelled them upward, angry at the great floating plates of the Earth's crust, crashing together, pushing them up as if reaching for the grandeur they had finally achieved, growing taller over hundreds of thousands of years as entire islands of sedimentary rock broken loose were pushed upward and collapsed on one another in huge tangles of rock and earth and sediment, which the sun and wind, heat and cold, had carved and shaped into stunning grandeur.

I am describing the environs of Tubac, a small village near the Mexican border in Southern Arizona which was founded in the 1740's and has seen five flags fly over it: Spain, Mexico, the US, Texas and Arizona. It was an arts and retirement community now, struggling with its identity, caught between those who wanted no change, those who wanted controlled change, and those who wanted unfettered development. Given the population pressures of a burgeoning retirement-age group of Americans, I suspected the future of Tubac would be a mixture of forces between those who wanted to preserve and those who wanted to develop. Those who wanted no change were foredoomed to failure. My family, which was now only my sister, Tanya, and I, had owned a home here for almost two decades.

The beauty of the evening was enhanced by the sorrow I felt from Layla's death. Life is made more precious by the loss of one so close, especially one so complex and intricate. I appreciated my boss' sensitive, though gruff, directive to take a few weeks off after Layla's death, and after the preemptive attack on Iran's emerging nuclear infrastructure left charred remains of shattered concrete and twisted steel, death, and, emptiness. The Middle East was temporarily quiet, but I fear, it was the quiet before the storm. The US and Israel were feared more than respected throughout the Middle East and, indeed, throughout the world. Our moral leadership had been lost, our 'soft' diplomacy a thing of the past.

I relived the intense experiences of December as they skipped randomly through my mind like a damaged DVD, picking up images here and there like a child picking flowers in a spring meadow. The escape from al-Tabari in Ramallah; the run across Jordan, Syria and Turkey; meeting Frank in Ankara; the return to Washington; the interviews with Robert Abramson and the Reverend von Saxon; the dash back to Istanbul to meet with al-Tabari and the joy of finding Layla, only to lose her again; the rescue of her brother Saeed and the tense hours in Washington before the decision to bomb Iran's nuclear infrastructure was made, over strong recommendations from me, Frank, and the national security advisor; and the ineffably sad moment when I learned of Layla's death.

The silence and my reverie were broken by the ringing of my private cell phone. Only two people had this cell phone number, Erin Cohen and Benjamin Franklin Pierce. Frank was special counsel to the national security advisor, and my boss and mentor, and Erin, a special friend of infinite complexity and no small amount of mystery with whom I had a personal relationship at one time, was a clinical psychologist in Dayton, Ohio. I had reached out to Erin after Layla's death, and our friendship had grown deeper through our recent shared experiences.

The call was from Erin, and I breathed a sigh of relief. A call from Frank would only mean that something was amiss. I am not quite ready to jump back into the hothouse of the Washington political scene, but in my gut I know the call from Frank is coming. US security, for which Frank carries an enormous amount of responsibility, in a world divided between Islam and the secular West, is deteriorating, not improving.

"How are you, Anderson?" came her gentle query. When Erin asked that, it really had meaning, not just a salutation.

"I'm well. I'm not ready to reenter the fray, but I'm doing well. I still spend far too much time reviewing the past, with too many, 'If onlys', but the mind has a wonderful ability to heal itself, and time is the greatest healer of all. Tubac is a good place to reflect. Erin, it's sad. Not even the grandeur of the Tumacacori Mountains can erase the realization that Layla's death was futile. When the Israeli Special Forces rescued Layla's brother, she was free, but she didn't know it, and I couldn't reach her. It was so damnably close. I try to think of ways I might avenge her death, but I can't settle on a target for my vengeance. No one individual caused her death. It was the fault of an entire culture, and of misunderstanding by both Islam and the West."

"Remember, Anderson, you're going through a really rough time. Mourning isn't easy."

"I know, Erin, the five stages of grief: denial, anger, bargaining, depression and acceptance. I think I'm hung up somewhere in between bargaining and depression. I spend a lot of time thinking about 'could have, should have, and if only,' but at least I'm beyond denial and anger. I know it'll get better, and, in fact, it has."

"Do you want me to come to Tubac?" Her voice was concerned and friendly.

I struggled, wanting her to come, but I was strangely afraid of being so close to someone for whom I still had warm feelings, even though I knew that hers was just a professional concern.

"Maybe not now, Erin. Can I take a rain check?"

"Of course, Anderson. Take your time. But it's important that you not get too removed. I know from what you've said that Tubac is lovely, but too much isolation is not a good thing. Clinically speaking, you remain conflicted between your affection for Layla and your feelings of guilt for not apprehending her early on. Those feelings, along with your feeling of loss, must be confronted and worked through."

"Yes, thanks, Erin. As always, your insights strike close to my heart. I take them seriously."

As the conversation wound down, I felt, despite, or perhaps because of, Erin's words, a growing sense of isolation, a distancing from human contact. Contact with Erin was really important to me, I realized.

The next day was poignant. I occupied my time caring for the property, grooming the grounds, cleaning the pool, all the while knowing that the make-work was just delaying the inevitable return to reality, when I would have to put my personal life on the backburner— into the compartment where I store issues I can't deal with at the moment—and get re-involved with national security issues.

Erin's offer to come to Tubac kept swimming around in my subconscious. Why not have her visit? I asked myself. It would be good to spend time with a true friend while I was trying to deal with my emotional traumas. Besides, it wasn't as if we were going to re-ignite the romantic relationship we once had. It would be an arm's-length friend-to-friend visit. She would sleep in the guestroom, and I would sleep in the master bedroom. What could be wrong with that? While I knew we would discuss my feelings about Layla, I also wanted her to relive with me the events leading up to the decision to strike Iran, which I had done a thousand times. I knew I was obsessing, but I wanted to hear her views formed with the passage of time, months after the events themselves. She had shown uncommon insights into the security ramifications of the actions of the main players of that saga: von Saxon, Abramson, al Tabari, and, indeed, the Israeli and US governments themselves. Another aspect of her mysteriousness and complexity, I suppose. How mysterious and complex I would soon find out.

The more I thought about it, the more appealing it became. I was far from having resolved my feelings for Layla, but having a professional psychologist, who was also a friend, nearby to discuss them had great merit. And, in addition to her professional interest, and her personal friendship for me, I was sure leaving Ohio in February wouldn't bother her either. I called her. I told her I had reconsidered her offer and asked her to come for a week. She said she needed to reschedule some appointments but could come early the following Tuesday.

The weekend passed slowly as I anticipated Erin's arrival. On Tuesday, late afternoon, I went to Tucson to pick her up. As the passengers exited the secure area and headed for baggage claim, I caught sight of her—tall, trim, with shoulder-length auburn hair. My heart skipped a beat as I felt a warm sense of well-being wash over me, and I was glad she was here. Our greeting was warm. Memories and feelings of the comfortable personal relationship we had had several years ago commuting between New York and Washington flooded over me. We exited the terminal where the air outside was a brisk but comfortable sixty degrees. The sky was a blue that seemed as if you could see forever into its depths, and cumulus clouds floated in white patches like ill-formed ships on an interminable ocean.

On the forty-five-minute drive to Tubac, we talked about neutral things. I asked her about her patient load and about Mary's progress. Mary Ansell was a patient of Erin's who had waived her own doctor-patient privilege to expose the evangelical preacher, James von Saxon, for the sexual predator he was in our failed attempt to limit his influence with the president. Erin, in turn, asked me about the area—about the hikes I had taken. I described to her the joy of going where a very small percentage of the population had ever gone, hiking Mount Wrightson, and the Elephant Head outcropping. I glanced at her in profile, at her strong cheekbones and smooth skin. I reached my hand across the seat and placed it on hers.

"I'm really glad you came, Erin."

Her hand was cool to the touch, and she returned my gesture with a pretty smile, but she didn't reply. Neither did she withdraw her hand.

We ate dinner that night at a local bistro before going up to Cerro Pelon, 'Bald Hill' in English, where my home was located. Evening comes early in Southern Arizona in February, and the colors rose vividly on the mountains. We had an exquisite view of Mount Hopkins and Mount Wrightson in the Santa Rita Mountain chain.

We talked for another hour or so before retiring, and I felt good about asking her to come, as I looked forward to a pleasant week.

I rose at dawn, the light silhouetting the Santa Ritas on the east side of the valley across the Santa Cruz River. The December and January freezes had taken their toll on the vegetation, but the skeletal outlines of the scrub mesquite inspired the senses even so. They spread across the Sonoran Desert, dense, but interrupted by patches of grass. It is said that much of this area was covered by grasses until the voluntary scrub mesquite moved in, but I am not sure if that's true.

My cell phone chirped, and this time it had to be Frank.

"Hello, Frank," I said into the phone before Frank had a chance to speak.

"Hello, Anderson, how are you feeling?" Frank's voice was halfway between a mutter and a growl, but I had gotten used to it, and he had spoken to me with genuine warmth and concern since Layla's death.

"I'm keeping myself busy, and reading a lot, writing some. What's up?" I could tell from Frank's voice that this was not a social call.

"I need you in Washington, Anderson. Something has come up and is developing fast. We really need to address it."

One of the many things I admired about Frank was his ability to accept defeat and then bounce back with his full sense of duty to public service and love of country.

"What is it, Frank?"

"I can't get into it in-depth on an open cell phone. That's why I need you to come to Washington for a full briefing. It's something called 'Electromagnetic Pulse', EMP for short. I have information from our mutual friend that an operation is to be carried out by a terrorist cell based in France which plans to use these things to disrupt communications, financial markets, and antimissile defense systems, among other things, in the West. That's about all I can say at this point. We have a lot more information which we need to jell into some kind of actionable intelligence. When can you be here?"

"I can leave tomorrow, Frank. There's a flight from Tucson to Washington. I have to wind up a few things here and close up the house, but I'll be on it."

"Good! I hate to interrupt your recovery, and I waited as long as I could. As usual, we have a lot of knowledge, but no operational plan to take out the threat. E-mail me when you know your arrival time, and I'll have a car at the airport to meet you." "Okay, sir," I said, and closed the connection. Despite our increasingly close relationship, my response to Frank always ended on a note of the highest respect. While Frank had begun to treat me as the son he never had, I never presumed on that relationship. I was constantly aware that he had the ear of the National Security Advisor (ANSA) and occasionally the president, and possessed enormous family wealth from Texas oil. His contract with the government—loosely defined—always lost him money, but without an heir of his own, money wasn't a great obsession for Frank. With his degree in physics from Caltech, EMP was something, I suspected, right up his alley.

Erin was waiting in the family room with cups of coffee. She recognized that when I talked with Frank the atmosphere changed and part of me became remote, no matter how attentive I tried to be. Since she also had privacy issues of her own to deal with, very significant issues I was to discover, she was respectful of mine.

"I'm terribly sorry, Erin. I thought I'd have more time, but I have to leave tomorrow. This was totally unexpected."

"I understand. Is there any of it you can tell me? Or is it too hush-hush?" she asked lightly.

"It's pretty sensitive. Frank wouldn't tell me much over the phone, but it has to do with electromagnetic pulse technology. This technology, if weaponized, threatens the current foundation of Western economies. It has the potential to render a computer inoperable, which means that the Internet, banking and financial markets in the Western world wouldn't work, not to mention our strategic defense. It's a threat from terrorists, which you might guess. I had thought such a pulse could only be generated by the detonation of a nuclear device at high altitude, but that doesn't seem to be what Frank was talking about. I've read about a simpler device which might achieve the same effect at a much lower technological level and therefore much lower cost. But I'm pretty much in the dark. At least we have all of today to enjoy Tubac before we have to close up."

"Anderson, you have to decide for yourself whether you're ready to 'reenter the fray' as you put it. I have my doubts. When one wrestles with the death of one as close as Layla was to you, one loses perspective. It isn't uncommon to see the conviction that 'all is well!' That 'I am over my loss; I am ready to resume life as before'. But life isn't like it was before. There's something really important missing.

To deny that fact is foolhardy. You may function more or less at the same capacity as before, but you aren't really there, and you're only delaying the confrontation of deep emotions that will become twisted and deformed if they aren't addressed. Your involvement with this terrorist threat will elevate your conflict to dangerous levels. If terrorists are set to use EMP to disrupt financial markets, they are also preparing to use it against national defense and space installations and activities, as well as against the psychology of mass populations."

I was taken aback by her knowledge of EMP technology and its possible use. We were both silent as I wondered about this side of this woman I only knew as a consulting psychologist. I also knew the wisdom of what she had said about my emotions. Indeed, I had turned it over and over in my mind these past few weeks. I really believed that I was further along in the process than she thought, but her professional insight gave me pause. I would think more about what her words in the days to come.

Instead of replying directly, I said, "You're undoubtedly right, Erin, but I must do what I must do, and right now what's right for me is to go where Frank wants me to go, to do what needs to be done. It gives me direction, purpose and focus, and I need that more than I need reflection, no matter what the consequences."

Erin gazed at me with an expression that was neither condemnatory nor forgiving, but rather understanding. "It's okay, Anderson. You'll be okay, but I'm here for you if you need me. Understood?"

"Right! Now, let's enjoy the day! It's already midmorning, so let's go to the resort at Tubac and have lunch. There's an excellent Mexican restaurant, then we can go to the Village for the art galleries and the bookstore."

We dressed for sixty-degree weather and headed directly for the resort. The resort was located on a tract of land given as a land grant to the Otero family as a cattle ranch during the period of the Mexican ascendancy. Its ranching history was long past, and it was now a first-class twenty-seven-hole golf resort with fine accommodations and two excellent restaurants.

After lunch we went to the Village and wandered from gallery to gallery, starting with local and regional artists, then to a gallery for western art, and then finally to a gallery for locally made jewelry. We visited the bookstore and several outdoor sculpture galleries before having an early cocktail at an outdoor bistro, then headed to Cerro Pelon and dinner.

I grilled two steaks on the grill and Erin prepared the accompaniments. I opened a bottle of Argentine Malbec, and we enjoyed a special dinner between two special friends on the patio. The moment was electric with promise, but we both knew that there were huge issues to overcome. Erin had just ended one relationship which was, to put it simply, not satisfying, and I was just overcoming, I hoped, a devastating loss, but the evening was enchanting. The night was cold, but we were warm beneath the heaters. Ten steps to the edge of the patio brought us to the incredible umbrella of the night sky. Because of the darkness in the valley the stars extended to the horizon. The stereo was playing soft music through the outside speakers. I turned to Erin and she responded; we danced slowly and dreamily to the music. The space was enchanting, and we were swept away to a land of 'what might be'.

However, far to the east, storm clouds were gathering.

Our mood was quiet and reflective as we rode in the limo to Tucson Airport the next morning. The interruption in our time together heightened our senses, raising our relationship to a new plateau of affection and curiosity. What was it that she was trying to find out about me? Our night together would be hard to explain, and, I believe, we both decided to leave it as a fond memory. I was subdued because I knew that Erin had made an extra effort to join me in Tubac, and I was mulling over her unusual comments.

Deep down I was excited to be in action again. I had reflected a great deal during my stay in Tubac, resolving little, and passing through most of the stages of mourning. One conclusion I had come to, however, was that Islam and the West could only live peaceably if individuals of all persuasions could strip the rags of religion from their minds and relate person-to-person. Unless the purveyors of religion, the ministers, the clerics, the priests, and the rabbis who benefit from its propagation could be banished to the background, honest and positive interaction would not be impossible. Could I nurture the process? Help it along? Or was I to be caught up in the maelstrom of conflicting beliefs, beliefs so strong their compulsions would have devastating consequences to me and to the world?

We drove to the departure terminal, Erin to United and I to American. She was dropped off first, and I turned to her to say goodbye. As I gazed into her eyes, I was drawn to her lips to seal our goodbye with a light kiss.

She responded warmly to my kiss but said, "Think hard about what you're doing, Anderson. Dealing with mourning in the bright sunlight of Tubac is one thing. Dealing with it in the midst of a full-action program is another. Despite what you think, you are not healed. The pressures of what you're about to undertake will test your equilibrium to the extreme. You must be able to keep things in perspective."

"Thanks, Erin. I think I can do that. Can I call you if I think I'm slipping off balance?"

"Of course!"

"Erin, I might make a layman's observation to you, if I may. You too have been under extreme pressure, torn between your personal life and your professional responsibilities. That isn't an easy place to be." I was genuine in my concern for her, but I was also probing her for some enlightenment about her mysterious questions.

"What are you trying to say?"

"I'm just saying I'm concerned for you as a person. I think you've reacted to your divorce by immersing yourself in your work, and obviously one of your last cases was very stressful."

"You're sweet, Anderson, but I'm a professional, and by asking me in that way you're revealing your gender bias. Don't worry about me. I'm stable."

"I'm sorry, Erin, I didn't mean to imply that you're anything but professional. It's just that I'm as concerned for you as you are for me, even if my concern isn't based on professional considerations, but rather personal ones. Enough said!"

Erin didn't say anything more but looked at me for a long time. At the time, I had no idea of the chasm in her soul; what pressures were even then motivating her actions.

Finally, she said, "Take care of yourself, Anderson. I want to see you again... in one piece." Then, she opened the door, and without looking back, she seized her carry-on bag and strode toward the terminal.

I felt her departure, as well as seeing it happen. My senses pounded at the coming isolation and loneliness. I wondered when we might see each other again, and I felt her absence immediately. My emotions tumbled within me. I was still mourning Layla's death, but despite the pull of my affection for her, Erin's departure was pure emptiness.

As I waited in the limo for the driver, and Erin walked away, I was wistful, as if something dear was slowly, softly, drifting away, and even if I were to reach for it, it would remain just beyond my grasp, unattainable, leaving me with the distinct feeling that I had decided something, but my decision was wrong. I wanted to reach out and draw her back, but as I reached, the soft, ill-defined image floated further away and eluded my touch. In some sense, I realized it was me floating away, like I was on an ice floe and Erin was the mainland. In dreams during nights to come, I would struggle with this image, seeking in the fitfulness of sleep a way to stop my floating, to regain the mainland.

CHAPTER THREE
***
WASHINGTON, D.C.

Itook the American flight from Tucson to Dulles International by way of Dallas. The MD80 took off smoothly in Tucson's heavy winter air, and the pilot pointed the plane's nose to the east for the eight-hour trip to Dulles and to the most dangerous encounter of my career.

I deplaned onto the American Concourse at DIA at about 3:45 p.m. and rode a 'people mover' to the main terminal. Frank's car and driver, Mark, were waiting when I exited the terminal, and I gave him directions to my townhouse in Alexandria.

We drove down the George Washington Parkway in the light counter rush-hour traffic until we passed Memorial Bridge and picked up outbound rush-hour traffic toward Reagan National and Alexandria. With consumer spending falling dramatically, the recession had deepened and spread rapidly throughout the entire economy. The dollar had crashed and inflation had risen to levels not seen since the seventies. The oil industry and Washington prospered, while the rest of the country lay prostrate.

The traffic in Washington continued to grow as the city, under the new president, initiated new programs designed to keep the recession from deepening into depression. These programs required more administrators, and they clogged the commuter routes in and out of the city, despite the increase in gas prices. Just before Reagan National, ironically, since Reagan was the last president to even try to shrink the growth in government, the traffic slowed to a crawl and we inched toward the exit to the airport, which I hoped would relieve at least some of the congestion on the Parkway.

"Was anyone expecting you, sir, other than Mr. Pierce, of course?" Mark asked me over his right shoulder.

"No, no one, why?"

"Well, sir, there's a black Porsche Cayenne that has been dodging in and out of traffic ever since we left Dulles, apparently trying to keep us in sight, and I don't think it's me they're interested in."

"Curious! How close are they?"

"They're about five cars back, and they're very aggressive with other drivers to make sure they don't fall further back. In fact, I believe they've jumped several cars in the last mile or so to get closer to us."

"Keep an eye on them and let me know if they get any closer. Does Frank keep a weapon in the car?"

"Generally yes, but, unfortunately, not today. His personal assistant asked me to take it to his office just this morning. His assistant said that Frank had asked for it. I did as I was told. Heads up! The Cayenne has moved up two cars."

"How far is the airport exit?"

"About two hundred yards, and it looks like traffic is open after that."

"Can he catch us before the exit?"

"The way he's driving, I think he can. He just jumped another car, and he might have creased a fender or two doing it. He obviously doesn't mind marking up the Cayenne a bit."

"So if he's going to try anything funny, the optimum time would be right at the airport exit, then hightail it in the open traffic beyond."

"It looks that way, sir. He just jumped another car and the driver is furious."

"Okay, it looks to me like there's some room on the right shoulder about fifty yards before the exit. When you get the chance, hit the shoulder and stay on it until you reach free traffic, then change lanes as fast and as frequently as you can. If the cops stop you for reckless driving, so much the better." I didn't have any illusions that Frank's Town Car was any match for the Cayenne, but the sooner we could drive defensively, the better off we would be. Right now, I was a sitting duck. Who knew I was coming? And why did Frank's assistant ask that the gun be delivered to the office? Was Frank's office compromised? If it was, who had compromised it?

The car took a violent jerk to the right as Mark took us up onto the shoulder and simultaneously gunned the powerful V-8, dropping the transmission to low from drive. The tachometer shot upward, and we surged forward in a hail of gravel, rocks, stones and trash. Cars flashed by on our left and the exit was only twenty yards ahead. It looked like we might make it until a gray Chevy Blazer decided to duplicate our maneuver. It pulled onto the shoulder just in front of us, going just a fraction of our speed. Mark had to brake to avoid hitting him.

I looked over my shoulder and stared right into the grill of the Cayenne. I just had enough time to duck before the back window exploded into thousands of fragments of splintered glass as a high-powered bullet plowed into the dashboard.

A grassy area to the right of the shoulder opened up, and Mark hauled the steering wheel around. The Town Car sloughed sickeningly to the left, and we scraped the right rear fender of the Blazer as we shot past him in a flash, just before he panicked and hauled his wheel sharply to the right, right in front of the Cayenne. Another wild round took out the front windshield simultaneously with the distinctive sound of four tons of steel coming together with no give in either car. Mark had a trickle of blood running down his right cheek, and the Town Car looked like a bare survivor of a demolition derby, but otherwise we appeared to be intact.

Mark maneuvered back into the right lane and as we limped on into Alexandria and up to my condo, I thought about the implications of the attack. I had talked to Erin and Frank about my flight time. Erin was out of the question, at least so I thought, so it had to have leaked out of Frank's office, maybe even the driver, Mark, himself. He certainly had the opportunity. If not him, it would have to be Frank's personal assistant or else the cell phone conversation had been intercepted. Mark had acquitted himself well with his driving skills, and I was inclined to rule him out. That left the personal assistant or an intercept. The intercept was certainly possible, but, on the other hand, the personal assistant had requested Mark remove the only defensive weapon from the car just before my arrival. I decided to make the personal assistant 'Agenda Item Number One' when Frank and I met the following day. Even if we identified the who and how, there was still the why. If the why were related to old antagonisms I had stirred up during the events of the unsuccessful female suicide bombers, I could understand, but I would have to exercise much more caution in the future. If the attack were related to the new operation, the EMP operation, it was much more serious because it would mean that security had been compromised and our knowledge, that is, Frank's knowledge, was enough of a threat to provoke extreme measures against me.

As we pulled up to the condo, Mark asked me if I wanted him to wait, but I said no. I got out of Frank's battered Town Car and walked up the steps with my light carry-on and laptop, alarm key in hand as Mark drove away. The street was well lighted, and I inserted the alarm key to turn off the alarm system before I realized that the alarm warning light wasn't on. The hair rose on the back of my neck and a chill ran up my spine.

I quickly stepped to the side of the door, out of the line of fire, and reached around to insert the lock key. The lock wasn't engaged, and I turned the knob as quietly as I could. The catch released and I gently pushed the door inward. With a sudden wrench, the door flew out of my hand and crashed against the wall as a burly figure hurtled by me in the darkness, followed by a lighter figure a few steps behind. I reached around the doorjamb, flipped on the light and stood back. Nothing happened. With every sense on full alert, I poked my head around the corner and snapped back. I didn't see anything alarming.

I waited in the darkness, lighted only by the streetlight, for what seemed like an eternity but was probably only a few minutes. My muscles were tense, ready for any further movement. I was leaning forward on the balls of my feet, but no movement came and my adrenaline receded. I stretched my foot out to the doorjamb without exposing the rest of my body and held it there. There was just the slightest rustle of noise in the living room and I went to full alert again, drawing my foot back. So there was a third burglar—for that is what I thought them to be. Why hadn't he left with the first two? Burglars wouldn't set a trap, so they must have some other purpose in mind. Maybe it wasn't related to the incident on the Parkway, but it seemed likely. It was time to call the police, but as I reached for my cell phone, the rustling sound came nearer the door and I had to stop. I put the cell phone away and readied myself to engage whoever it was. I had had plenty of self-defense training, but all of the rules abandoned me, and I prepared to get down and dirty. I would wait him out. He seemed to be coming closer to the door. If he were going to leave, this would be the logical route.

I sensed rather than heard movement, but it was definitely closer. Waiting was excruciating! Every fiber of my body was alert, trying to determine his location. He seemed to be everywhere beyond the door, moving left, moving right, but one thing I gave him grudging respect for, he was really light-footed. Finally, when I could hardly restrain myself any longer, the movement was just at the door opening. I raised my right hand in the classic judo chop... waiting. Then a shadow appeared, then the foot... of a cat? Tension left my body and relief flowed over me like a waterfall. A nervous giggle escaped me. It was my neighbor's tabby cat, who must have entered the house when the burglars picked the lock and opened the door. Evidencing no fear, he gingerly stepped over the jamb and disappeared into the night.

I moved back out of sight and again waited for any signs of movement. There were none. I reached around and killed the lights. Then I stepped across the threshold and moved to one side to avoid making a silhouette. I closed the door and shot the bolt. If there were any more visitors, they would have to pause for a moment to release the bolt upon their exit. That would give me an opportunity to get acquainted.

I waited for a few minutes in the dark before moving across the carpet to the foot of the stairs. All was quiet. I found the light switch and flipped it on for a few seconds. The living room and dining room were intact and hadn't been burgled. I turned off the light, let my eyes adjust, and then started up the stairs. At the top of the stairs, I backed against the wall and turned on the light. It looked like a tornado had gone through my library and bedroom. Books had been pulled off the shelves and were lying on the floor. Drawers had been pulled out and turned upside down, the contents scattered, then apparently examined. They hadn't discovered my in-wall safe in the library, where I keep a spare .38 and a box of hollow points, but the most disturbing thing was the defacing of images of Layla, some of which I had brought to Alexandria during my last mission, when I was in Washington for a few days only, and some of which they had apparently brought themselves. The intruders' foreign origin was evident in the spelling of 'beech' and 'hore'.

My anger reached a fever pitch when I saw a picture of her face with a bloody shape of a red crescent splattered in red paint across the image. It wasn't a picture I had placed, so they had brought it with them. What were they trying to tell me? And what were they trying to find out? It was obviously an extreme warning. It didn't appear that they had taken anything. Picture albums of my family were lying on the floor. My file cabinet had been opened and file contents were strewn, almost in a pattern, as if a file has been read and tossed, the reader then moving on to the next one, only to toss that one in turn.

The anger at the violation of my privacy was added to by the anger at the defilement of Layla's image. I would track these bastards down if it took the rest of my life. The pledge was formed silently in my brain as I surveyed the mess. I swung the door of the library closed behind me, looking for clues inside the room itself. It seemed they weren't interested in theft, as I couldn't immediately see that anything had been taken. Were they trying to learn more about me, my motives, my habits, my idiosyncrasies? It seemed so. Why else would they peruse my file labeled 'writings', or the one labeled 'schedules', or the file labeled 'US Bank accounts'? I had made many enemies from Amman, Jordan and Ramallah, the West Bank to Istanbul, Turkey. My lack of affection for extreme Muslims was reciprocated in their dislike of me, but those general enmities were not enough to explain the actions here. This would appear to be the work of someone or ones whom I had especially offended. Whoever it was, they were familiar with and angered by my past relationship with Layla, evidenced by the defacing of her photos.

I heard a scratching sound outside the door, as if someone were trying to find a keyhole to the doorknob lock. As with most interior doors, the lock on the door to the library was a simple one. Any fine-pointed object would unlock it, but I hadn't even locked it. I watched, mesmerized, as the knob slowly and quietly turned to the right. hyper-alert to the slightest movement, and my anger made me tremble. Every nerve was screaming for action... but I waited! Finally, the doorknob reached its furthest point on the arc of its turn. There was a slight hesitation before the door began to move inward.

I grabbed the knob and violently jerked it towards me. The intruder virtually fell into the room, his body at a forty-five-degree forward angle. From my strategic point just behind the front edge of the door, I thrust my right knee into his chin as he fell forward. His head snapped back, but his arms and knees caught his fall. He was quick and strong.

He rose to his feet, shaking the cobwebs from his brain and turned toward me. He was about my height, maybe a couple of inches taller. We were face to face. I jerked my head forward, dropping the angle so that my forehead made contact with the bridge of his nose, bone on cartilage. The cartilage gave way and blood spurted from his nostrils, leaking from his eyes. His beefy hands sought, and found, my throat. Blood was streaming down his face as his hands found purchase on my neck, and he tightened his grip. I began to feel lightheaded and knew that I had to break his hold. I brought my knee up sharply into his testicles, and there was a sharp intake of air. His hands loosened their grip as he bent forward to lessen the pain in his groin. I doubled my fists and hammered the back of his neck. He fell like a pole-axed steer.

I gasped for air and picked up the letter opener from the floor where I had dropped it. The intruder was lying on his side in the fetal position, holding his groin and bleeding onto my carpet. In a rage, I grabbed his shoulder and turned him over on his back. He was wheezing and moaning. I must have entered a different mental zone, as I forget what I did next, but when I calmed, I found myself astride him. His eyes were wide in terror and his breathing labored. His head was pinned to the floor, my letter opener speared through the lobe of his ear and stuck in the wooden base beneath the carpet. He didn't move his head, but his eyes shifted back and forth as he sought to comprehend what had just happened. I couldn't have explained it to him.

Blood began to collect in his throat, and he coughed as he struggled to breathe. I jerked the letter opener out of the floor and the razor edge severed the lobe from his ear. He looked improbably like van Gogh. I pulled him to his feet, grabbed his right arm and twisted it behind his back. I then forced his head forward so he could spit out the blood. My carpet was already a mess, but I gave him my handkerchief anyway. After he seemed to start breathing more normally, I loosened my hold on his arm and turned him around to face me. He immediately took a swing, wild and ineffective. But he wasn't quite ready to quit. I gave him a quick punch to his unguarded solar plexus, and he bent over with a gasp. I rabbit punched him again and he went down. This time, I let him lay there. I hacked off a length of the draw cord from the window curtains and tied his hands behind his back. Then, just for good measure, I tied his feet firmly together at the ankles.

My return to Washington was anything but boring. Someone knew I was coming and had enough resources to pull together a serious greeting party. That someone had to have had a pipeline into Frank's office, to someone Frank trusted. My guess was that it was someone who was close enough to Frank to know the existence of the EMP operation, was aware that Frank was bringing me in to mount a counter operation and had decided to simultaneously get rid of me permanently, learning everything they could about me in the process in case they failed to kill me. Fortunately for me, they were unsuccessful.

I rolled my assailant over. His bleeding had stopped, and the blood was beginning to dry on his face. He was of Middle Eastern or South Asian origin, no surprise there! Was he Pakistani, Israeli or Iranian? Did it matter? Whoever directed him was likely to try a little misdirection by hiring his ethnic enemies anyway. I couldn't assume that his boss would be his ethnic brother. I spoke a few phrases of Arabic to him and got the reaction I expected. Anger twisted his face, and he spat more blood onto my carpet, but he didn't say anything. What to do with him? Since I had no official position with the US government after I left the State Department to join Frank's loosely organized consulting service, the local police would be the best place to start. I called them and asked that they come quietly, without sirens blaring. I told them that my intruder was secure and I didn't want to disturb the neighbors.

I double-checked the cord on his hands and ankles then went downstairs to let the police in. While I waited, I could hear some commotion upstairs, but I didn't think the intruder could possibly escape his bonds. I would regret that conclusion.

I let the police in and we went upstairs, reaching the library just in time to see the broken glass of the window over the desk settle to the floor. The sergeant immediately radioed his downstairs backup to search the side of the house, but all he found were two deep footprints in the rain-softened soil and no other usable traces of the intruder.

I spent several hours with the police explaining the circumstances of my return and trying to recreate what probably happened while I waited downstairs. The most likely scenario, suggested by fresh blood on the windowsill, was that he managed to get erect and hopped to the window. He subsequently turned around, broke the window with his hands and sawed the cord on a broken piece of glass, cutting his wrists in the process. His bear-like strength enabled him to withstand a fall from the second story and move quickly into the night.

The police launched a patrol to search the area, but he was long gone before they could get any serious coverage. Finally, at midnight, the police left and I turned to the task of repairing the damage to my condo. I restored the files as best I could and made a mental note to call the cleaning lady, as well as the carpet cleaners, in the morning. Finally, at two a.m., I double-checked the locks on all the external doors and collapsed on the bed, my body and mind flat from the precipitous drop in the adrenaline flow.

I had called Frank when I landed at Dulles, and we had agreed on nine a.m. for a meeting in his office in the Foggy Bottom area of Washington. I hadn't reckoned on how tired and beat-up I would feel in the morning. I awoke at seven a.m., showered and shaved and prepared myself mentally for the meeting. I intended to meet all of Frank's associates as soon as possible when I arrived at his offices. I wanted to evaluate their responses to me when I confronted them, alive and reasonably fit. I planned to act as if nothing had happened and see if one of them exhibited any signs of surprise or concern. At 8:30 a.m., after having called the cleaning lady and the carpet cleaners, I answered the front doorbell to find Mark, Frank's driver, ready to drive me to Foggy Bottom.

CHAPTER FOUR
✳✳✳
FOGGY BOTTOM

The office building where Frank's offices were located was pre-war, that is, the big war, World War II. After many renovations, including at least one to accommodate the CIA, the current décor exuded a quiet serious air. It was a little more than a stone's throw from the Department of State, between the Department and the Potomac River.

When I got off the elevator on the third floor, I looked out the west window of the vestibule and could see Roosevelt Island and the Iwo Jima Memorial beyond. American history doesn't get any more real than that. I gave myself a full two minutes to reflect on the significance of what I was seeing: Roosevelt Island, now the home of the FDR Memorial, honoring the man who single-handedly led the country out of depression and into war; and the Iwo Jima Memorial, where Marines fought one of the bloodiest and most vicious contests of the War in the Pacific. Anyone who is not humbled, nor proud, of identifying with the sacrifice of one's forebears has to be numb, insensate, or ignorant—perhaps all three.

I moved to a door marked 'Pierce Consulting Services' and entered. I sensed that I was stepping into a new paradigm, one whose lines and contours were foreign to me, whose character would prove terrifying.

An attractive receptionist awaited me. She looked up, blue eyes framed by long dark lashes, and asked me if she could help me. A long list of things entered my mind, but I said, simply, "I'm here to see Frank Pierce."

"And you are?"

"Anderson Wyeth. I believe he's expecting me."

"Oh! Yes, Mr. Wyeth. We're expecting you. I've seen your name on many documents, and Mr. Pierce and others have spoken highly of you, but I haven't had the pleasure of meeting you. My name is Angelina Markey. Welcome to Pierce Consulting Services. I'll let Mr. Pierce know you're here."

She turned and spoke into her headset. I could barely hear because of her soft voice when she said, "Mr. Pierce, Mr. Wyeth is here. Shall I show him in?" Then, "Yes, sir." She turned back to me and said, with a smile, "I'll show you in, Mr. Wyeth."

I followed her gently swaying long skirt down a narrow corridor until we reached a door marked 'Pierce'. She knocked once, then turned the knob and swung the door open.

I stepped into the office of one of the most powerful men in Washington, a man the public doesn't know, but whose ability to influence events in Washington is legendary. Benjamin Franklin Pierce, six feet five, and named after our fourteenth president and was some shirttail descendent of his, rose from behind his desk and stepped around to the side. He approached me and spread his arms to embrace me. It was a genuine expression of affection, a sentiment Frank didn't indulge casually or without thinking seriously about beforehand. Frank's attitude toward me is fatherly. The last survivor of an enormously wealthy Texas oil family, Frank was without an heir. His interest, dare I say affection, for me dated from the time he was deputy chief of mission in the US Embassy in Cairo, and I was a newly minted foreign service officer, at which time he focused on me and began to promote my career. Frank left the Foreign Service shortly after that assignment, and I left the Service not long after. "Anderson, how are you, my boy! It's really good to see you. How was the flight?"

"It was fine, sir. A few complications on arrival, which we can talk about later."

"Why? What happened?"

"I'll tell you everything, sir, but first, I'd like to meet the other members of your senior staff. Would that be possible?"

"Of course. As a matter of fact, I decided to combine yours and my meeting with our regular weekly senior staff meeting. We have a guest from the Department of Defense. You can get acquainted with everybody." With that, we left Frank's private office and walked into the adjacent conference room.

Frank's staff was already assembled, getting coffee and finding seats. It was an unusual group, certainly nonconforming. Frank sat at the head of the table and motioned me to sit at his right. I did, foregoing the coffee for a bottle of water.

Frank started by introducing me to the five members who made up his senior staff. On my immediate right was Giovanni, who had responsibility for Europe; Oleg, who had responsibility for Eastern Europe and Russia; next to him was Andreas, who had responsibility for Latin America; Chou Li, across the table, had responsibility for all of Asia, including Japan, China, Pakistan and India; and next to him was Gordon Rhoads, who had responsibility for North America, including Canada, Mexico and the Caribbean. Each of them gave their background in some depth, except for Gordon. Gordon proved to be an enigma. He had long blonde hair and narrow slanted eyes that were almost Slavic in appearance. He never looked at me directly, but rather alternately looked down at the table and at his colleagues with a defiant air. He said he was American by birth, Canadian by choice, a lawyer by training, and a real estate developer by experience.

I had carefully repaired the bruises to my face so that from the length of the table it would not appear that I had been assaulted. None of the senior staff exhibited any reaction to my appearance until Frank introduced Gordon, who looked at me with such intensity that it was clear he expected me to have a much-altered appearance to that which he was presently observing. An irrational anger grew within me, and I struggled to maintain my composure. I broke the stare he had fixed on me and looked out the window.

The building was surrounded by trees, some of which I recognized and some of which I did not. But one grabbed my interest. An ancient black locust tree, thorny, its limbs bare in the late winter, seized my attention, and as I stared at it, my calm returned. I looked back at Gordon, who again stared at me with intensity and hostility. I needed no additional evidence to identify the person behind the assaults I had experienced on my return to Washington. Was Frank aware of this person in the midst of his senior staff? Most likely not.

I stared back at Gordon with all the calm I could muster and forced him to commit with words. Finally, he said. "I'm surprised that your return to Washington was so uneventful, Anderson. I'd have thought that it would have been more, shall we say, filled with 'unexpected' events."

"One might have thought so, Gordon, but it was really quite tranquil."

He stared at me as I had him. Silence pervaded the conference room.

Finally, Frank broke the silence by saying, "Well, enough of that. We have a representative from Defense Intelligence to talk to us about something that came up within the last month or so. Information has reached us from a very reliable source, one which Anderson knows very well, that there's a radical Islamic terrorist cell working in Casablanca, Marseille and Paris which has designed a weaponized version of a fairly simple device that operates on a basic, but well-established, principle of physics. The theory behind this device was proposed in 1925 by physicist Arthur H. Compton—not to build weapons, but to study atoms. Compton demonstrated that firing a stream of highly energized photons into atoms that have a low atomic number causes the atoms to eject a stream of electrons. This is known as the 'Compton effect'. This stream of electrons, when focused, wrecks havoc on any electronic device it strikes. The potential of this operation can have unimaginable effects on our electronic society. Let's be very clear! One possible impact of this threat is no less than the paralysis of the Western financial system and/or our strategic defense systems. I should say not only paralysis, but the possible destruction of the system because it may be impossible to accurately reconstruct the data once it has been compromised. Now, welcome Dr. Vicram Gangehar, a physicist and an expert on the effects of electromagnetic pulse technology, or EMP, as it is known, from the Department of Defense."

"Thank you, Mr. Pierce. Gentlemen, the Western world is facing an unprecedented threat to its technological infrastructure. Electromagnetic pulse technology, EMP, can bring the Western, in which I include India, China and Japan, high-technology social order to its knees—a blow from which it would take a long time to recover, if ever." He stopped speaking for effect, and it worked. The room was silent. All of the participants were on the edge of their seats, waiting.

"Let me start from the beginning. In 1958, we, the United States, exploded a thermonuclear device over the Pacific. This led to an unexpected demonstration of the power of the Compton effect. The detonations created bursts of gamma rays that, upon striking the oxygen and nitrogen in the atmosphere, released a tsunami of electrons that spread for hundreds of miles. Streetlights were blown out in Hawaii, and radio navigation was disrupted for eighteen hours as far away as Australia. The power surge, the EMP effect, was felt thousands of miles away. The implications of this effect are unfathomable. As a simple illustration of its consequences on you, your computers' motherboards would be fried. Your Blackberries would, frankly, melt. The smell of cordite would be overwhelming as all of the wiring in your electrical appliances burned to a crisp. At the simplest level, you would try to access your bank account and find that it had disappeared. The ones and zeros of modern technology would have evaporated. You would go to your bank in hopes of finding your deposits and find instead blank stares as the bank personnel tried to grasp what had happened. You'd go from wealthy to bankrupt in milliseconds."

I had read some of the literature on EMP, but the effects, as described by Dr. Gangehar, far exceeded anything I had heard about.

Dr. Gangehar passed out a ten-page document going into great detail on the EMP technology. He then proceeded to summarize the main points for us.

"What I would like to do today is start with the broad picture of cyber attacks and gradually narrow it down to the subset of what I think you are most interested in, which is the use by terrorists of EMP, highly focused operations designed to destroy computer systems and other electronic media, and thereby disrupt, damage or destroy important financial markets and, or, military installations.

"For the broad picture of cyber attacks, I quote liberally from a paper posted by Robert Lemos on Net News sometime ago. 'Cyber attacks come in two forms: one against data, the other against control systems. The first type attempts to steal or corrupt data and the data services. The vast majority of Internet and other computer attacks have fallen into this category, attacks such as credit card number theft, website vandalism and the occasional major denial of service assault.

'Control system attacks attempt to disable or take power over operations used to maintain physical infrastructure, such as distributed control systems that regulate water supplies, electrical transmission networks and railroads. While remote access to many control systems have previously required an attacker to dial in with a modem, these operations are now using the Internet to transmit data or are connected to a company's local network—a system protected with firewalls that, in some cases, can be penetrated.

'Many power companies and water utilities are operated with networks of computer-controlled devices known as supervisory control and data acquisition (SCADA) systems, which could be hacked. More than 80% of such critical infrastructure is privately owned, and in many cases the companies have not been sufficiently educated about information security until recently. Many utilities have an indirect path to the Internet from their SCADA master terminals.

'There have been a number of large cyber attacks against US infrastructure over the last decade, but none has resulted in death or mass destruction. For example, in 1988 a man named Robert Morris released a worm that infected between three and four thousand of the Internet's approximately sixty thousand servers (at that time). In 1989, the 'Legion of Doom' hacker group took control of the BellSouth telephone system and was able to tap telephone lines, route calls and pose as technicians. In 1994, a hacker known as Merc managed to dial into a server at the Salt River Project and explore computers used to monitor water canals in the Phoenix region. In 1997, a teenager disabled a key telephone company computer servicing a small airport in Massachusetts. The control tower lost critical services for six hours. Fortunately, airplanes were still able to get information from radio and other airports in the vicinity. Finally, keeping in mind that this list is not all-inclusive, in 2001, a Nimba virus wormed its way into servers and networks Internet-wide, hitting the financial industry especially hard. Recently, hackers from Russia or China have hacked into defense and air traffic control systems.

'The lesson to be taken away from these examples is that the threat is real, but so far the attackers have been unable to derive any benefit from the attacks, or conversely, create large-scale disruption over any extended period of time. Undoubtedly, there are many more attacks that have been mounted but have been detected either by government or private security systems and stopped before they were able to accomplish their ends. I think it is also fair to say that these cyber attacks mentioned have been designed to take over existing computer systems and networks and SCADA systems, with the objective of employing those systems for their own purposes. They were not, it seems to me, designed to destroy the systems themselves or the hardware on which the systems operate.

"Now let's turn to another variant of cyber attacks. This one I guess we could call a good one because we, the West, are in the forefront of its development, and most probably its use. This involves the development of the electromagnetic bomb; let's call it a weapon of electrical mass destruction, or e-bomb.

"I will rely on the expertise of Carlo Kopp, a defense analyst from Melbourne, Australia, from a paper he wrote in the early nineties. 'The Electro-Magnetic Pulse (EMP) effect was first observed during the early testing of high-altitude airburst nuclear weapons. The effect is characterized by the production of a very short (hundreds of nanoseconds) but intense electromagnetic pulse, which propagates away from its source with ever-diminishing intensity, governed by the theory of electromagnetism. The electromagnetic pulse is in effect an electromagnetic shockwave. This pulse of energy produces a powerful electromagnetic field, particularly within the vicinity of the weapon burst. The field can be sufficiently strong to produce short-lived transient voltages of thousands of volts on electrical conductors, such as wires, or conductive tracks on printed circuit boards.

'It is this aspect of the EMP effect which is of military significance, as it can result in irreversible damage to a wide range of electrical and electronic equipment, particularly computers and radio or radar receivers. The equipment can be irreversibly damaged or in effect electrically destroyed. The damage inflicted is not unlike that experienced through exposure to close proximity lightning strikes. Wounded devices may still function, but their reliability would be seriously impaired. Any cables running in and out of the equipment will behave very much like antennas, conducting the electromagnetic pulse into the equipment itself.

'Computers used in data processing systems, communications systems, displays, industrial control applications, including road and rail signaling, and those embedded in military equipment, such as signal processors, electronic flight controls and digital engine control systems, are all potentially vulnerable to the EMP effect. Receivers of all varieties are particularly sensitive to EMP, as the highly sensitive miniature high-frequency transistors and diodes in such equipment are easily destroyed by exposure to high-voltage electrical transients. Therefore, radar and electronic warfare equipment, satellite, microwave, UHF, VHF, HFN, low-band communications equipment and television equipment are all potentially vulnerable to the EMP effect.

'It is significant that modern military platforms are densely packed with electronic equipment, and an EMP device can substantially reduce their function or render them unusable.

'The technology base which may be applied to the design of electromagnetic bombs is both diverse and in many areas quite mature. Key technologies are explosively pumped Flux Compression Generators (FCG), and a range of High Power Microwave (HPM) devices, such as the virtual cathode oscillator or 'vircator'.

'The explosively pumped FCG is the most mature technology applicable to bomb designs. The FCG is a device capable of producing electrical energies of tens of megajoules in tens to hundreds of microseconds of time in a relatively compact package. To put this in perspective, the current produced by a large FCG is between ten to a thousand times greater than that produced by a typical lightning bolt.

'The central idea behind the construction of FCG's is that of using a fast explosive to rapidly compress a magnetic field, transferring much energy from the explosive into the magnetic field.

"I will come back to the construction of the FCG's because I believe this is the device in which you will have the greatest interest in terms of your present focus. However, I want to expose you to some of the higher level weaponized versions of electromagnetic bombs which are currently within the capabilities of advanced countries, and you should presume that these have been used or are ready for use in an actual warfare situation. Please don't ask me any questions about these bombs beyond what I'm about to tell you because your level of classification will not permit me to expand on what I say. But let's return to Mr. Kopp as he speaks about lethality.

'Lethality is a measure of how much power is transferred from the field produced by the weapon into the target. Only power coupled into the target can cause useful damage. There are two principal coupling modes. Front door coupling occurs typically when power from an electromagnetic weapon is coupled into an antenna associated with radar or communications equipment. The antenna subsystem is designed to couple power in and out of the equipment, and thus provides an efficient path for the power flow from the electromagnetic weapon to enter the equipment and cause damage.

'Back door coupling occurs when the electromagnetic field from a weapon produces large transient currents or electrical standing waves on fixed electrical wiring and cables interconnecting equipment, or providing connections to main power or the telephone network. Equipment connected to exposed cables or wiring will experience either high-voltage transient spikes or standing waves, either of which can damage power supplies and communications interfaces. A low-frequency weapon will couple well into a typical wiring infrastructure.

'Because microwave weapons can couple more readily than low-frequency weapons, and can in many instances bypass protection devices designed to stop low-frequency coupling, microwave weapons have the potential to be significantly more lethal than low-frequency weapons.

"With that introduction, suffice it to say that weapons development in the advanced countries has been done on a high-frequency basis. In the current period of international relations, we do not see the likelihood of advanced countries utilizing weaponized EMP devices against one another. It is much more likely that an advanced country will use such a device against a lesser-developed country whose defenses against it are virtually nil. Or, terrorists from less-developed countries might use EMP devices with great effect against developed countries with a more advanced electronic infrastructure.

"Now, since your interest is in terrorist groups from lesser-developed countries which might pose a threat to US security, I'll return to the CFG, since that is the device in which you will likely have the greatest interest. And well you should! Compression flux generators, CFG's, are cheap and efficient, thus making them accessible to poorly financed groups from less-developed countries. Furthermore, the potential payoff, in terms of destructive power, is enormous, thus leveling the playing field between developed countries and their adversaries. Usually, CFG devices do not require detonation by a suicide bomber, but rather can be detonated remotely, thus conserving one of the limited resources of terrorist groups, individuals willing to sacrifice their lives in the war of Islam against the West. Again, Mr. Kopp:

'CFG devices are easily constructed. All it takes is a tube to contain the detonation charge, copper wire to wrap the tube, a coupling device, and a timer. They are easily detonated remotely, by implanting a receiver in the charge which recognizes a signal from a cell phone or other remote transmitter. They are easily portable, being small and lightweight. In short, there is an incredible cost-benefit to a terrorist organization.'"

CHAPTER FIVE
***
KHALIDA

The meeting lasted until noon, and when it was over, Frank showed me into his private office and called his personal assistant. When she entered the room, the atmosphere was so cold it could have snowed. She had an icy demeanor, formal and reserved, and a presence that emanated from her that affected anyone it came in contact with. She was South Asian, Pakistani or Indian. She wasn't particularly tall, but she seemed so; again, the presence thing. Her gray eyes smoldered as Frank introduced us.

"Anderson Wyeth, Khalida Azmat," he said as we shook hands.

She was dressed in a sari. I had risen out of courtesy, and stood a full head taller so that I had to look down at her, but her amazing presence seemed to raise her to my height. She asked what I would like for lunch, and I stammered like a schoolboy until I finally said a sandwich of any kind would do, unfortunately adding then, "A ham sandwich would be nice."

Her smoldering eyes and her icy composure congealed into a withering look at me, then a glance at Frank, who said, "Anderson, she's Muslim; she won't serve you a sandwich made from the flesh of swine."

I was nonplussed and unsteady, rocked by the presence of the drama queen—Pakistani or Indian, I still knew not which, already having committed the sin of asking for a sandwich made of a forbidden meat, and reeling from the intensity of her gaze into my eyes at the first moment of being introduced to her. I felt like I was gasping for air, groping for purchase on something solid before I collapsed into a chair like a spent balloon. My obvious confusion and unmooring actually penetrated her hardened countenance and a twitch in her lower lip revealed her controlled sense of humor, but there was an undefined aura about her, not evil, but not good either.

Finally, out of desperation, I managed to say, "Just bring me anything, anything at all."

She turned and walked out of Frank's office, obviously knowing from experience what Frank's choice would be.

I turned to Frank and said, "What was that?"

"That was Khalida, possibly the best personal assistant I've ever had. She's brilliant, efficient, and tireless. I couldn't do half of what I do without her. While I initially hired her for administrative things only, I increasingly ask her opinion on matters of substance. She's invaluable to me."

Was this the personal assistant who had Mark remove the gun from Frank's Town Car the day I arrived, I wondered? Or, was my arrival purely coincidental with some other non-threatening duties she was carrying out?

While we waited for our sandwiches, I told Frank about the threat on the Parkway and the break-in at my condo. I omitted the detail about the removal of the gun from the car. Until I had more background, I didn't want to cast any aspersions on anyone. I was just finishing up my abbreviated account of the incidents when Khalida returned with lunch. I stopped talking and watched her closely as Frank assigned some routine tasks to her. She totally ignored me except for placing my sandwich on the table between Frank and me. She avoided eye contact and made a graceful exit.

"That's alarming, Anderson. Who knew about your arrival?"

"That's just it, Frank, no one knew except Erin and you. I'd trust Erin and you with my life, so there had to be a leak by someone in your office, or there was an intercept of our cell phone conversation. If the latter, either it was random, which is highly unlikely but remotely conceivable, or else your cell phone is compromised. And if it is, who'd be in a position to best facilitate that compromise? It gets us back to someone in your office, I think."

"I think that's highly unlikely, Anderson. All of the people working for me have been thoroughly vetted by an outside, independent, security firm, GSI Security Inc. I've used them for over ten years and have never been disappointed. They also do work for sensitive government agencies, and have been held to the highest standards. One mistake could ruin their reputation, and in their business, one mistake would put them out of business."

"How about Khalida, where did you find her? She certainly has a commanding presence, and she's definitely not a shrinking violet." I again avoided the issue of the removal of the gun from the car, a gun which might have given me better odds if the attacker on the Parkway had been successful in getting alongside. "Was she fully vetted by GSI?"

"She came to me, in a way. She was recommended by a friend of mine at a very high level in the Pakistani intelligence services, the ISI. I asked Gordon Rhoads to arrange for GSI to vet her. Gordon has very strong ties with Pakistan. In fact, I asked him to make sure that their investigation was extra thorough. I reviewed the report and saw nothing that would cause alarm. She's quite well connected in Pakistani ruling circles. She's from Sindh province, where the Bhutto family is from, and may in fact be related to them in some distant way. She went to a private boarding school in London, then to the University of Pennsylvania, where she earned a bachelor of science with a dual major in physics and math and graduated cum laude. She's fearsomely bright, Anderson."

"Is she as anti-American as the average Pakistani?"

"If she is, she keeps it under control. It is not in evidence around here. She's deadly serious! There's no joking around. My friend said she could be the next Benazir Bhutto. What's bothering you Anderson? Something about Khalida jars you, doesn't it?"

"I can't put my finger on it, Frank, but Khalida is from a religion and a culture that has not been terribly friendly to us. My experience, of course, is recent and very personal. But nonetheless, almost all of the terrorist threats of any significance come from members of the Muslim religion, and members of the clergy of Islam haven't exactly gone out of their way to condemn or otherwise discouraged such threats. I guess it just eats on me a little. I have to admit that I don't subscribe to the 'no stereotyping and no profiling' philosophy. Nor am I an adherent of the school of thought that says extreme diversity is an absolute good."

Frank didn't respond, and I had said all I intended to say. So we sat quietly for a while until I got up and asked him where I could work in private. He indicated a direction and said I would find privacy and accommodations there. He said I could ask Khalida for anything I might need, but it seemed that criticism, overt or implied, of Khalida would not be encouraged. A very slight chill seemed to have crept into our relationship.

On my way out, Frank said we should get together after I was settled.

CHAPTER SIX

***

GORDON

I went to the office Frank indicated. It was comfortably appointed but not extravagant. I had brought my own laptop computer and I logged on to the secured wireless network. In seconds, I was connected.

I had a great deal to think about since my arrival in Washington. A near miss on the Parkway coming in from Dulles Airport, combined with a breaking and entering in my condo in Alexandria was certainly enough to put me on notice that my return was not universally welcomed. I was certain that the knowledge of my arrival time had to have come from Frank's office, and furthermore, that whoever received the information had arranged the two incidents. Was it Gordon Rhoads or Khalida Azmat, or both?

No sooner had I begun to enter Khalida's name and address, which I had found out from the receptionist, into Google than a knock on my office door announced the arrival of Gordon Rhoads.

"May I come in, Anderson?"

"Of course. Have a seat. What can I do for you, Gordon?"

"It occurred to me, Anderson, that we didn't get off to a very good start. I am passionate about what I do for Frank, and sometimes my intensity gets in the way of my natural instinct to be friendly. You're new here, or at least new to the Washington office and one is naturally somewhat reserved when dealing with the new variable in what has been a complete and finely tuned operation. I hope you understand."

His explanation was weak, but it was at least minimally descriptive under the circumstances.

"No hard feelings, Gordon. I can understand that I'm the 'new variable' in Frank's operation. How long have you been with Frank?"

"Well, not all that long really. Frank sought me out about a year ago to join the firm, with a focus on North America, including Canada and Mexico, and the Caribbean."

"What is it that you do?"

"My primary focus, as with others, is security. I've developed a number of contacts within the Department of Homeland Security. I read the current press extensively, analyze trends, seek out vulnerabilities, and collate all of the information into a type of analytical framework which can tell me where potential threats are developing. By its nature, I'm focused on the long term, not the day-to-day development of threats. Frank and I talk extensively, frequently and in considerable depth on developing trends."

Gordon's demeanor appeared to be relaxed and casual, with obvious self-possession. But he seemed furtive and his eyes kept shifting from my face to something behind my head, or perhaps to nothing behind my head but away from my face and my eyes.

"What's your background, Anderson?"

"I was born and grew up in the Midwest, went to a state university then the School of Advanced International Studies at Johns Hopkins. I spent some time in the Department of the Army then USAID, and then the US Foreign Service. That's it in a nutshell. How about you?"

"Different, but similar I suppose. I grew up in Winnipeg, Canada, but my family originally settled in a Midwestern state in the US. They migrated to Canada shortly after I was born, and I grew up there. After college, I went to law school, and then I had a number of assignments with private security services in various parts of the world. On the side, I dabbled in organizing investment partnerships and developed some real estate. When Frank found me, I was living in Switzerland and tending to some personal investments."

"If you don't mind my asking, what's your ethnic background?"

"I don't mind your asking. My lineage stretches back several millennia to the Aryans who settled the Indus Valley in what is now Pakistan. I suppose that's why my family found it comfortable to migrate to Canada, a part of the British Empire, whose glory is now long gone of course. I imagine this is of little interest to you."

"On the contrary, it fascinates me. I've always had an interest in history, both modern and ancient. The Mohenjo-daro civilization was in the Indus Valley, wasn't it? One of the oldest in the world, on a par with the civilization of Ur, and of Egypt. The Aryans, I believe, settled in the Indus Valley sometime in the 1500 B.C. era. The current Pakistani state has a proud tradition, tracing its roots back to that era. So your family didn't emigrate directly from Pakistan?"

"No, as I said, my family initially emigrated from Pakistan to London, which was the normal route of emigration in the 1800s, when Pakistan was still part of the British Empire. Because of our fair complexion, courtesy of the Aryan lineage, we assimilated readily in the UK. However, my grandparents were not satisfied with the opportunities there, notwithstanding the considerable wealth they brought with them, and saw far greater opportunities in the US, which they realized, then moved on to Winnipeg."

Our conversation slowed to an uncomfortable silence. I wanted to ask him more about what he did on his various travels, but it seemed to me that I would need a better relationship before I could ask him that, one based on more shared experiences and time together. He appeared to have the same challenge. We both started to speak at the same time, stopped, and offered the other the opportunity to continue, but neither did. We didn't have enough confidence in one another to pursue the discussion. Finally, Gordon rose from his chair, said he had a morning flight to catch and excused himself.

CHAPTER SEVEN
***
CALGARY, MONTREAL, PARIS

Gordon left Washington Reagan on a nine a.m. flight to Chicago with connections to Calgary on Air Canada. He was dressed in a gray tweed jacket over black slacks, with a black T-shirt. He had cropped his blond hair short and was unremarkable, even if anyone had happened to pay attention to him for whatever reason, which they did not. Comfortably and discreetly seated in the Red Carpet Room in O'Hare's 'B' Concourse, Gordon used a prepaid cell phone to dial a number he knew from memory. When a heavily accented voice answered, Gordon spoke in short, terse sentences. "You failed! Why?"

"I was not expecting someone who fought as ferociously as this one did. He almost cut my ear off. I nearly had him, but something caused such rage in him that he fought like a wild animal. I was barely able to get away alive."

"Did you leave anything that might be traced to you?"

"I don't think so. I returned to New York as soon as I could travel, and there's no evidence I'm being followed."

"Well, then! Keep under cover. You might have to go back to Washington soon. We must eliminate him. He is developing a good nose for some of our activities, and I think we might have had some indiscretion in our African unit. We must stop this before it gets out of hand."

"I understand! Is there anything else?"

"No! Allahu Akbar!"

"Allahu Akbar!"

When he deplaned in Calgary, he went to the line for 'Returning Canadian Citizens' and offered his Canadian passport and accompanying immigration and customs forms.

"Welcome home, sir, anything to declare?"

"Nothing," Gordon said.

"Any checked baggage?"

"No, I'm just traveling with the carry-on."

"Thank you! Please proceed to customs."

Exiting customs, Gordon sauntered in the direction of the men's room. He casually turned around, and seeing nothing out of the ordinary, entered the room, which was only occupied by two other men. He entered a stall with his carry-on bag, hung up his jacket and sat on the stool. He placed the bag on his lap. He casually looked up to be sure there were no cameras designed to capture improper sexual conduct and, seeing none, unzipped the bag and withdrew a black galabiya robe, and a thaqib—turban hat—clothing resembling that worn by a Muslim cleric. He carefully folded the jacket and placed it in the carry-on. He stood, turned, put on the galabiya and the thaqib and flushed the toilet for effect. Enough time had passed for the other occupants to have left the restroom. Indeed, he had heard the steps of two men leaving, and one man entering. So no one would know that Gordon Rhoads had entered the stall and Salman Rahman, cleric, had exited. He went to the sink and washed his hands, looked into the mirror and stared at the Muslim cleric looking back at him. The only resemblance to Gordon Rhoads was his light-colored skin and his gray eyes.

Wyeth is naïve, but he must be handled carefully, he thought. *I've worked long and hard to get into a position where I can keep my finger on the pulse of the Western economies.* Gordon had actually done a stint on Wall Street working for Bear Stearns long before its collapse. As a management trainee he had spent months in the Bear Stearns Information Technology Department, where he was schooled on how to access the various exchange intranets through the Internet, as well as how to build websites for the exchange of data and information.

Salman strode to the embarkation terminal and went directly to the Air Canada counter. As he stood in line for economy, he unzipped the front pocket of his carry-on and slipped out a passport issued by the Foreign Office of the Sovereign Republic of Pakistan in the name of Salman Rahman, address Zamzama, 115 Defence at Main Khayaban-e-Shabaz, Sindh Province, Karachi, Pakistan. The fact that the address was an espresso bar in Karachi did not concern Salman. He asked for a ticket to Paris and was told there was a flight leaving within the hour for Montreal, where he could connect to an overnight flight to Paris on Air France. He paid for the ticket with a Visa card issued by Citibank from its bank in Karachi in the name of Salman Rahman. Both the passport and the credit card were counterfeited from the stolen identity of the real Salman Rahman, a Pakistani banker residing in Karachi.

Other than maintaining two identities which could only be discovered by a complete search of all documents in his possession, Salman Rahman was 'clean' from a security standpoint. The plans he carried in his carry-on could only be deciphered by an expert. He carried the approved amount of liquids, less than three ounces, and had no metal that could be detected by security. He put his Koran into a round plastic basket and sent it through the x-ray machine. As he was cleared through x-ray, he smirked at the security agents carefully wanding a seventy-year-old gray-haired lady who had transgressed security procedures by having two titanium knees surgically implanted to replace her worn-out original issue.

He was inside the security perimeter and would have no further interaction with security until he was ready to re-board in Paris two weeks later. By that time, the devices that would trigger security alarms at commercial airline terminals would be on their way by land and air and passage would be arranged to pass borders where security would be cursory.

CHAPTER EIGHT

***

MONTMARTRE

Salman Rahman deplaned at Charles de Gaulle Airport at eight a.m. Paris time. Since he had nothing but his carry-on, he bypassed baggage control and went directly to Customs and Immigration where the procedures were quick and painless. He exited the airport and hailed a cab, in fluent French, for the 18th Arrondissement, close by Montmartre. He was relaxed but observant, as he always was, but he saw nothing out of the ordinary. No cars pulled into the traffic behind his taxi, and the Paris police, liberally stationed around the airport entrance and exit, were more interested in bulkier cargo vehicles, trucks and vans, rather than a simple Muslim cleric who gave off a decidedly less-threatening presence than the myriad of colorfully dressed citizens from the far corners of France's former far-flung empire.

One dutiful officer did put down in his black notebook the terse observation: "Muslim cleric in religious dress left de Gaulle airport at 8:10 a.m. and hailed a cab." But after discussing it with his partner, they decided not to approach or follow him, seeing nothing threatening in his behavior.

Salman's cab took the Autoroute du Nord to the Peripherique then jumped to the Rue de Damremont, which took them southwest into the 18th Arrondissement. The traffic was suffocating and the trip took a full hour and a half to complete.

Finally, just to the east of Montmartre, on a narrow side street, he told the driver to stop in front of a nondescript townhouse. He paid the fare, walked calmly up to the front door and knocked softly. There was a click and the door swung inward, revealing blackness within. Hesitating for an instant, Salman stepped into the darkness and stopped, waiting for his eyes to adjust. It was quiet, so quiet that

Salman's ears thumped a deafening drumbeat in tune with his heart. He wasn't accustomed to being alarmed, let alone frightened, and the darkness weighed on him like a heavy cloak. His muscles, normally so alive and vibrant, couldn't seem to react. And so he wasn't ready when the knife, glinting from the soft light outside, came down in a slashing motion from above his shoulder directly toward his chest.

He had scarcely begun to react, when he was confronted with a bloodcurdling scream. "Allahu Akbar! God is great! The great Mogul empire of Pakistan and northern India greets you!" This was followed by deep barrel-chested laughter from a darkened figure who even now was putting away the knife into its sheath. "You must be more careful, Salman, my brother. Even though we are in a friendly city in a friendly country, we have enemies everywhere. If you aren't careful, you will be carrying your head in your hands."

"I must admit to a certain lack of care, Ahmed, my brother. Please let me get my breath." And with that, the two figures put their arms around each other and alternately bumped, pushed and jostled one another, Salman pulling his carry-on, into the main room of the townhouse, where the light was only slightly brighter than the light in the corridor. In the center of the room stood a table, bare but for a yellow pad and pencil midway down one side. There was also a laptop computer with a long cord leading to a telephone jack just above the baseboard.

Salman couldn't help but expostulate, "My God, Ahmed, you're still using dial-up? That's primitive!"

"I know it appears so, Salman, but with the various accelerators and whatnot, it's much better than you think."

"How long have you been here?"

"I've been here since December, shortly after the decision was made to proceed on our project. Since that time, I have been acquiring the right materials necessary to build the devices. I am about done."

"Really, Ahmed, are they all complete?"

"No, not all complete, but three of them are, except for the critical timing devices, which Shahid is arranging to ship from Karachi. All the other materials are available here in Paris, but I've been careful to avoid too much concentration in my acquisitions, lest it lead snooping authorities to become suspicious. I really need the plans, which I hope you brought. The information I have is incomplete."

"Yes, I brought the plans. What about our targets, Ahmed? Have they been selected? Have they been surveilled? What do we know about them?"

"Slow down, Salman. They haven't been determined yet. They will be determined by people above us."

"Well, we'll probably have a test project first, to ensure that the devices work."

"But we know they will work. They've been used everywhere in the Middle East. We built them in college."

"Yes, Ahmed, we did. But seeing them work in a harsh and difficult environment is different than it is in a college lab. We have to know how close we need to be to the target for one thing, and we have to know that the timing devices will work as planned. The key to the whole project is to have precise timing."

Ahmed looked at Salman curiously, just beginning to realize that he and Salman were talking about entirely different devices. He was working on bombs a suicide bomber could strap on his body. What was Salman talking about?

CHAPTER NINE
***
ISLAMABAD

Shahid Kureshi sat in the dark and dingy café just off a back street in Islamabad. It was late in the evening, and the lateness of the hour increased his apprehension. The back streets of Islamabad were not a place to be wandering about late at night. He toyed with the cup that had recently contained his third cup of tea since arriving over an hour before. Shahid wasn't squeamish or afraid of the dark. In fact, quite the opposite, he was comfortable operating in the dark, but he was also a realist and knew that the chances of something unfortunate happening were increased after dark. He was, after all, not without enemies. Some of his enemies were jealous of his successes; some were jealous of his freedom of operation; some were jealous of his close relationships with certain members of the Pakistani Inter-Services Intelligence (ISI). All of his enemies were formidable, most of whom were outside of the ISI, but the most fearsome were those on the inside.

His enemies inside the ISI were most dangerous because they were political and believed that those who didn't agree with their politics were endangering the very life of the state. The ISI reflected the divisions of the Pakistani people, a large share of which distrust the West, especially the United States, and believe that the future of Pakistan rested with their Muslim brothers. Another faction believed that Pakistan was culturally allied with the West, and indeed was a close ally of the United States. Very little public information was available on the ISI, he mused, less than on the Indian Intelligence Agency, and the Research and Analysis Wing (RAW) had been his implacable foe for every one of his twenty years in the intelligence business.

His reflections were interrupted by a dark shadow that materialized seemingly out of nowhere. The shadow wore a keffiyeh over a turban and a simple galabiya. The keffiyeh was pulled forward on both sides of his face, which served to obscure his identity, but Shahid recognized him immediately. He was the individual who had been Shahid's lifeline to the ISI for the last ten years. From him, Shahid received his instructions, his money, and his reporting requirements. To him, Shahid delivered the results of the best work he could perform, whether it was the collection of information from sensitive sources, or the execution of a directive, which may or may not have included 'wet' operations.

Shahid knew that his contact was a senior military officer, but he had never seen him in uniform. Shahid felt a curious bond to this individual, but it wasn't a bond of loyalty. It was more like a bond of security, of shared interests, of shared secrets. Shahid didn't truly trust his handler, but rather knew that their relationship was based on mutual self-interest and that both parties needed each other. His handler had given him directives that Shahid knew were unlawful. And his handler knew that Shahid had performed acts that were outside the law, and sometimes even outside of his own directives.

The handler sat down heavily in the booth opposite Shahid, keeping his face hidden in the shadows of the keffiyeh.

"Our Fatherland is in a difficult period, my brother. The balance in the ISI is shifting to the right, recognizing the increased opposition of the people to the West and beleaguered by the disastrous state of our economy. My colleagues are also sensing the increased power of the Taliban and Al-Qaeda and the decreasing ability of our government and Western forces in Afghanistan to do anything about it. Those who maintained a firm position right in the middle of the fence are now slipping over to the right, and those who were more favorable to the West are now climbing on the fence. It comes at a most inopportune time, as our project is reaching its maturity."

"I fail to understand why the unsettled political condition in the country should have an impact on our project."

"It assuredly does, my friend. I have spent the last several weeks, arguing about the appropriate targets for our devices. We have enough resources in terms of manpower, and matériel, to strike five targets. In our initial deliberations, we targeted Surat, Mumbai, Hyderabad,

Bangalore, and Delhi. Now, I am being pressured, no, told, to select four targets in the West, and only one in the home of our historic enemy, India. They have generously advised me that I can select the target in India, but that I must select New York, Chicago, London and Paris. This will, according to the logic in the ISI, inflict maximum damage in the heart of Western economies, and thus advance the cause of Islam everywhere."

"And what is your personal preference?"

"In these matters, I have no personal interests."

"My brother," Shahid said. "I have no doubt that we can inflict damage on the economies of the West, but if we were to focus our resources on India, we could bring its 'Silicon Valley' in Bangalore and Hyderabad to its knees, stop or at least slow its most rapidly growing city, Surat, disrupt its significant outsourcing industry in Delhi as well as its financial markets in Mumbai. It would be a success and an operation with measurably fewer risks than spreading our resources all over the Western world. I hope you realize the difficulty of trying to shape an operation with such diverse goals. Focusing on India alone, we would be able to operate much more efficiently, without the distractions of operating in five geographically and culturally diverse areas. I must warn you that the risks of exposure and failure will go up geometrically if we attempt to accomplish such a broad mandate. Why can we not concentrate on four targets in India and one in New York if you absolutely must hit the West? I have a particularly talented operative, who lives and works in Washington D.C., but who has worked in the financial markets in New York. Once given the objectives and the resources, he can act quite independently. That would allow me to focus the efforts of the rest of my team on India, where we know the culture and the personalities. Such a strategy would have a far greater chance of success. It is clearly much more within our, that is Pakistan's, national interest to disrupt and slow India's growth than it is to use our pitiably small resources to enlist in the war between Islam and the West."

"I won't say it publicly, but you are right, Shahid. Pakistan's national interest is to lessen the threat from India, whose economy is many times larger than ours, and whose primary foreign-policy goal is to render us ineffective against her. It's an argument that I've used confidentially in one-on-one meetings in the ISI, but my arguments have fallen on deaf ears. You know there is a virulent debate raging in the ISI, the military, and among civilian leaders about the possibility of a nuclear first strike against India. Perhaps I shouldn't be telling you this, but it could have an effect on the use of your resources in the cell in Paris, and you should be prepared for a change in direction."

"I would welcome such a change, but why now?"

"Because our nuclear deterrent is becoming less effective daily in deterring a nuclear first strike from India. Israel, which has a highly developed aerospace capability, is now the largest supplier of defense equipment to India. They now exceed Russia at a billion dollars a year. Some of the systems they are selling will directly reduce our effectiveness in a first strike, and even worse, in a second-strike response to their first strike. India is buying an enhanced version of the SPYDER surface to air missile system from Israel, and contracts have been signed for three and possibly six new Phalcom Airborne Warning and Control Systems, AWACs, and has agreed to joint development of medium-range surface to air missiles. They are already cooperating in satellite launches. In January, 2008, an Indian military Polar Satellite Launch Vehicle lifted off from Sriharikota Space Launch facility carrying an advanced Israeli satellite, the Polaris. In short, India's defense is growing exponentially while ours is static. If we do not do something rapidly, our window for a first strike will disappear. But there is one wild card that will be a trump. Our weapon can be a trump!"

"How can our weapon be a trump? I thought we were going to use suicide bombers simultaneously on five targets. While they are effective and will achieve our limited objectives, they are in no way a trump card. We plan to use off-the-shelf technology in making the bombs, but there's always the possibility that some of the parts might be defective, so out of the five, we may only achieve success with four."

The handler started to speak, but at that moment, the waiter approached the table. He first gave a menu to Shahid then he carefully placed his right hand on the table and laid the menu for the handler on the top of his hand before he withdrew it. He asked the handler if he would like a cup of tea, and when the handler said no, the waiter looked around casually then left the table. There was a moment of silence before the handler slid his hand under the menu and pulled out a piece of paper. It was soiled from cooking grease that had apparently spattered on it from the kitchen.

As he looked at the note, the handler's face sagged. "Those bastards must have followed me. A friend tells me there's one across the street facing the door, and one three doors down the street. If we go out the door we came in, we will be caught in a crossfire. There is a back door through the kitchen that leads to an alley. If we get out that door before they realize there is a back door, we might have a chance."

"Who are they? And why are they targeting you?"

"I'm not sure they are targeting me," the handler said as he rose slowly to his feet and began moving toward the kitchen. "They may be targeting you. I don't really know. I do know there are two members of your team you must watch very carefully. I also know they will stop at nothing to make sure the devices I have already arranged to deliver to you in Paris are used according to their instructions. Salman Rahman will join you in Paris, and he has the initial plans. Plans for their final assembly and specifications for their use and effectiveness will be included with the delivery of the devices, along with the specific targets in the specific cities mentioned. Now let's get out of here!"

"Wait! Who are the two members I must watch?" But there was no time to wait or to answer. The handler started to move very quickly, and Shahid sprang up to follow him into the kitchen, where they found a door hidden by a large storage rack, which was now moved out of the way. Standing beside the door was a chef with a meat cleaver at the ready. He pushed open the door and Shahid and the handler sped through it. They ran down the alleyway to a one-way street leading to the right, up to Sadar Road. At Sadar Road, they turned right again and ran toward the Melody Market, approximately one block away.

Shahid was in better physical condition, and his handler began to fall behind. They turned left into Melody Market, and right toward the car repair area. Shahid sensed rather than saw someone following them and dove in front of an ancient British Leyland truck, his heart beating furiously, and waited for his handler, but the man never arrived. He heard a brief scuffle, and then the sound of a body falling to the street, followed by a gurgling sound as air and blood exhaled from a body.

Shahid remained where he was for the better part of half an hour. Finally, hearing no further noise on the street, he stood up and slipped quietly between broken cars until he reached Bazaar Road, where he hailed a taxi.

Returning to his temporary rented room, he moved a heavy wardrobe in front of the closed door, lay down on the bed and tried to get some sleep. He slept fitfully until three a.m., when the ancient phone in the room rang. He tried to force a calm he didn't feel when he lifted the receiver and said, "Hello."

The voice on the other end of the line was muffled and harsh.

"We are finished with debate. Do you understand what is required of you?"

"Yes, I do!"

"Good! Do not forget it. You are to proceed to Paris immediately and follow the instructions that will be communicated to you there. Do you understand?"

"Yes."

CHAPTER TEN
***
GEORGETOWN

The address was as good as an address can get. The townhouse was in Georgetown next to Dumbarton Oaks, where post-World War II negotiators set up the framework for the United Nations. The invitees matched the address. It was a typical Washington power reception. I had been invited by Frank, who had seen more than his share of such parties and was hosting this one. The guests were all recognizable, and were from different levels in the Washington power structure. Near the piano, ambassadors from Eastern European countries were in animated debate, while their wives stood languidly by, sipping white wine and trying to look at least minimally interested. Next to the buffet table, Middle Eastern diplomats from Muslim countries stood serenely in their thawbs, wearing simple white keffiyehs, carefully sampling the hors d'oeuvres to ensure that they would not be ingesting any pork products, and drinking club soda until they could return to the privacy of their own homes where they could drink liquor without fear of condemnation.

I had earlier introduced myself to the Jordanian ambassador, Prince Maktoum Hamid Sharaf, and we had exchanged stories of the tumultuous times in Jordan when I had been kidnapped and escaped from the souk in Amman. I had also spoken briefly with the Pakistani ambassador, who was completely noncommittal about events in Islamabad. *He has every reason to be evasive*, I thought. Knowing who was riding which horse in Pakistan was a full-time job, let alone being able to fulfill the task of representing the country's interests in the best possible light, knowing full well that those lights might change at any moment. I looked around as someone tapped me on the shoulder. It was Frank.

"Pakistan," I said quietly as I glanced discreetly at the Pakistani ambassador, "has to have one of the most challenging governance tasks in the world. It's nearly a failed state, despite its enormously rich history and tradition and its educated elite. Its traditional enemy, India, now has industrial power and a defense industry, as well as an energetic and increasingly well-educated population, which has most likely dwarfed Pakistan's capabilities in all aspects of statehood."

"That's true, but Pakistan, like a wounded lion, is more dangerous than ever. We worry about Iran's development of nuclear weapons, but Pakistan already has them, knows how to deliver them, and it's a profoundly Islamic country. Pakistan has been a battleground for the intensifying conflict between the Shia and Sunnis. Fifty percent, or a shade more, of the Pakistani population is Shia and the Shia/Sunni conflict is deeper and more enduring than the conflict between Islam and the West. It can only be compared with the Thirty Years' War in Europe, between 1618 and 1648, in which Protestants and Catholics fought each other bitterly and remorselessly until Europe was a wasteland. The laid-waste countryside lingered like a cloud for generations. This internal civil conflict bears watching," Frank drawled.

"Anderson, there's someone I want you to meet, Joan Singer-Taylor." He took me by the arm and guided me into close proximity to a shapely blonde who was facing away from us talking to another guest. Frank tapped her on the shoulder and said, "Joan, this is the Anderson Wyeth I've told you about."

Joan turned fully around to face me and my breath caught in my throat. She too gasped for breath as we stood, face-to-face, Erin and I, for it was Erin Cohen who faced me; the same Erin Cohen I had last seen in Tucson Airport less than a week before.

Oblivious to our astonishment, Frank continued, "Anderson has extensive experience in the Middle East and has been working for me for about a year, but I've known him since we served together in the US Embassy in Egypt several years ago. Anderson, Joan was a lobbyist for the ill-fated Fannie Mae here in Washington. She still commutes regularly to New York to interact with counterparts in investment banks, now commercial banks, I guess. She's very knowledgeable about the markets and of course about banking law and regulation. Capital is currently a major issue with banks, and she is exploring the possibility of approaching sovereign wealth funds in Dubai and Qatar. You might have some thoughts you could share with her."

I could forgive Frank for he had only met Erin briefly several months ago in Washington, and she had then been a brunette and had been introduced as a practicing psychologist. It was a totally different person from the one who stood before me now.

As I struggled to regain my composure, 'Joan' more quickly regained hers and said coolly, "Hello, Anderson."

She waited briefly for me to speak but then began telling me about her background as if we had just met. As she described herself, she was one of those great products from the Midwest. Born into a middle-class family in Ohio, she graduated at the top of her class in high school, received a scholarship that took her through Ohio State, and with some help from her family and student loans, she cruised through Columbia Law School, graduating in the top 20% of her class. She was married, briefly, to a classmate, got a job with a Wall Street firm, and then was enticed to a lobbying firm in Washington. She was junior counsel for several years, she said, then, when the senior lawyer on the account left the firm, she inherited the entire Fannie Mae account. She was totally immersed in Fannie Mae's credit default swap operations in New York and in the regulatory and legal environment in which Fannie operated. Since Fannie and Freddie were taken over by the government, she was doing lobbying work for other, lesser clients, but still in the financial arena.

There was just enough similarity with Erin's and this other person's background, even down to the brief marriage, so that, as she was talking, I was trying to integrate the parts. And, since Frank was still standing beside me, and as I hadn't figured out the game plan, I played along.

"Tell me more about your interest in obtaining capital from a sovereign wealth fund," I said haltingly.

"Well, obviously," she said acidly, "people on the Hill wanted what they called, for lack of a better term, 'accountability' from current stockholders and executive management of Fannie Mae. Fannie Mae is history. Now we have to find capital for banks. Capital is not readily available in the US, since we have exported it to oil-producing countries, and China, through our oil and consumer goods imports, so one way to get it back is through sovereign wealth fund investment. The fact is that things are really unsettled right now. Everyone is on the edge of their seats, waiting for the next rumor. The latest rumor was a real whopper, something about a total computer hardware meltdown."

I had been half-listening, still trying to figure out what was going on, but as her words sunk in, I asked, "What did you just say?"

"I said people on Wall Street are focused on rumors about regulatory steps that might be proposed—"

"No, after that! Something about a meltdown."

"I'm sure it's just another stupid rumor, but it's apparently been circulating in some backrooms that there is some kind of a bomb that will fry the wiring in computer hardware, which would really create chaos in financial markets."

I tried to keep my voice calm when I asked, "Do you have any idea who might have started the rumor?"

"No idea, other than it might have been someone of foreign extraction who used to work on the Street but now works in Washington."

An image of Gordon Rhoads formed in my mind. My hands were beginning to get clammy, but I forced myself to change the subject because I didn't want her to see that I was very interested in the rumor she had mentioned. "How interesting that there's a rumor a minute on Wall Street, and it seems like if it's in a down market, it's a rumor about some kind of impending disaster. If it's in an up market, it's a rumor about some incredible deal that will make everybody richer."

Her eyes probed mine as I asked her how she liked Washington. She was slow to reply, adjusting to my rapid change of subject.

"I've liked Washington since the first day I arrived. It's a city that gets into your blood. It exudes power, even when that isn't the intention. People go through their daily lives here, doing normal things, going to the supermarket, going to the dry cleaners, going home to the family, all the while their mind is back-grounding the fact that they live in the city that is the capital of the most powerful country on the face of the Earth, now and in all of history. That's a pretty heavy feeling, you know, whether you like the administration or not. The most popular, prevalent phrase is that life here is hectic, high-pressure and people are stressed out. That's true, of course, but it's also true in every major city in the United States. It's just that here the decisions that are made have not only citywide, statewide, and nationwide effect, but also international significance and implications. I think anyone who fails to sense that reality is missing one of the truly great 'awarenesses' and excitements of the 21st century. This city is incredible, you know, from art collections to all of the museums on the Mall. From the huge bureaucracy to the White House and the Capitol, from the ridiculous to the sublime, to reverse Napoleon's famous phrase. What about you?"

"It's nice to talk to someone who recognizes the importance of the moment and the importance of the place," I stated, still playing the role for anyone who might overhear.

"Washington truly is a magical city. I've spent a great deal of time here, and when I haven't been living here, I've traveled here on a short-term basis. I love the city, from the almost unendurable hot humid days of summer to the beauty of the cherry blossoms at the Tidal Basin in the spring. It's no wonder when congressional representatives are elected they manage to find a way to remain here even after their mandate from the people has long expired. The city grows and grows, not caring which party is in power."

'Joan' had managed to maneuver us away from the densest part of the guests into a semi-private area.

"That's all very interesting, Anderson, but I can tell when someone is changing the subject. What is it that you didn't want to talk about?"

"Okay, Joan," I said. I couldn't believe I was addressing her as Joan. It was surreal, as if I were in another place and time. "I was in fact changing the subject. I apologize! The rumor you mentioned interests me a great deal because it isn't the first time I've heard reference to such a 'bomb'. I know that such a device exists. I suspect it's been used in situations where aggression, but not physical damage, is intended, probably by the Russians, the Israelis, and ourselves, maybe others. I fear that its practical application could have consequences beyond anything we've been able to imagine. Is there anything else to the rumors you know of?"

"What I mentioned is pretty much everything I know. No one seems to know how it works or what its impact would be, except that it would melt the wiring in our computers. In fact, when it was related to me I found it humorous."

"Is there any indication of how many computers could be affected? Or where the bomb might be placed—geographically speaking? Would it be placed in Lower Manhattan, in the NYSE itself? Or on one of the trading floors of one of the major investment houses—Morgan Stanley for example? Or even Goldman?"

"No, nothing so specific. It was a trader from Goldman who first mentioned it to me, however."

"First mentioned? That sounds like you've heard it more than once."

"It does, doesn't it? And maybe I have. As we're talking about it, it seems like it was referenced in another conversation I had, maybe another trader. When I was counsel to Fannie Mae, we traded through all of the major investment banks. Maybe I heard it from a broker from another bank."

"Do you remember who it might have been, specifically? Either time?"

"Let me think. One time was during a luncheon at Goldman. I was sitting beside a broker making small talk, and I said something about our information systems 'blowing up', metaphorically speaking, and he said 'don't make jokes about that!' I remember specifically saying, 'Whatever do you mean?' And he said, 'There's a rumor going around about a bomb that could melt our hardware like butter on a hot waffle iron.' I joked that such a bomb could accomplish more in an hour than the Communists were able to accomplish in decades, 'Who would have an interest in doing that?' I asked, and he said, 'The Muslims.' I was about to ask what he meant, but at that moment the luncheon speaker was introduced and we ended the conversation. Who was he…I've forgotten! I can easily find out, though. Someone set up the luncheon and we had name cards, so someone knows we were sitting together."

I politely excused myself from 'Joan', still unnerved by her being at one and the same time Joan and Erin, and looked around the room for Frank. He was removed from the crowd, standing in a secluded alcove which served as his library. It had wall-to-wall, floor-to-ceiling bookshelves that were crammed full of volumes. I knew from prior visits that the titles ranged from aesthetics to zoology, with physics, philosophy and political economy in between. And even more impressive, I knew that Frank had read all or parts of all of them. He was talking with a tall slender man, whose back was to me, dressed in a white thawb and a keffiyeh. From his stature and body language, there was something familiar about him to me, but before I could approach more closely, he raised his hand in a half-salute to Frank and moved quickly toward the second door of the library.

"Frank, who was that you were talking with? He seemed very familiar to me seeing him from the back, but I can't place him."

"He should be very familiar to you, Anderson. That was al-Tabari!"

"My God, Frank! Why didn't you tell me he was going to be here?"

"I didn't know it myself until the last minute. Al-Tabari moves according to his own time schedule and place. I have, of course, arranged to have an appropriate passport and travel documents for him, but he does not advise me in advance of his travel plans."

I called out to the disappearing figure of al-Tabari, but he either didn't hear me or didn't want to acknowledge me. I took a step in the direction of his departing figure but realized that this wasn't the time or place to chase him. I stopped as memories and images flooded my mind. Memories of when I first met him. It had been less than a year before in a half-finished house in Ramallah on the West Bank. Our positions were much different then. I was captive, and he was captor. He had, I first assumed, arranged the capture of Layla and I in Mexico and had caused us to be transported to Ramallah for the purpose, we assumed, of interrogation of me and punishment of Layla.

He was a striking figure then, as now. I could almost see him as I first saw him in the dim light of the room under construction. He was my inquisitor then and he was silent. I could see his outline in the dim light. He sat with a doorway behind him as the only source of light, and I could barely see his face. He was slender, severe in a black faux turtleneck sweater, expressionless, and handsome. At that time I guessed his age at forty-eight. He wore a mustache and goatee so common among Middle Easterners of Arab descent. I remember that I could just make out a scar on his right cheek, high on the cheekbone. I thought about the propriety of such a scar. Given his demeanor, he may have once fought in a duel, but I had concluded that this was the wrong century—right man, wrong century. Dignity, pride and severity shrouded him like a cloak.

I had asked him then who he was and why he was holding Layla and I. He responded forthrightly. "My given name is Khalid, he had said, but you shall know me as Ali al-Tabari. I am a Palestinian of the Shiite branch."

"Are you an ayatollah, then?" I had asked.

"No," he told me. "In the Shiite sect, ayatollah's must have direct lineage to one of the Imams. There were eleven Imams in the Shiite sect, all direct descendents of Ali, who was Mohammed's paternal cousin and son-in-law, married to Fatima. My lineage is from Muhammad ibn Jarir al-Tabari, who was one of the earliest, most scholarly, and most famous commentators on the Koran. He died in Baghdad in 923 A.D. My family has tried to follow his tradition for 1100 years. Some are successful, some are not. I do my best."

It was clear to me then from the sound and timbre of his voice that he was a man of enormous pride and ego, and the respectful way in which he referred to his ancient forebear reflected his scholarly inclination.

I grew to respect, fear and love al-Tabari, as he in turn helped Layla and I, astounded me with his connections in the shadow world of intelligence, and grieved with me as I sought, in vain, to free Layla from her sinister bond to Islam.

As I stood there in Frank's house I tried to come to grips with the various crosscurrents affecting me. In the other room, a woman whom I had known as Erin Cohen, a practicing clinical psychologist in Ohio, was now representing herself to be an attorney living and working in Washington and New York, deeply involved in the upper reaches of financial management for some of the world's largest financial institutions. And through the door to the room in which I was standing, had passed an enigmatic figure, complex, multifaceted, at times ominous, who had in turn caused fear and optimism in me.

I returned to the room where Erin/Joan was still standing, talking to someone who looked like he was about to leave. My approach hastened his departure.

"Erin," I said. "When are you going to tell me what's going on? I'm trying very hard to respect this dual personality of yours, but I need to know where it's all going, or I'm going to make a mistake at an inopportune moment. I don't want to do that, but you owe me an explanation."

Erin looked around her, and as she did so, I did the same, half-expecting someone, or multiple someones, to be watching us because that was what Erin's actions conveyed.

Erin's shoulders sagged and she sighed, as if under a great weight. "It's complicated, Anderson."

"I can understand that. Try me."

"Anderson, I've become involved in something very, very difficult. I can tell you a little bit about it, but now is not the time nor the place. Will you trust me on this? I really, really do need you to be Anderson to my Joan, not to my Erin. I don't know for sure when, if ever, I'll be able to give you a complete explanation. Perhaps even worse, I'm not sure you want a complete explanation, or, if you were to understand the implications completely, you'd want a complete explanation."

CHAPTER ELEVEN
✴✴✴
WASHINGTON – NEW YORK

Erin, what's going on?"

"I'm sorry to have surprised you, Anderson, but I must say, you surprised me as well! Obviously, I didn't expect to see you here, and please, my name is Joan."

"But who are you? I've known you for years. We were lovers, you and I. You were just in Tubac. Who are you now? Why are you playing this game?"

"Anderson, this is not an easy thing to explain at a noisy cocktail reception. I'm involved with a variety of organizations, some of which do not relate organically to the others. Because of that, sometimes I have to assume a different persona in order to keep the lines of communication clear and direct between the different organizations. Please trust me on this. There is nothing more I can say here. Please accept me for who I am here now, a lobbyist for New York financial firms."

"I'm totally confused, but I respect you because of our long-standing relationship, and I will play your game, and I assume that you wish me to refer to you in public as 'Joan'."

"You must!" 'Joan' said, almost weeping with the intensity of her plea.

"Okay then, but you'll have to cue me when I should recognize some aspects of your persona and not others, like when you're an attorney versus when you're a psychologist, or I'll make a blunder for sure. Would you do that for me, Erin…I mean, Joan?"

"Of course I will, Anderson. As you might surmise, I must, I have to be, totally aware of who I am and where I am 100% of the time. I will not let you slip."

I looked at her for what seemed like a long time, with respect, but also with curiosity, as if gazing at her face would yield clues about this new person being revealed to me, but ultimately I gave up and said, "I've been thinking about our discussion of the rumor you heard during your Goldman luncheon. As I told you, I've also heard of such a device, but I'm not sure it's ever been 'weaponized', at least at the level of individual terrorism. Would you be willing to help me out by tracking down the broker you were having a conversation with and setting up a luncheon for the three of us for the next time you go to New York?"

She looked at me with a puzzled expression. "Do you often make trips to New York just to track down what's probably just a goofy rumor?"

"Not often." I found it curious that she thought my behavior was eccentric given what she had just revealed to me. "This particular rumor does intrigue me, however, because of its economic and security implications."

"Of course, I'd be happy to. My personal assistant should be able to determine my seatmate with a couple of phone calls tomorrow. I'm scheduled to go to New York the day after tomorrow. If I can arrange it, would you be available to go then?"

"I certainly could. I assume you go up and back the same day?"

"Yes, I take the eight thirty Delta shuttle to LaGuardia, and I'm usually in our New York office by ten thirty or eleven a.m. We should be in plenty of time to have lunch at noon. I return to Washington whenever my work is done. Do you have a number where I can reach you tomorrow?"

"Yes, I have an office in Frank's office complex. You have his number I'm sure. Just call his offices, and the receptionist will put you through to me. Thank you for this. It is appreciated." I also gave her my home number.

I said good night to 'Joan' and on my way to find Frank, I said good night to several other people I had met during the evening. My head was spinning from the information I was trying to assimilate. I found Frank in the hallway having an animated conversation with a dapper Pakistani deputy chief of mission in the Pakistani Embassy, whom I had met earlier in the evening. I said good night to Frank, nodded to the Pakistani and stepped out into the chill, damp Georgetown night.

At 7:15 the next morning I was back at my office researching the physics of electromagnetic pulse technology. The day passed swiftly, and at two p.m., Joan's personal assistant called to tell me that we had a luncheon set up for noon the next day. On my way out of the office, I stopped by Frank's office.

"Just curious, Frank, but I haven't seen Gordon all day, or for the last several days as far as that goes. Is he off on assignment somewhere?"

"Yes, he is. He flew off to Alberta several days ago. We have a friend up in Edmonton who keeps an eye on the Athabasca tar sands. You know, when the price of oil exceeds fifty dollars a barrel, extraction of oil from the tar sands is quite profitable. It's an enormous deposit, placing Canada second only to Saudi Arabia in oil reserves. The tar sands themselves cover an area the size of the entire state of Wisconsin. So it becomes a security issue for the US. I like to keep an eye on what's going on up there. He should be back in a week or so."

"Just wondered. I'm off, and I'm going up to New York tomorrow to check out a rumor about what might be a flux compression generator device. Seems as though some traders have been talking about the possibility of one being placed on one of the trading floors of an investment bank. Probably just a rumor, but I'll check it out."

"It might be more than that, Anderson. That's why al-Tabari was in Washington last night. I told you he has information that there's a terrorist cell, mostly made up of Pakistanis, operating out of Paris, with operatives in Casablanca and possibly Marseille. He obviously won't tell me his source, but he seems to think it's fairly reliable. According to his information, they're at least talking about the use of a compression flux generator, which they call an 'e-bomb', for electronic, or electron, bomb, I guess. He didn't have any indication of what the target or targets might be, but if successful, an EMP weapon could do serious damage to computer networks. Even though the information on most computer systems is backed up on a regular basis, networks rarely have totally redundant hardware and frequently not operating systems. If a piece of hardware in the network is damaged but not destroyed, it presents an almost greater problem because it brings into question the reliability of the information being processed. God knows electronic information is frequently questionable anyway, and if people believe there's a glitch in the information technology itself, it would produce paralysis. So take all of these rumors seriously."

"Okay, Frank. I'm off."

When I got home, there was a message from Joan on my recorder. She would meet me at Reagan National at 7:30 the next morning. As I looked around my living room, the thought briefly occurred to me that since Gordon was out of town my life had become more tranquil, but I didn't dwell on it. I called a cab and arranged for a pick up at 6:30 a.m., then went to the kitchen and thawed a frozen pizza, which I took into the library, where I booted up my laptop.

I went to the New York Times home page and my eye was drawn to an *Associated Press* story about a glitch in the FAA's air traffic control system.

An electronic communication failure Tuesday at a Federal Aviation Administration facility that processes flight plans for the eastern half of the United States caused massive delays around the country. The Northeast was hardest hit. At one point, an FAA website that tracks airport status showed delays at about three-dozen major airports across the country. An FAA spokesperson said there was a failure in a communications link that transmits the data to a similar facility elsewhere in the country. She also said there was an unrelated hardware problem at another FAA facility about a week ago which delayed the departure of at least 134 flights.

The story set off alarm bells. I tried to convince myself these were normal computer glitches in the enormously complex air traffic control system, but I kept saying to myself 'yes, that's right, but what if?' At peak traffic times, there are between four and six thousand planes in the air, far too many to be flying on VFR—visual flight rules—in an unclouded sky. In inclement weather, without the air traffic control system operating properly, or more accurately, without the computers of the air traffic control system operating properly, the volume of air traffic would become a nightmare, with planes flying through congested airspace with no indication that they were on a collision course with another aircraft until onboard collision warning alarms warned them, giving the pilots only seconds to avert a disaster.

After exhausting all of the information I could glean from the Internet, I shut down the laptop, checked the locks on the doors, and went upstairs to bed.

I awoke at 5:30 a.m., as usual, and was ready for the taxi at 6:30. I arrived at Reagan National before 7:30 and bought my ticket for the Delta shuttle. I only had my briefcase since I fully intended to be back in Washington that evening. I wandered around the area in front of the Delta desk, waiting for Joan.

At precisely 7:30 a.m., she strode briskly up to the counter, acknowledged me with a light wave of her hand, bought her ticket, and walked over to say hello. She was dressed very conservatively, in a tailored beige suit with a delicate Hermes scarf tucked into her blouse. She had spent some time on her hair, and her makeup accented her hazel eyes. She was stunningly attractive. She too only had a briefcase. We went through security with scarcely a second look and found ourselves in the Delta concourse waiting for the shuttle.

"Did you happen to see an article from the *Associated Press* regarding an FAA computer glitch yesterday?" I asked.

"As a matter of fact, I did. I really couldn't make heads or tails of it, so at first I put it out of my mind. However, our discussion about some kind of a device which would render computer systems unreliable kept intruding on my thoughts, so I went on the Internet and did some research on electromagnetic pulse technology, and it's really rather alarming. Do you think that the FAA computer glitch could possibly have been caused by some kind of terrorist device?"

"There's no question about whether it *could* have been caused by a terrorist e-bomb. The only question is whether it *was* caused by a terrorist e-bomb. At this point, we're only speculating."

The gate attendant called our flight, and we moved toward the line which was forming to get onto our plane.

"I'm boarding area number one, how about you?"

"I am as well. What's your seat?"

"2A."

"I'm 2B. Excellent!"

As we boarded, we found our seats and jostled next to one another. I felt the soft pressure of her breast and immediately said excuse me, and she said, just as promptly, that it was all right.

After the safety instructions, the plane was pushed back from the gate and we began to taxi to the head of runway 19, which roughly parallels the Potomac River. After many years of flying, I was attuned to the movement of aircraft, and as we approached the turn, I felt an unusual slowing. We came to a stop, and after a minute's silence, the pilot came on the air and said we had been given a 'hold' for a few minutes. He apologized for the delay, but said it was mandated by air traffic control procedures and that it should not last long. Joan and I looked at each other but said nothing. An hour later, we were still looking at each other. The pilot had apologized twice more but still had no information as to when we might take off. We had been first in line for takeoff, and now it was apparent that there were many planes behind us, possibly as many as twenty or thirty. Something was obviously wrong, and it was not simply a case of an air traffic control slow down.

"I'm trying very hard to think of this as a normal air traffic situation," Joan said. "I've been through countless numbers of these. There's really no reason to be concerned. The weather is beautiful, and I looked at New York weather last night and it was fine. If it weren't for our conversation, I'd think nothing of it."

"I absolutely agree," I said. "Nonetheless, I have to say that this is somewhat bizarre, especially in light of what we both read in the *Associated Press* article. How long have we been here? I think it's at least an hour."

"It's been just an hour. It is 9:30, and if we sit here much longer, we're going to miss the luncheon. Apparently they aren't giving the pilot any information either. Have you noticed? I haven't seen any planes landing during the entire time we've been sitting here."

"Yes, I did notice. It appears that all flight operations have been suspended. That certainly implies that some systemic failure has occurred, at least with regard to operations at this airport."

Finally, the pilot came on the intercom and in a measured voice said, "Ladies and gentlemen, we're going to have to sit here for another half-hour or so. There has apparently been some interruption in the air traffic control communications system, and the FAA is unable to coordinate all of the flight plans in the system. Many flights will have to be canceled in order to reduce traffic on certain high-density routes. That would enable a few flights to fly VFR, that is, visual flight rules, on routes where the traffic has been reduced. Weather between Washington and New York is clear, and a number of flights have already been canceled on this route. We will not know if we are among the lucky ones for another half-hour. As soon as I get any information, I will pass it along to you."

"I'm not sure whether being able to fly VFR means that we're among the lucky ones. I confess to certain reservations, but it doesn't look like we're going to have much choice in the matter either way," I said.

Joan nodded. "Unfortunately, I agree with you on both points. It really highlights the fact that we're captives. That hasn't been a bad thing when you have no real reason to distrust the pilots or the air traffic control system. But now, when we at least have reason to believe that the system may be a target of a malevolent act, it really makes me uncomfortable."

We waited in silence for another fifteen minutes until, finally, the pilot came on again. "Good news, ladies and gentlemen, we've been cleared to fly to New York on visual flight rules. I want to assure you that this does not compromise our safety in any way. The number of flights on this air corridor has been reduced substantially and the weather remains clear up to New York. The first officer and I learned to fly on visual flight rules, so it's nothing new to us. We'll keep you informed as to any developments." With that, the CRJ 700 slowly moved onto the runway, powered up and began its roll. We were airborne in less than a minute.

We both took reading material from our briefcases and settled in for the short flight to New York. I was seated by the window, lost in my reading. I came to a break in the text and looked out the window to think about what I had just read. It took a second to sink in, but I suddenly realized that the clear weather we had been enjoying since our departure from Washington had now become a haze and seemed to be getting thicker by the minute. I watched out the window for a full five minutes then turned to Joan and said, "You should be aware of this!"

"Aware of what?" Joan asked.

"We're flying on VFR, but we have no 'V'. The haze is getting thicker by the minute, and I can't see more than a hundred feet outside the window. I don't want to be an alarmist, and I'm sure everything is okay, but I do sincerely hope the traffic in this corridor is very, very light."

"My God! It's impossible to see anything. Shouldn't we be turning back? Or doing something? This is really unnerving!"

I started to reply, but the air was forced from my lungs as the plane took a sickening dive. The oxygen masks dropped from the overhead and people whose seat belts weren't fastened took an immediate surge toward the top of the aircraft. Joan and I both had our seatbelts fastened, but she seized my arm with a death grip and I could see the blood drain from her face. Throughout the plane, women were screaming and men were swearing.

After a drop of what must have been at least five thousand feet, the plane stabilized and the passengers were able to recover some equilibrium.

We flew relatively flat for almost a minute before the pilot came on the intercom. "I'm truly sorry about that, ladies and gentlemen, but our cockpit collision alarm system sounded, and we had no time to waste. We were in the immediate vicinity of another aircraft which we were unable to see. We're safe now and will be flying at this altitude until we have visual sighting of New York's LaGuardia Airport. By our reckoning, that should be within the next ten minutes. We were taken by surprise by this heavy haze, which was not forecast when we left Washington. We're now at ten thousand feet, and we believe the haze does not extend below eight thousand feet. In the next five minutes, we'll descend to eight thousand feet, where we expect to get a visual sighting of New York. We will keep you informed."

I could sense the aircraft descending and could only hope the instruments in the cockpit were not somehow damaged by the same e-bomb which I was now totally convinced had damaged the air traffic control system. Only later would I learn that our near disaster had been the result of a test by a cell in Paris, codenamed 'Broken Spark'. I continued to look out the window, and I could sense that Joan was looking across me and out the window as well. Five minutes seemed to drag, and I knew we must have descended below eight thousand feet, but I could still not see anything beyond a hundred feet. Another five minutes passed, and I could only guess at how much altitude we had lost. The pilot wasn't saying anything, and the tension in the cabin was palpable.

The strain was about to approach breaking point, with the oxygen masks dangling from the overhead, and the smell of overused air sickness bags wafting through the cabin, when I saw the first break in the dense haze and could make out Lower Manhattan, which looked like it was no more than three thousand feet below us. A cheer went through the cabin as other passengers, who were also keeping a close eye on the weather outside, realized the pilots would be able to 'see' us into LaGuardia. I turned to Joan and patted her, paternalistically, on her thigh. She grabbed my hand and squeezed it hard as she stared wordlessly into my eyes. Her mouth opened as she attempted to speak, but no words came.

"That was a little more dramatic than I like to experience," I said.

Joan only nodded and squeezed my hand even tighter, but she was still unable to speak. I shifted in my seat so that I could take her other hand, and we sat that way as the plane made a 180° turn and landed toward the south. As soon as the wheels touched the landing strip, the pilot reversed thrust and gently applied the brakes. We rolled to a stop before exiting the landing strip and a cheer rolled through the cabin. Applause broke out. It was a spontaneous release of tension and a recognition of how close we had come to a disaster in the air.

We left the Delta concourse and walked out of the terminal. Joan was just recovering her ability to speak, and I was scarcely better. We stood still, hand in hand, at the taxi stand, gathering strength from one another. We got into the taxi and gave the driver Goldman Sachs' address at one New York Plaza. Joan suggested we take I-278 south to the Brooklyn Bridge and cross into Lower Manhattan from there. The taxi driver, who had a dark South Asian complexion, nodded in agreement. However, as we left LaGuardia, it quickly became apparent that he had his own preferred route which led to the Queensboro Bridge and the FDR drive down to Lower Manhattan. Joan tried to suggest to him that I-278 to the Brooklyn Bridge would be a better route, but he switched to Urdu and effectively terminated communication. By the time we had reached the Queensboro Bridge, our anxiety had risen to a fever pitch. When another taxi cut in front of him, the driver went into an absolute rage, waving his arms and expostulating in Urdu. Joan and I looked at one another and held our tongues as we double-checked our seatbelts.

We arrived at one New York Plaza in one piece but seriously frazzled. I paid the cab fare without comment as we exited and stood on solid ground, looking at each other. I opened my arms and Joan moved into my chest in a dramatic expression of relief. We stood that way for a full thirty seconds, not saying a word. Between the plane ride and the taxi ride, our tolerance was stretched to the limit. Our embrace was filial, not sexual, but with our bodies pressed together we found calm and strength in one another.

"What time is it?" I asked.

"It's preciscly twelve o'clock. We agreed to have lunch on the private dining floor, and it will just take us minutes to get there, so we're in good shape."

"Well, that may describe you, but I'm just holding on. I don't feel like I'm in good shape at all."

Joan laughed, a giggly, nervous type of laugh, and said, "I'm no better! I was referring to the time."

"I know!"

We entered the glass doors of the Goldman Sachs headquarters and found an elevator to take us to the private dining floor. When we left the elevator, a young man in a pinstriped suit was there to greet us.

"Andre," Joan said. "How nice of you to meet us. We've had an interesting trip from Washington. I want you to meet Anderson Wyeth." We exchanged formalities, and Andre led us into a private dining room just off the main area. We ordered before opening the main subject.

Joan began the discussion. "I asked for the luncheon because Anderson has a very strong interest in the rumor you and I talked about when we were last together at a luncheon here."

"How interesting that you should remember that discussion," Andre said. "I think I presented it to you almost as a farce, and that's what I believed it to be. However, since we talked, there have been further developments. Mr. Wyeth, who do you represent and what's your interest in this rumor?"

"I work for a private contractor to the US government who consults at the highest level on matters of national security. Joan can vouch for my employer. If you wish any further verification, I'll be happy to supply it."

"No, no! If Joan can vouch for you, I have no concerns. I'm just a little jumpy because this is so far out of my normal orbit. I'm a trader. My life involves buying and selling securities on behalf of clients. I have no reason to get involved in politics, especially international politics of this variety. It's really kind of spooky. Something I'm not equipped for."

"You mentioned new developments, Andre. What kind of developments?" I asked.

"After I mentioned the rumor to Joan, the rumor was discussed by a number of traders. You know, traders are on the phone all the time, and a new idea, a new joke or a new rumor is grist for their mill, but everything about the rumor died down and the chatter turned back to jokes and economics, which are sometimes the same thing. But then, out of the blue, a trader I know very well called me and asked if we could visit over a cocktail after work. He's South Asian by extraction, an Indian who was born in this country and was educated here. His parents are from Bangalore, and it was extremely difficult for them to leave India and resettle here. You know how important family relationships are there.

"Anyway, Sanjay Singh, 'Sanj', has an excellent education, physics, I think, always at the top of his class, etc. I said sure. So when we had a cocktail, and after some light chitchat about some trades, he sprang this rumor on me. He asked me if I'd heard it, and of course I said I had. He tried to probe me on any further details, but I didn't have any. I simply said all I know is that it was brought up to me in several phone calls by several different traders, and the gist of the rumor was that some foreign entity, person, government, movement, I don't know which, had developed something like an electron bomb that could take out all of our computers and all of the telephone switching mechanisms with an electromagnetic charge. I'm probably describing this badly, but I studied finance, not physics. Anyway, my friend was intensely interested in the rumor, and who was spreading it. He asked for the names of the traders I'd talked to, but I could only remember several. I didn't see any harm in giving him their names, so I did.

"Then, he started talking, and the way he talked was unlike any chatter I've had with traders. He talked about electromagnetic pulse technology with such familiarity that you'd think he knew physics better than he knew finance, which is pretty awesome. Maybe he does. Anyway, since I obviously didn't know much about electromagnetic pulse technology, he started from the beginning, or rather the elementary level.

"He told me that the US exploded hydrogen bombs high above the Pacific Ocean in the late fifties and that these detonations released enormous bursts of some kind of rays that, when they hit oxygen and nitrogen in the atmosphere, released huge quantities of electrons that spread for hundreds of miles, destroying streetlights and disrupting radio navigation systems. He said, and I found it pretty difficult to follow here, small electromagnetic pulse devices could be constructed to have a similar effect, but even more devastating if somehow they were placed in close proximity to computers or other electronic devices such as telephone switching systems.

"I scoffed at that and said I didn't know what he'd been smoking, but this seemed pretty far out to me. That's when he really scared me! 'What if I told you, Andre,' he said, 'that the chief Indian intelligence agency, the RAW, the Research and Analysis Wing of Indian intelligence, had discovered evidence that the Pakistani intelligence services had prepared an operation directed against the Indian 'Silicone Valley', in and around Bangalore, contemplating the use of exactly such a device or devices to destroy or render unreliable the extensive use of computers and computer networks used for research there?'

"I was flabbergasted! I asked how he'd know about something like that? 'I was there!' he said. Apparently, according to Sanj, the operation was uncovered before it had a chance to do its damage, but two Indian intelligence officers and one Pakistani were killed, and four other Pakistani intelligence officers were taken into custody. He told me that the Pakistanis had a very sophisticated knowledge of physics, gained not only in their own universities, but also by studying abroad in Britain and the United States.

"They were jealous and suspicious of Indian advances in technology and wanted to damage or cripple those advances, he told me. I asked why he'd be involved in an Indian intelligence operation. 'I didn't say I was involved,' he said, 'I said I was there and that's probably enough about my interest in that operation,' he said. He said he only mentioned it to convince me of the seriousness of the rumor. Well, believe me, I was convinced. I am convinced. I'm glad you contacted me because I didn't know where to go. I thought about going to the FBI, but I didn't know what to tell them about Sanj. I don't want to get him in trouble. I really don't know what his role is, but he's certainly more than a floor trader."

"It's a fascinating development, Andre," I said. "There's certainly nothing wrong with going to the FBI. The information that Sanj gave you, if nothing else, adds credibility to the information that's come your way in the form of a rumor. I will certainly leave it up to you to decide whether to go to the FBI. With your help, I would like to pursue it myself because this is an area in which my employer, who regularly consults with the ANSA, the national security advisor, and I, have a very strong interest. Just so you know, we've obtained information from another source that corroborates the rumor you heard. Would you help me by arranging a meeting with Mr. Singh, maybe after working hours for a cocktail nearby? You'd be welcome to join us if you have an interest."

"I don't have a particular interest in meeting with the two of you, but I do want to know how this thing is developing. Obviously, whatever happens on the floor has implications for the way I make my living."

"I'll certainly tell you what I can," I said. "But what I can't do is tell you information, the disclosure of which might compromise another source of the information. That's as true of Mr. Singh's sources as well as my own."

"I understand," he said.

During the conversation, Joan had remained quiet, but followed it with intense interest. Finally, she said, "What you're suggesting, both of you, is the possibility of an event which if successful would freeze up the credit markets worse than they were frozen in 2007 and 2008. Such an event would be intolerable for the major credit institutions of this country; commercial banks, investment banks, and fixed income investors. We're only now just beginning to recover from the last crisis. Surely it can be stopped!"

"There's no disagreement there," I said. "The question is how. It always is. What we must do is find out the how, plus the who, what, when and where. I think we know the why. Their motivation is to cause the greatest damage to Western financial markets and therefore to Western economies and Western culture. We have one indication they intend to strike the New York Stock Exchange. We can't be so naïve as to believe that that's the only target they have. Remember, it takes less than two thousand dollars each to construct these e-bombs, and they have an unlimited numbers of fanatics who are ready and willing to sacrifice their lives in order to explode bombs at the most opportune time, from their point of view.

"We must assume there are additional targets that have already been selected and that preparations are underway to strike them. We also must assume that we don't have very much time. The rumor surfaced here in New York. Rumors generally don't surface if they relate to something that's months in the future. I'm thinking we only have days, or possibly weeks, before they make their first attempt."

Andre had been staring intently at me, hanging on my every word. He shook himself and came alert. "Let me call Sanj right now." He pulled his cell phone out of his pocket and dialed.

"Hello, Sanj, this is Andre. You know that rumor we were talking about the other night, the one about the electromagnetic pulse device. I'm talking right now with somebody from Washington. No, he's not with the government, but the firm he's with consults with the national security adviser, so it's very high-level communication. He seems to know almost as much as you do about the e-bombs, and he's intensely interested in our rumor. He'd like to meet with you, tonight, if possible. Yes. Yes. Yes, okay. I'll tell him. Yes, I might join you. I do want to stay informed as things develop, if they do. Okay, thanks, Sanj."

Andre hung up and without saying anything redialed his phone. "Yes, I'd like to make a reservation for four for this evening, any time you have available. Great! The name is Andre. Thanks, okay, bye. What luck, we got into Delmonico's at 5:30. That's a little early, but it's the only time they have available. It's just around the corner on Beaver Street."

"I'd like to join you, if you don't mind. I don't often get to have dinner at Delmonico's. Given the subject matter, and the opportunity to eat at Delmonico's, I'm not going to miss the opportunity," Joan said.

"Excellent!" I said. I turned to Joan and said, "I know you have meetings this afternoon, so I'll find a way to use my time productively, and I'll meet you at Delmonico's at 5:30 unless you finish what you have to do and want to go back to Washington."

"I wouldn't miss this for the world! Not only do the firms I represent have a stake in this, but I'm intensely interested personally. It isn't often I have an opportunity to meet a representative from Indian intelligence and discuss electromagnetic pulse technology. What's not to like?" I wasn't sure whether she was laughing at me or not, but we were soon to find out it wasn't going to be a laughing matter.

"I'm not sure when the last shuttle flight goes back to Washington, but I'm quite sure Amtrak runs trains late into the night. We, or I, can catch one of those trains after dinner. That is if you decide you're going to stay in New York," I said.

We finished our lunch; Andre went back to the trading floor, Joan went to her meeting on the twelfth floor, and I went to the street. As soon as I went outside, I made a fateful decision. I called Frank and told him I was having dinner at Delmonico's.

I didn't know for sure what I was going to do for the next four hours, but I wasn't worried. Any place in Lower Manhattan was fine with me, even though it was a chilly March day. I could always take the ferry to Staten Island, something I hadn't done since being in New

York as a young man, or take a tour to the Statue of Liberty. I opted for the ferry. I walked down Broad Street to Water Street and on down to the Staten Island Ferry Terminal. It would be a good opportunity to see whether anyone was trying to tail me.

The Staten Island Ferry is the greatest value in the world. When the ferry gets on the bay, you have the most spectacular view of the downtown skyline, the Statue of Liberty, Ellis Island, and the Hudson and East Rivers. It was a gorgeous day in New York, with blue skies and only intermittent clouds. I was prepared for the chill with a trench coat over my suit. The twenty-five-minute ride on the open deck was spectacular, and when I got to the Staten Island terminal, I immediately went to the dock for the ferry back to Manhattan. I looked around, but I saw nothing unusual or threatening. Another twenty-five minutes and I was back on Manhattan. It was almost four o'clock.

CHAPTER TWELVE

***

PARIS

It was a chilly March morning in Montmartre. The safe house wasn't heated because the current occupants didn't want to go to the Gaz de France office to start the gas flowing and heighten the risk of being identified. They had paid for two months water and electricity in advance because they were told that both might be needed in the process of assembling the devices.

Salman and Ahmed were dressed in heavy coats and stocking caps to ward off the cold. They rubbed their hands and pushed them into their pockets to keep warm. They were expecting Taufig and Ibrahim sometime before noon. Taufig was flying to London Heathrow from Casablanca, and then on to Paris. They were fairly certain of his arrival that morning. They didn't know Ibrahim, but were assured they didn't have to worry about him, as he was well able to take care of himself. He would be in charge of security.

There was a knock at the door. Both men sprang up, but Salman said, "Ahmed, my brother, don't repeat the greeting you gave me. Remember that Taufig is of a gentle temperament and the shock might be too much. Given Ibrahim's responsibility for security, we may not want to startle him."

"All right!" Ahmed said, but it was obvious he was disappointed. He was in charge of operations. His job was to make the bombs and to make them work, and he was really good at it. He had a cheerful disposition, and it was clear that life for Ahmed was a dinner and practical jokes were his entrée. He slid his hand under his tunic and gently grasped the handle of the 9mm Glock, but left it in place. The two men moved quietly toward the front door through the same dimly lit corridor Salmon had passed not long before. Salman stood on the back side of the door while Ahmed grasped the handle and opened the door a fraction of an inch, peering out.

"Taufig, my brother," he roared. "We have been expecting you." He jerked open the door, grabbed Taufig by the arm and dragged him into the corridor. Taufig was only a little less startled than he would have been if Ahmed had swung the knife in the same way he had greeted Salman. With that, the three young Muslims made their way through the dark corridor and into the room where the stark table with a laptop and a yellow pad stood.

The three men had been to university together in Islamabad, Salman as an exchange student from North America, and the other two had studied graduate-level physics in the US and one in England. They knew each other well. They had been recruited by the ISI and had many assignments behind them, all in the field, but this would be their first operation on the same team. Taufig's slight nervousness offset Ahmed's ebullience, and Salman's calm gave him a remote and detached air.

"What are our targets, Taufig?" asked Ahmed. Seated on one of the cheap table chairs, Ahmed leaned forward with an air of expectancy, much as he had shown with Salman. After being disappointed that Salman hadn't divulged solid information, he thought Taufig was the messenger, although that would be a little surprising given Taufig's temperament.

Taufig was taken aback, as if no one would entrust him with such a responsibility. "I don't know, but I assume they will be here in France or in Morocco. It's strange that you ask that, since I recently received a very unusual phone call which also raised the question about the goals of the Moroccans I trained. It would seem odd that their purpose would be changed at this late date. I can only guess that the reason I recruited and trained the Moroccans would be for an operation in a French-speaking country. They are ready to die with the explosives we will give them."

Ahmed settled back, clearly disappointed with Taufig's answer. "It's curious Taufig. I've been assembling the explosives, and they seem to me to be rather weak, not like explosives I've assembled before. I'm not even sure they have enough force to destroy whatever our targets are."

At this, Salman sharply turned his head toward Ahmed. "I thought you said three of them were assembled, save the timers, which Shahid would bring."

"They are, but they are of a very different design. I think I'm still missing part of the concept. There is an explosive, which is set in a copper coil—" he was interrupted by a knock on the door.

Ahmed opened the door, prepared to give a warm and generous welcome to Ibrahim, but when the figure emerged from the light behind it, Ahmed gave a sharp intake of breath, almost aghast, for the gaunt shape that stood before him could have been Satan himself. Cloaked in a black robe, with a black keffiyeh, the man's face was totally hidden until he reached the large room. In the still dim light, his eyes were so intense they seem to add light to the room, but only where he focused them, which at the moment was on Taufig, who shrank and felt a tremble he failed to conceal.

"Ibrahim, meet Taufig. He has trained—"

"I know what he has done, and I also know he has committed serious security breaches which endanger our operation. From this moment on, he is to be in the company of one of us in this room at all times until I say otherwise. Furthermore, your own security procedures are seriously lacking. You open the door for me as if I were the only possible person who could be coming to the door at this time. What if I'd been from the Surete, the French police?"

"But, but there was no reason to, to…" Ahmed tried to say.

But he again was cut off by Ibrahim. "If you don't want to end up in a French prison, you had better think like the French and believe at all times that there has been an information leak somewhere, and that your very lives are in danger. I am here to make sure that doesn't happen if it is within my control. Now, who are we missing? We are missing Shahid, are we not?"

Ahmed, barely recovering from the viciousness of Ibrahim's attack, said, "Yes, other than Shahid, we are all here. We have not begun our discussions. I have begun to assemble several of the bombs, but information is missing and some of the parts for the bombs are missing."

"I don't think anything is missing. You are attempting to assemble parts which if complete would make a conventional explosive. However, the operation we are about to undertake will be completely different from anything you have ever done before. The detonation of a conventional explosive, if done properly, will kill ten, twenty, possibly thirty people, most of whom will be civilians that have no part in the struggle we are engaged in. If we are lucky, we may get one or two leaders of the opposition. The impact of the explosives we are going to build, distribute and detonate will be far, far broader and destructive to the economies and the morale of our enemies. It will make them easier to kill." And with that, Ibrahim stopped talking and an evil smile, a rictus even, seized his face.

Ibrahim sat down at the table and was joined by Salman, who displayed the least amount of concern or fear of Ibrahim. Taufig remained standing, almost cowering, near the door, his nervousness apparent with every move he made. Ahmed's naturally sunny disposition, damaged by Ibrahim's sharp attack, was replaced with a scowl and silence.

"What time is Shahid due to arrive?" Ibrahim asked. No one answered, whether because they didn't know or because they simply didn't feel cooperative toward Ibrahim. Ibrahim appeared to be comfortable with silence and settled in for the wait. The others didn't speak and accepted the silence as a part of being around Ibrahim.

The silence went on for an hour until finally there was a knock at the front door.

Ahmed turned to look at Ibrahim but did not move toward the door. Ibrahim got up from the table, said, "Wait for my knock, three quick and two slow, before you open the door!" and went back through the kitchen to a backdoor. He slipped silently out and sped down the alleyway to the street and around to the front of the row houses so he could see the front door of the safe house. Determining that it was Shahid standing there, he sauntered up to the door, taking care to remain at Shahid's back.

"Allahu Akbar!" he said.

Shahid turned around slowly and wearily and replied, "Allahu Akbar!"

He made no move to embrace Ibrahim, knowing that no bond of friendship existed or would ever exist between the two. Ibrahim knocked three times quickly, followed by two knocks separated by a pause.

Salman opened the door. "Hello, Shahid, my brother. We've been expecting you. Please enter."

The three conspirators went down the dimly lit corridor to the large room. Shahid greeted the other two warmly and sat at the table with the air of a man who had endured much just to get there.

Ahmed was the first to speak. "What news do you bring, my brother? I have started to assemble bombs, but I'm missing something, and I don't mean materials. There's something about the concept that isn't right. What I'm assembling wouldn't blow up a newsstand. I assume you brought the timers, but even with the timers we won't be able to do enough damage to justify the time we've spent in planning and preparing."

"You're right of course, Ahmed. I'm sorry to have deceived you, but I thought it best if you had something to occupy your time rather than sitting here waiting and wondering. I do have the parts, the timers and other materials for the assembly of the bombs. The copper wire can be procured here in Paris. Salman has the plans, don't you, Salman?"

"Yes, I do. They are safely packed in my carry-on. I'll get them when we're ready to move forward, but before we do, what information do you have for us relating to the targets and the date and time?"

"The targets remain problematic at this point. We were told to target financial markets in Western European countries and in the United States. It was thought, rightly, that disruptions of data communications in the central computer systems serving the financial markets in primary financial centers would disrupt Western economies, deflect their interest in campaigns against our Muslim brothers and injure the morale of Western countries' populations. As you have witnessed, all of that has been taken care of for us by the collapse of Western financial markets by their own internal contradictions.

"What has arisen, and I must say this very confidentially, is a serious debate within the higher levels of our government relative to a possible first strike, nuclear strike, against our historic enemy, India. It's no surprise to any of us here, although Ibrahim is Egyptian by birth, that Pakistan's nuclear arsenal is static in the face of an enormous buildup by Indian offensive capability and defensive capability for nuclear warfare. At one time it was sufficient to have the capacity for a nuclear first strike. The assumption was that the objective of that first strike would be to severely damage, politically, militarily and economically, the enemy. Now it's not so clear. We know that with India's defensive weapons capability, much of which they have acquired from the Israelis, India could very well survive a first strike and be able to launch a devastating retaliatory strike. The longer we delay, the more likely this is to happen. In November of last year, India successfully tested the Shaurya, a medium-range surface-to-surface missile which can be mounted on a highly mobile platform and has a range of 640 km. It has a payload capacity of approximately one ton of conventional weapons, but one would have to assume that the payload could be changed to a nuclear device. It could easily deliver its payload directly into Islamabad from Amritsar. This does not count their arsenal of missiles having a range of four to six thousand miles, as well as some that could be launched from submarines.

"There is an intense debate at the highest levels of our government as to whether we should strike now while our nuclear capability still has some maximum force versus waiting until India's defensive capability could very well neutralize our first strike advantage. These are very difficult decisions with no easy answers. I personally believe in an immediate first strike. Waiting will gain us nothing! We aren't likely to become friends with the Indians, and they aren't likely, with their far greater economic resources, to desist from further strengthening their defensive capability.

"So, we are in a temporary holding period. It shouldn't last long, for either we will go forward or not. If the decision is made to go forward, we have a new and difficult challenge, but it's one which is in the highest interest of the Pakistani state. Our mission, should a first strike be decided, will be to disrupt communications at Indian launch sites, such as Sriharikota and Balasore in Orissa Province. These launch sites will be heavily guarded, and it must be expected that we will remain on the ground for one to two weeks before activating the devices. We do have some logistical support in India, and that will be communicated to us when the time is right. In the meantime, we will, Ahmed, finish assembling the devices so that we will be ready, and we will do a test of the CFG on air traffic control here in Europe. We have already done a test in the United States against FAA facilities, and, although we used a small device, the effects were dramatic. Once we receive our instructions, we will move out in ones and twos to our targets.

"The weapon we will use, chosen by the wisdom of our superiors, is what is called an electromagnetic pulse bomb. The potential for this bomb is enormous, for it can destroy the confidence of those immediately affected in the reliability of the functioning of their computer systems. Ibrahim, or Salman, do you have anything to add?" Shahid stopped speaking. He appeared to be exhausted.

"Perhaps I can add my humble information to our brother Shahid's news," Salman offered. "I have indeed been able to procure the plans for electromagnetic pulse bombs from the Internet. I was requested to do so by our superiors in Islamabad, and I was directed by them to keep such information secret until Shahid arrived. Electromagnetic pulse technology, as Ahmed knows, is a phenomenon of physics. The Americans discovered the impact of the electromagnetic pulse way back in 1958 during the early testing of high-altitude airburst nuclear weapons. The electromagnetic pulse is in effect an electromagnetic shockwave. This pulse of energy produces a powerful electromagnetic field, particularly within the vicinity of the weapon burst. The field can be sufficiently strong to produce short-lived transient voltages of thousands of volts on exposed electrical conductors, such as wires, or conductive tracks on printed circuit boards. Commercial computer equipment is particularly vulnerable to electromagnetic pulse effects. What's significant is that very little energy is required to permanently wound or destroy computer equipment. Anything in excess of tens of volts can produce an effect termed gate breakdown which effectively destroys the device.

"What can that have to do with us, you ask? We don't have a thermonuclear weapon. We cannot explode it in high altitude. Yes, that's true, my brothers. However, there is an interesting device, which is called a flux compression generator, which Shahid mentioned. This device can be constructed with readily available materials for less than two thousand dollars and can reliably produce an electromagnetic pulse capable of destroying, or rendering inoperable, computers and other electronic devices necessary for the operation of the launch sequence of missiles. It is this device for which I have the plans. It is this device for which Shahid has the materials. It is this device which we will use to destroy the reliable functioning of military defense systems and the morale of the enemies of Pakistan."

"Salman, is this the device you were referring to when you said that it was something we'd studied in our beginning physics courses? I thought you were referring to the bombs I was trying to assemble. I do remember reading something about generating an electromagnetic pulse, the so-called Compton effect I think it was called, but I've never seen it work. Can we actually build them? How can we be sure it works? How close to the computers do we need to be when we explode the devices? What kinds of risks are we taking? Of course, I'm talking about risks of failure, not about risks to our lives."

"Ahmed, the flux compression generator is actually rather simple to construct. It is an explosive-packed tube placed inside a slightly larger copper coil. It's detonated by a chemical explosive. Immediately before the explosive charge detonates, the coil is energized by a bank of capacitors, creating a magnetic field. The explosive charge detonates from the rear forward. The tube flares outward, and as it does so, it touches the edge of the coil, creating a moving short circuit. The short circuit has the effect of compressing the magnetic field while reducing the inductance of the coil. The result is that flux compression generators will produce a ramping current pulse which breaks before the final disintegration of the device. Ramp times of tens of hundreds of microseconds and currents of tens of millions of amps have been observed. The pulse that results makes a lightning bolt look like a flashbulb by comparison.

"So, yes, we can make them. You asked how close we need to be to the computers when we explode the devices. There's what is known as the 'late-time EMP effect'. It occurs in the fifteen minutes after detonation. The EMP that surges through electrical systems creates localized magnetic fields. When these magnetic fields collapse, they cause electric surges to travel through the power and telecommunication infrastructure. This means we do not have to place our bombs directly on our targets. Telephone switching centers and electronic funds transfer exchanges can be attacked through their electric and telecommunications connections.

"You asked whether they will work. All of you understand English. I'm going to read you a report from an *Associated Press* article that appeared in yesterday's *International Herald Tribune*, which I purchased at the airport. 'An electronic communication failure Tuesday at a Federal Aviation Administration facility that processes flight plans for the eastern half of the United States caused massive delays around the country. The Northeast was hardest hit. At one point, an FAA website that tracks airport status showed delays at about three-dozen major airports across the country. An FAA spokesperson said there was a failure in a communications link that transmits the data to a similar facility elsewhere in the country. She also said there was an unrelated hardware problem at another FAA facility about a week ago which delayed the departure of at least 134 flights.'"

Salman paused for effect. "Both of those hardware and software failures, my brothers, were the result of two tests of very small devices which we built in the United States for test purposes. Another, larger one, is scheduled to be detonated tomorrow morning. It will be, as the others were, wired into, or simply plugged into, electrical outlets in the bathrooms of FAA facilities and the timer will be set to explode well after our Muslim brother has had time to leave the facility. Yes! They will work."

There was silence in the room. Finally, Taufig spoke quietly. "I am impressed, Salman, by the potential of the CFG's. I know enough physics to know how vulnerable computer and other communications networks are to being damaged by an electromagnetic impulse. And I am impressed by the methodology of coupling the electromagnetic charge into such networks.

"However, I am most excited about the possibility of an effort to cripple a second launch capability by the Indians in the event our leaders should decide to launch a first strike. That is the mission to which I am willing to commit my skills, my resources, and, yes, my life, for the benefit of our Islamic peoples against the infidels running India. Shahid has correctly identified the reasons why this must be done now. In addition, I would add that the administration in Washington has yet to catch its breath and focus its foreign and defense policy. They continue to wrestle with the severity of the downturn in their economy. Their reaction time at this point would most likely be slow, which is another reason why the decision should be made now.

"I am not opposed to using our resources in the great battle of Islam against the West. However, the internal decay and weakness of the West has now been manifested, and chaos in India would contribute further to that decline and be a manifestation of it."

It took great effort for Taufig to assert himself, and beads of perspiration developed on his smooth brow. He avoided looking at Ibrahim while speaking and glanced furtively at Salman before fixing his gaze on Shahid, whose eyes were directed toward the floor.

Finally, Shahid looked up and locked his eyes on Taufig before speaking. "Whatever the outcome of the discussions in Islamabad, being a part of Islam's struggle is an important part of our purpose in—"

He was interrupted by Ibrahim, who stood leaning against one of the walls cleaning his fingernails with a stiletto, his face bent forward, mostly covered by his keffiyeh. "It has been decided that our efforts are to be merged into the great struggle with the West. There was an individual in Islamabad who disagreed with that decision. He was in a position of high authority in the ISI. He and I disagreed personally. You will note that I refer to him in the past tense. There is only one mission, and one mission alone. Those who disagree with that mission are simply excess baggage."

With that, he looked directly at Shahid, who returned his stare with all the intensity he could muster, which wasn't much. Ibrahim finally broke the stare and turned to look at Salman, who gave a slight shrug. Ahmed looked in turn at Taufig and Shahid at Ibrahim and Salman.

Salman stood quietly, looking from one member of the cell to the next. Something needed to be done to focus the energies of the cell members on a specific doable task, one that would galvanize their activities in a common cause. Without it, the cell could very well disintegrate through centripetal forces.

He felt his cell phone vibrate in his pocket and stepped into the entry room to answer it. It was a woman's voice and she spoke without formality.

"Wyeth is to be at a dinner in New York on Thursday night at a place called Delmonico's. He's meeting with an Indian spy. I think you know what that means. You must not fail again."

"I understand that very well. Goodbye." He reached into his pocket for another prepaid cell phone and entered the number he had called from O'Hare. The call was answered immediately with a simple 'Yes'.

"Our target is to be in New York on Thursday night at Delmonico's. It's a restaurant. Do you know it?"

"Yes, I do. I know where it is, but I haven't eaten there. It is a little rich for me."

"Do not fail this time! Do you understand?"

"I will not fail!" The connection was broken and Salman returned to the main room. The other members of the cell looked at him expectantly, but Salman revealed nothing and said nothing.

CHAPTER THIRTEEN
***
DELMONICO'S

I walked back up Water Street to Broad and then up Beach Street to number 56. I entered Delmonico's through the original Pompeian columns and the opulent portico. Delmonico's has been in business since 1827, then as a pastry shop and then in 1930 it was listed as a restaurant. The expensive wood paneling on the walls, however, could be no more than a few years old. The rich dark woods of the tables and chairs and booths reflected the recent half-decade of prosperity in the markets. Delmonico's could only exist in a city where its principal patrons were making lots of money. I went into the bar and took one of the high chairs, facing the mirror behind the bar. I ordered a drink, watching the people coming into the bar and restaurant from their various duties in the financial district.

They came in ones and twos, the guys generally coming straight to the bar, and the ladies taking a table in the bar lounge. The market must have been down because as the guys walked up to the bar, they loosened their neckties and affected a resigned air. As I sat at the bar I had one of those sixth-sense feelings, the kind when you know something is wrong, but you don't know exactly what it is. I sensed a pair of eyes boring into the back of my head and did a quick one-eighty, pivoting with my right foot on the step rail of the bar. I caught one guy quickly shifting his eyes away from me, and I thought he looked familiar. He was big, so big he was bursting out of his suit. Was this one of the guys who broke into my townhouse in Alexandria? Or was I just jumpy from the intensity of the last week?

Andre came in with a tall slender man of South Asian extraction. When Andre saw me, he acknowledged me with a slight wave of his hand and walked over. He introduced me to Sanjay Singh, who was very cordial, though quite reserved. I asked him where he was from, and he said he was born in New York City but had close ties to India. His family was from Bangalore. His father taught physics at Columbia University. As new immigrants to New York City, his mother and father were homesick and went back to India as often as they could, so he felt a close kinship to Bangalore, as if it were a second hometown. He said he went to CCNY for his bachelor's then to Columbia for a master's in physics. At graduation, he was hired to develop mathematical trading models at Goldman Sachs, which he did for several years, but he wanted the excitement of the trading floor and so transferred to trading.

"And you, Mr. Wyeth? Where are you from and what do you do?"

I told him I was born in a Midwest city and had grown up in rather unremarkable circumstances. I told him my father was a senior executive with the eighth largest bank in the country, with a major presence in the city where I grew up. I explained I went to a public university, then to Johns Hopkins, SAIS, and on to the Wharton School of Finance at the University of Pennsylvania.

At that moment, Joan arrived and was introduced to Sanjay. Andre signaled the waiter, and we were escorted to our table. We ordered drinks and our entrées before resuming our conversation. "Mr. Singh, I'm fascinated by Bangalore, but I know very little about it, except that it's known as the 'Silicon Valley' of India. Could you tell us a little about it please?" I forced a quick glance again at the bar and the big guy was still there, trying to fit in but looking like a bull in a china shop.

"Of course, Mr. Wyeth. You are correct, it is known as the 'Silicon Valley' of India due to the presence of extensive investment in research in the hardware and software industries. It was at one time known as the 'Pensioners Paradise' in India because of its salubrious climate, located at about three thousand feet. Nehru decided that it should become the intellectual capital of the country, and in many respects it has become that. It is also one of the wealthier Indian cities, with much of the population engaged in information technology research and biotechnology research industries. It is also the home of ISRO, the Indian space research organization, which employs almost twenty thousand people. It's the headquarters of the Indian

Astrophysics Institute, which grants graduate and doctoral degrees as well as funding research. And it's the home of three universities."

"That's impressive," I said. "If you don't mind my mentioning it, Andre indicated that you might have some connection with Indian intelligence."

"I don't mind talking about it, Mr. Wyeth, because my links with Indian intelligence are intellectual more than institutional. Indian intelligence is naturally interested in the Bangalore area because of the level of research and the amount of infrastructure that is dedicated to high technology, in which India intends to advance and maintain its leadership position. You are doubtless aware that Pakistan has a well-established position in nuclear research and development and has a substantial higher education infrastructure in physics and mathematics as well.

"Unfortunately, Pakistan and India have a natural enmity which both countries can trace back literally hundreds of years to when the Muslim Mogul emperors dominated the existing Hindu culture in India. The separation of India and Pakistan in 1947, when the British left, only partially resolved the conflict between Muslims and Hindus. There was a massive resettlement of Muslims from India to Pakistan, and while there are very few Hindus in Pakistan, there remain many Muslims in India, and they are intertwined in the daily life of the country. It's hard to definitively separate the two cultures. It is perceived by some, inevitably perhaps, that the Muslims in India comprise something of a fifth column. India's government, and especially the RAW, is especially sensitive to the possibility of covert operations launched by Pakistan, one of whose objectives would be to damage the high-tech infrastructure in India, particularly in Bangalore.

"The tragedy in Mumbai late last year demonstrates India's vulnerability to terrorist attacks. One of the ways in which Pakistan could inflict immense damage would be to destroy or render inoperable a significant part of the high-tech infrastructure in Bangalore, or to disable communications facilities at the missile launch sites at Sriharikota and at Balasore. Because of my father's ties with India, and because of his expertise in physics, the Indian government does, from time to time, seek his counsel. I have been privileged to be a small part of those conversations.

"As you are aware, Mr. Wyeth, suicide bombers with conventional explosives can do a lot of damage. However, the damage, however terrifying, is limited in scope to a defined number of human beings or to a defined installation. It is the current thinking, I believe, in the Indian government that a device which would destroy or render unreliable the hardware and software so widely used in Bangalore and in the missile launch facilities would be a significant tactical victory for Pakistan in the struggle between the two countries, and conceivably could damage India's missile launch capability.

"I believe the Indian government perhaps has a better understanding of this threat than our American government. Of course it's obvious that in the long run, as India is even more able to manage its technological superiority and its vastly more significant resources, the struggle between Pakistan and India will become more of an irritation than a national threat. But, for the time being, it's an irritation they believe must be taken seriously.

"I'm speaking completely off the record, as I'm sure you will understand, since I have no official relationship whatsoever with the Indian government. Now that I have laid my cards on the table, may I ask you, Mr. Wyeth, what's your interest in the rumor which occupied the conversation between Ms. Singer-Taylor and our friend Andre?"

"Of course, Mr. Singh. I've spent all of my adult life in the service of the United States government, and the people of America. Most of that time has been dedicated to the US Foreign Service and to the protection of the national security interests of the United States. My current employer is a consultant to the national security advisor, whose current incumbent is Alex Woods. Our office has received information, completely independent of the rumor we are now discussing, which suggests that there are representatives of radical Islam, primarily from Pakistan we are told, planning a multifaceted attack on India and the West, targeting the financial markets and/or the missile launch facilities of both, primarily using EMP technology. Our information does not reference any focus on Bangalore, but such a target would be reasonable in the twisted logic of terrorists."

"Where did you get your information, Mr. Wyeth?" Sanjay burst out. "This is of critical importance to my...er...to friends of mine in India."

"I'm sorry, I cannot and will not jeopardize the source of my information until I know more about you, but I can tell you that this source is extremely reliable. I don't have the exact date of the attack, but we believe it to be planned for sometime in the next month or two."

"Mr. Wyeth, you must give me your source! It is a matter of the utmost importance! I can promise you absolute confidentiality, and even more importantly, the cooperation of very important elements of the Indian government in support of your efforts in India as well as cooperation in other countries where their targets might be."

During this exchange, Andre was watching us both with eyes wide and intense, his gaze shifting back and forth as the discussion shifted. Joan was quiet, her face concentrated as she focused on what she was hearing.

I decided neither of them should be put in danger by knowing more than they should, and I suggested to Sanjay that perhaps we should move to the bar and let them finish their meal. He was in agreement, and we rose to leave the table amid protests by Joan and Andre. I told Sanjay I would make a men's room stop and meet him at the end of the bar where the barflies were less dense.

Although it was evening, I knew Frank would be available by cell phone, so I called him. He answered on the first ring and I explained the situation. Basically, I wanted to know if I could trust Sanjay and if I could tell him what we knew about the information we had received from al-Tabari. He said, "Leave your cell phone on and I'll get back to you." I proceeded to the bar and found a chair next to Sanjay.

"Mr. Wyeth," he said. "Let's be clear. This may be one of many attacks directed against the West by Muslim fanatics from your perspective, and I understand that. But to my people, that is, the people of my parents and my ancestors, this is a life-and-death struggle between ancient suppressors of our spiritual origins and the Mogul emperors who ruled us. We expect no quarter, and we will give none. Every attack against us is personal to me. If you will not tell me who is planning this attack and when, I will find out from someone else. I don't intend to rest idly by while you wrestle with your conscience. Do I make myself clear?"

"Yes, you do, Sanjay," using his first name for the first time. "And, if I were in your position, I'd have the same frame of mind and do the same thing as you are threatening now. However, I am not, and I am not going to place my source in danger until I am comfortable that I will not betray him through you. Do I make *myself* clear?"

There was a deep silence while we stared at one another. I don't know how long we would have remained thus, but my cell phone rang, and I saw it was Frank.

I answered and Frank's gravelly voice said, "He's okay. He's well known to my friends in the RAW. He's very deep, so treat his cover with care and don't blow it. You can trust him and his information. We're on the same side, at least in this operation."

"Got it, Frank. Thanks!" I turned back to Sanjay and told him everything. I told him everything I knew about al-Tabari, and how we had worked together in Ramallah and Istanbul, and how I suspected he had attempted to save Layla in Las Vegas. I told him al-Tabari had moved to Casablanca and that he had, because of his erudition as an Islamic scholar, been able to establish relationships with a local cell and its trainer, a Pakistani named Taufig Hosain.

When I was done speaking, Sanjay stuck out his hand and said, "We are on the same side, Anderson. Where do we go from here? I've told you just about everything I know. There's a little more, and this may be important. We know the ISI in Pakistan very well. I think I can find out who's directing this operation, and who's responsible for carrying it out. I think that might be helpful for both of us.

"Perfect," I said. "First, you should know who my superior is. His name is Frank Pierce, and he operates out of Washington, D.C. in Foggy Bottom. Who do you report to?"

"I report to Sunil Dandekar, who's an assistant to India's ambassador to the UN. I will immediately communicate your name to him." He took out his Blackberry and punched in a text message.

I waited patiently and looked over at the table Sanjay and I had just vacated. Andre and Joan were in an animated conversation, and I looked back at Sanjay just in time to see his face disappear and his head become an empty cavity where his skull had been. Blood splattered against the top of the bar and on the tables behind. The bartender dropped to the floor and the other customers left their seats and ran screaming for the exits.

I was numb! I reached for Sanjay to keep him from falling to the floor, and his body slumped against mine. Blood ran down the front of my shirt and suit as I looked over my shoulder in the direction the shot had come from. Most of the restaurant's customers were on the floor, but a small group was crowding the exit door, and it was to them I looked. One guy caught my attention as he violently shoved people out of the way in order to open his exit path. Was it the same guy I had seen earlier? Was it me he was trying to kill, not Sanjay? Had I ducked my head when I turned to look at Joan and Andre?

There was nothing I could do for Sanjay, so I leapt from the chair and ran for the door. People crowding out slowed me down, but when they saw the blood on my front, they moved aside and gave me room. I burst out the door and looked left and right just in time to see the guy running down Broad Street. I ran after him, but traffic on the sidewalk and the street prevented me from catching up, so I slowed to a walk and turned back in the direction of Delmonico's.

By this time police and ambulance sirens were screaming all over Lower Manhattan. As I walked back into Delmonico's, the police were already taking statements from people who had been sitting close to Sanjay and me. Joan and Andre were still at their table, although they were standing, waiting until the police, inevitably, got to them.

I walked up to the police and told them who I was, which they confirmed by my ID. As I talked with the detective in charge, my eyes wandered to the place where Sanjay had been sitting and to the floor beneath his chair. The face of his Blackberry caught my eye, and I remembered that he had been texting his contact in the office of the Indian ambassador to the UN. Since the face of the Blackberry was still lit, either his message was still trying to get through or his contact was trying to text him back.

I decided maintaining his cover might be of more importance under the circumstances than blurting it out to the police. I moved carefully around the detective until I stood directly between him and the Blackberry. I casually lifted my foot and planted it squarely on the device, effectively concealing it. Because of my curious movement, the police detective looked at me quizzically but made no comment.

I told the police of my relationship with Sanjay, which was honest in its brevity. When I had satisfied them that it was my first meeting with Sanjay, the detective turned to other witnesses to verify the facts of the shooting. As he turned, I casually reached down to retrieve the Blackberry, slipped it into my pocket and walked to the table where Joan and Andre were still waiting. Their faces were colorless and their voices reflected their concern.

I assured them I was all right and the three of us stood uncomfortably waiting for the police to approach us. Joan insisted on taking me to the water fountain in front of the men's room. She took a handkerchief out of her purse and wetted it down. She then wiped the front of my suit and shirt, removing the blood as best as she could. The Blackberry was burning a hole in my pocket, but I resisted reaching for it until I could be alone. The police investigation was thorough, and they weren't satisfied, but there was little to go on and it was approaching midnight.

"I'm afraid we have a problem, Joan. I'm quite sure Amtrak doesn't run this late, and the last shuttle left hours ago."

"You're welcome to stay with me," Andre said. "Unfortunately, my apartment is only six hundred square feet, and I don't have anything that even resembles a guest bed, even less two."

"Thanks, Andre, but we should be able to find a hotel. My main concern is to get clean clothes. I don't know if this shirt and suit can ever be saved."

"I have a tailor in Chinatown," Andre offered. "I'll bet I can get him up, and with enough cash, maybe he can fix you up. It's worth a try." Andre turned his back and began paging through his contact list.

Joan and I looked at each other and shrugged our shoulders. "Any ideas where to start?" I asked.

"Let's start with the Marriott on the West Side Drive. I'll call."

While she was on her cell phone, Andre turned back, his eyes sparkling with his triumph. "What are your sizes, Anderson? My tailor can modify a suit he has on the rack, and he has a shirt and tie on the shelf, if they fit."

I gave him my sizes and he related them to his grumbling tailor.

"They'll be at your hotel at seven a.m. tomorrow, but it will cost you. What's your hotel?"

"That's okay, Andre, whatever it takes."

At that moment, Joan turned and said the Marriott had two rooms, and I relayed that information to Andre, who in turn confirmed it to his tailor.

I sagged with exhaustion. I felt like I was making some small progress in unwinding the objectives of this 'Broken Spark', but in the back of my mind, I knew the big picture was getting more diabolical and ominous.

CHAPTER FOURTEEN
***
DOWNTOWN MARRIOTT

Joan and I took a cab to the Marriott. Fortunately, I had hung up my trench coat at the restaurant and it was untouched by the blood covering my front, so I was able to pull it closed when we registered in the lobby, and although I looked a bit geeky, I at least didn't look like a serial killer readying myself for a long weekend in the city. I told the clerk to expect a delivery of a new suit in the morning and to put it on my bill. I put Joan's room on my card as well. "It's the least I can do to repay you for what's been an extraordinary evening."

She didn't object. We went to our rooms and I took a shower, letting the hot water run so long I thought I might exhaust the entire hotel supply. I put on the robe supplied by the hotel, sent my underwear to the hotel's special overnight service and settled down on the couch to reflect on the day. My mind was going at a hundred miles an hour, and there was no way I was going to sleep, at least for quite a while.

The phone rang, and it was Joan. "Anderson, do you want to go down to the bar for a drink? It's open for another forty-five minutes. I feel a need to talk."

"You forget, Joan, my suit and shirt are covered with blood, and I sent my underclothes to the laundry. I don't think they'd appreciate me in the bar in my robe."

"Oh! Right, Anderson. I wasn't thinking. I'll see you in the morning."

"Wait, Joan! I doubt I'll be able to sleep for at least another hour. Do you want to come over? The minibar seems to be well-stocked, but we can also order something if you like."

"Okay, I'd like that! Give me five minutes."

Ten minutes later, Joan was at my door in her hotel robe. As she passed me, I smelled the fresh shampoo from her dampened hair and I guessed, based on the way she clutched her robe, that she had sent her undergarments to the overnight laundry as well.

She took the single formal chair and sat primly in the center of it. I asked her what she would like to drink and she opted for a white wine. I already had a scotch.

"The weird thing, Anderson, is that I don't know what to feel. I didn't know Sanjay, so I guess it's just shock at seeing someone you've just met murdered in front of your eyes. On the other hand, I feel like I knew him because we share the same business connections. Is that weird? It must be shock!"

"I agree that shock is a big part of it, but why shock? I suspect there aren't many patrons of Delmonico's who feel the same as we do right now, so there's something more. Sanjay was a decent guy involved in an honorable mission for his ancestral homeland. We can identify with that. I suppose if he'd been a thug working for the mob, or dealing drugs, we wouldn't feel his brutal death as intimately. But whoever his assassin was, he was a savage—yes, savage is the right word. Uncivilized!"

"Have you considered, Anderson, that it might not have been Sanjay he meant to kill, but you? It seemed to me that you turned to look at Andre and I just as the shot was fired. Perhaps you threw off his aim just enough, or you moved out of his aim just enough for him to miss you and hit Sanjay."

"I wish you hadn't mentioned that, Erin, I'm sorry, Joan, because I've considered it. In fact, I've thought about it a lot. As you know, my interaction with Islam has been quite confrontational, and in some cases violent. In fact, it's involved conflict with the highest levels of the Iranian government and the Palestinian authorities, and their respective intelligence services. I do have enemies. Al-Tabari, you've heard me talk about him, is a decent human being, but his life is a dangerous game played for high stakes offered by three competing governments, the Iranian, the Israeli and the American. He saved Layla and me from the hands of fanatical conservative Muslim clergy, at the risk of his own life, when we were imprisoned in Ramallah. So I've made enemies, and they are not afraid to kill. When I returned to Washington just last week, I was attacked on the George Washington

Parkway on the way to Alexandria, then my condo was broken into and violent and insulting images of Layla were strategically placed in my office for maximum shock effect...."

"Could these incidents be related, Anderson? How exactly did Layla die?"

I had a sense that 'Joan' was reverting to her role as Erin, a psychologist. Her gentle questioning was less lawyerly than that of a counselor.

"She killed herself in Las Vegas to avoid killing innocent people. Her death was unnecessary, but she didn't know it...." I trailed off as memories crowded into my consciousness, battering my barely healed spirit with vivid images of Layla, all of my senses struggling to put her back together in my mind but failing.

"How well did you know her? What makes you so certain she took her own life, Anderson?"

"I didn't know her long but intensely. She was selected and trained to become an Istishhadiya, a female suicide bomber, by al-Tabari himself. She was inserted into the US through our porous border with Mexico at a place just south of my home in Tubac. She lost her way and collapsed of hunger, dehydration and exposure not far from my house. I rescued her, but as she was gaining strength, she took the backpack nuclear device she was equipped with, defective as it turns out, and left for Las Vegas, her target. I tried to stop her; she shot me, but in an astonishing and dramatic change of heart, she saved my life, after nearly taking it, and nursed me back to health. There's more to this story, but that tells you the essentials."

"But you still haven't told me why she took her own life."

"Fanatical Islamic clergy kidnapped her brother and ransomed his life in exchange for her carrying out her mission in Las Vegas. In her mind, the only way to free her brother, by making his life useless to the clergy, and avoid killing innocents was to take her own life. Part of my sadness is that we, Frank and I, had obtained her brother's freedom thanks to an Israeli Special Forces rescue not twenty-four hours before she committed suicide, but she was taken to Las Vegas by a female guard and was prevented from receiving the information. She struggled with her guard, presumably killed her, then killed herself. If there were some way to avenge her death, I could more easily move on, but there is no one person responsible. It's the entire fanatical mindset of the culture, and it's that fanatical cultural mindset that I'll fight against as long as I live."

"That's sad, Anderson, but from what you say it isn't certain that she took her own life. Unless you've omitted something, the possibility exists that the same people who attacked you in Alexandria, and possibly here, are the same people who might have killed Layla. Who knew you were coming back to Washington to investigate a plot involving EMP technology? And who knew you were coming to New York?"

"Only you and Frank's office knew I was going to Washington, and only Frank knew I was coming here. Frank knew the purpose of my trip, the meeting with Sanjay. I suppose others in Frank's office knew I was coming here. I made no secret of it."

Like a tiny dark cloud in a clear sky, the image of Khalida floated into the back of my brain. Frank trusted her implicitly. It was possible he mentioned my travel plans to her.

"Anderson, given the violence that's followed you, are you absolutely certain Frank's office is secure? Unless you suspect me, most of the knowledge of your whereabouts seems to be focused in Frank's office. Is there anyone in the office who would have a motive for limiting your effectiveness? Is there any connection with anyone in Frank's office to the terrorist cell which is presumably plotting an attack with an e-bomb? Think hard!"

"I really hate to accuse anyone in the office. After all, even though I've worked with Frank for a long period of time, I've been in his office a very short time and barely know his other associates. There are two individuals who have links to Pakistan. One of them, Gordon Rhoads, is of ancient Aryan-Pakistani lineage. I have no idea whether he's even a Muslim, but I suppose he is. The other is Khalida, a beautiful Pakistani woman who was recommended to Frank by one of Frank's associates in the powerful Pakistani intelligence service, the ISI. The ISI's political and religious orientation is ambiguous at best. Frank believes that she wants to work in the US as kind of a networking experience with people connected to the power structure in Washington. He believes her motives are honorable, but I have no way of knowing. Either Gordon or Khalida might know of my schedule, and either of them might have reasons for wanting to limit my effectiveness with regard to the Broken Spark plot. You do understand, I don't tell you this story to elicit your sympathy, but rather to help you understand what you've innocently gotten yourself into. There's is still time to get you out."

"Perhaps not, Anderson. I saw the face of the assassin! I'm not sure, but if they're as violent as you portray them to be, and as violent as the religion is, they aren't going to let me be."

"Did you tell the police?"

"Yes, of course, although I was somewhat vague. But I promise you, his face is not vague to me. I'll remember it forever. His left temple is caved in and a hideous scar is there were his hair should be. He had a scraggly beard and was very unkempt. He looked right at me before he shot Sanjay."

"Mohammed!" I exclaimed.

"What?"

"Layla was kidnapped from my home in Tubac by two enforcers from Islam. They took her into Mexico, and I caught up with them in León, Mexico. I was able to free Layla, but I had to shoot the kidnappers. One was named Mohammed. I shot him in the left temple, and I would have sworn he was dead. What a brute! He would not, I suppose, think kindly of me."

"Anderson, one thing I don't understand. How do these people move about the world so freely? How does a Muslim from Palestine, I guess he was from Palestine from what you've said, how does he move from the West Bank to Arizona, then to Mexico, get medical treatment, then enter the US and shoot at you and mistakenly kill poor Sanjay? That just seems impossible to me."

"You have to understand, Joan, that the advances in more complex and refined security procedures are offset measure for measure by advances in ways to defeat them. Just as developments to defeat counterfeiting of passports improve, technologies to improve counterfeiting of passports advance. It's the old 'Spy versus Counterspy' of *Mad Magazine*. People who get caught with a counterfeit passport have been supplied by a second-rate source. We don't, by definition, hear about the ones who are not caught. We may wish to think of our adversaries as possessors of inferior intellect and resources, kind of like Sgt. Schultz and Col. Klink in *Hogan's Heroes*, but that is totally incorrect. Their leaders are possessed of first-rate intellects, and by our purchasing their oil at elevated prices for years we've given them the ability to acquire superior resources. Radical Islam is an adversary who is our equal in many ways, and its representatives are innovative, remorseless and indefatigable in their mission."

"Anderson, does it make sense that this Mohammed is a Palestinian? I thought this cell you were pursuing was made up of Pakistanis."

"The leadership appears to be Pakistani, but the foot soldiers are drawn from Muslims in any country where the locals have been radicalized. It's not unusual."

"What do we do next?" she asked.

We were sitting on the bed and Joan placed her hand lightly on my knee.

"Do I go back to lobbying as if this never happened? Do you go back to whatever you do? A man has died here. It could have been you. I'm glad it wasn't obviously, but it could have been. It could be tomorrow. What are you going to do differently?"

"It isn't quite the 'sea change' event for me that it is for you. I've been here before, and life goes on. The first thing I must do tomorrow is talk to Sanjay's contact at the UN."

"How are you going to do that?"

"Sanjay was in the process of texting him when he was shot. I have his Blackberry. His contact was trying to text him back when he died."

"What's the big picture here, Anderson? Where are you going to go and what are you going to do? Surely life doesn't just return to normal for you, does it? Is this normal for you?"

"In the world I live in, Joan, there is no normal, there are only varying perceptions of normal, and probably none of them would fit your perception of normal. Americans like to think that there's an objective standard of normalcy, but there isn't. During the 1950s, we read of the return to normalcy under Eisenhower after World War II.

But we know, or we should know, that during the 1950s the Soviet Union was developing the tools for a competition with the US which would unfold for decades of intensive Cold War hostility. In the 1960s, we had the Vietnam War in tandem with the coming of age of the baby boomers, our generation, tearing apart the American social fabric. In the 1970s, we had the resignation of President Nixon and an economy in stagflation. In the 1980s, we had the incredible and disruptive drop in the stock market in 1987 and then the unraveling of the Soviet Union in 1989, and the aging of President Reagan. The 1990s were assumed to be a period of dramatic economic expansion and growth in new technology, but in retrospect we see that it was an incredible speculative bubble which nursed another speculative bubble in housing loans and toxic securitized loans, and that brought us the incredible collapse of the credit markets in August of 2007. And, since 9/11, we've been threatened by terrorism from fanatical Islam unprecedented in our nation's history. This threat has enabled our federal government to impose limitations on our constitutional freedoms which we never dreamed would be imposed. Which of those periods do we choose to identify as the period of normalcy in America? Which decade defines the spirit and nature of the American people? Which period would we want to return to? I'm not sure I can answer that. Can you?"

Joan was silent as her eyes searched my face, and she reflected on my challenge. Her strong face was drawn from the stress of the day, sitting alone in her hotel robe, the fingers of her left hand nervously plying the fingers of her right. I was glad I had invited her over.

"It's something of a litany of horrors, isn't it, Anderson? I'm not sure there's any one of those decades I'd like to return to. I grew up in the 1980s, in Ohio, and the challenges of the world were very far away from me. It was a happy time, perhaps not for me personally, but for the country. Maybe that's what makes the present seem so abnormal. There's no place we can go to hide. Current affairs and the world itself are thrust upon us on a daily basis, either through the media, or more significantly now through the Internet. We're totally engaged, unless we, purposely, in one form or another isolate ourselves. I guess that's the answer to your question. There is no time to which we can return, so this is the new normalcy. I have no way of really knowing what it was like to live in the US in the 1950s, nor do you, do you? We can only try to understand what it was like by talking to our parents or our parents' peers, and reading historical accounts of the 1950s. We live with kind of a fantasy legend of what the 1950s were like, and the legend is always told as if it was a kinder, gentler time, but maybe it wasn't, maybe it was because Americans simply didn't know much about what was going on in the world."

"I think that's right. And, don't forget, the kindler gentler legend of the fifties usually doesn't include the McCarthy hearings, which sent a chill through the entire educated class of the country. What's normal in the country is a moving concept. It evolves in response to the pressures of the times."

We stood, now facing one another. Joan's head came up to my forehead. She looked into my eyes and searched for meaning there. I touched the fingers of her left hand with my right and an electric shock ran through us both. Somehow, in the act of standing up, Joan's bathrobe had come undone. In my modest way, I tried not to look down at her nude body, but my courtesy was inhibited because my robe had also come undone. I could tell by her eyes as they widened ever so slightly that she felt the same electricity I felt. There was a force so strong it was irresistible. We leaned toward one another a little until I felt the tips of her breasts pressed gently against my chest. Her hard nipples felt like gentle electrodes against my sensitive skin, sending a shock through my entire body.

We leaned as one against one another in defiance of everything we knew we should not do. The effect was ethereal. We were as one and time suspended itself as if it too recognized the exquisiteness of the moment and wanted to help it along. We resisted as one person, but the combined force overwhelmed us both, our eagerness winning over our sensitivity.

Afterwards, we lay as one, spent in the consummation of the passion we were afraid to acknowledge.

As I escorted Joan to her door I turned to face her, and I could tell from the honest intensity in her eyes that our lives were more intertwined than ever. It was hard to say goodbye, and we stood for a long time simply holding hands and being a part of one another.

CHAPTER FIFTEEN

✳✳✳

THE UNITED NATIONS

My new suit, shirt and tie were delivered to my room at 6:30 a.m. The hotel had provided me with a shaving kit, and by seven a.m. I was ready to meet Joan for breakfast. The short night's sleep had refreshed her, and she obviously felt more self-assured than she had at one a.m., but she was still somewhat reserved compared to her demeanor twenty-four hours earlier. She was dressed in the same dark blue business suit she had worn the day before. She had done her long hair in an upswept style, the shorter hairs at the nape of her neck escaping from the pins capturing the rest. She looked younger and more vulnerable than she ever had, but when she spoke, her voice was firm.

"Are we going to talk about last night?"

"You mean about the murder?"

"No, you ass! About making love. Does it mean something, or is it just what two emotionally overwrought people do to relieve tension?"

"I hope it's the former, but I don't think we have time to get very far into that right now, so maybe we ought to go with the latter until we can give the love thing the time it deserves." To Joan's credit, she didn't hit me or throw her coffee cup at me, instead settling for a grimace.

"What do you expect to learn, or accomplish, by going to see the Indian ambassador? Isn't it quite possible that he, or she, will not speak candidly with you?"

"That's certainly a possibility. However, since I have Sanjay's Blackberry, and since I was with him when he was killed, and since I have privileged information that he conveyed to me, I think it's a better than average possibility that I'll be able to establish some kind of communication, if not rapport, with his colleague. Besides, he was in the process of texting information about me to his contact. I don't know how much information was actually sent, but some must have been."

"I don't know, Anderson, last night when we were talking about this in your room, I thought I had it pretty well worked out in my mind, but this morning it again seems surreal, unconnected to real life. You seem to be living and functioning in a parallel universe, one that only comes in contact with the universe I know from time to time." Despite her projection of naïveté, there was something about her tone and demeanor that suggested she understood more about my life than she pretended.

"I understand, Joan. Yesterday, you experienced some shocking things you've never experienced before. It's a lot to assimilate in a short period of time. I'll get a cab to take you to LaGuardia, and you'll be back in Washington by ten thirty. I apologize for involving you in this whole thing." By her silence, I thought Joan had acquiesced. I was, of course, wrong.

After breakfast, we picked up our meager belongings and returned to meet in the lobby. I called a cab for Joan, and we stood on the sidewalk waiting for it. Out of habit, I scanned up and down the sidewalk and street and the adjacent buildings for any unusual activity. It was quiet, but I did note movement in a darkened doorway two doors to the south.

I moved slightly on the sidewalk so that my body stood between the doorway and Joan. The cab seemed to take forever, but it finally drew up to the curb in front of the Marriott. I stepped toward the cab, and in that instant I heard the muffled sound of a silenced revolver. I stood back up and looked at Joan. Her eyes were open wide and her left hand was holding her right arm. A very slight red discoloration began to appear between the fingers. Her mouth dropped open as she tried in vain to say something. I roughly pushed her into the cab and followed behind her, pressing her down on the seat. I yelled at the cab driver to go to the UN, and he peeled away from the curb going up West Side Highway.

After about two blocks, I cautiously lifted up and looked out the back window, but I saw nothing. "Are you all right, Joan?" I asked.

"Yes, I'm okay. I believe the bullet just singed my arm. I feel a sting, but nothing worse." I was a little surprised because her voice was strong and emphatic.

"Are you sure? We can get you to a doctor or we can go straight to the airport."

"No way! This has just become very personal! It's one thing to see you get shot at and to see somebody else get killed, but when someone shoots at me personally, I take offense! I don't know where this is going to lead, but I intend to go with you until there are at least a few answers to go with the questions I have."

I smiled, or perhaps it was a grimace. "I'm glad to have you along."

The cab driver took the West Side Highway through its various name changes up to 42nd Street and went across town to First Avenue. Traffic was extremely heavy and it took us almost an hour to get to UN Plaza just off First Avenue. Half the time I was turned around in the seat to see if I could spot anyone following us. If there was, he was very careful because I didn't see him. The driver dropped us in the circle in front of the Secretariat, and we entered the soaring building overlooking the East River.

We went directly to the receptionist and I gave my name and asked for the Indian ambassador. The name of the Indian ambassador did not match the name Sanjay had given me, but when the receptionist called the extension, the person answering the phone had apparently received instructions to accommodate me. The receptionist hung up and said someone would be down momentarily to collect me.

While we waited, I asked Joan about her arm, and she said that was only a scratch and resisted any effort to have it attended to.

A diminutive young Indian woman in a sari exited the elevator and approached us. She asked if I were Mr. Wyeth, and when I said yes, she turned toward Joan with a quizzical expression on her face. I introduced her to Joan and said, "Ms. Singer-Taylor was with me last night when Mr. Singh was killed. She's a trusted colleague of mine."

The young woman nodded her head in acknowledgment but did not give her name. She turned toward the elevator and said, "Please follow me."

When we stepped off the elevator, we saw that the entire foyer was a reception area for the Indian delegation. The windows on the east side of the building offered a spectacular view of the East River. We were asked to take a seat in two leather chairs in the reception area while the young woman went to her desk and dialed an extension. She turned away from us so we could not hear what she was saying.

Joan turned to me and said, "So I'm now a trusted colleague of yours, am I?"

"Well, after what we've been through together, I certainly trust you, and I hope you trust me. That takes care of the trust part, and I guess we're colleagues through our connection with Frank. Does that bother you?"

"No, of course not! I just hope you realize this is all pretty new to me. I'm not sure how much I can help you, and I certainly don't want to hinder you in any way. My worst nightmare would be to reveal to inappropriate parties something you wish to keep concealed. I'm sometimes accosted by the press and forced to answer questions that I must answer truthfully in order to protect my credibility. Here we are in the midst of a financial crisis, and I'm a lobbyist for what were investment banks which no longer exist. What if I'm asked about the possibility of electromagnetic pulse technology and whether such technology could have been a factor in the black hole of information that represented the balance sheets of some of these highly leveraged investment banks? I'm at the offices of the Indian delegation to the United Nations. What if I'm asked about the connection between the Indian military and the Mossad in satellite spy technology? Does the Indian intelligence organization have an interest in electromagnetic pulse technology? You know, the wrong answer to any one of these questions might reveal more than you want me to reveal. I'd do it unconsciously, of course, but it still might be harmful."

We had been speaking to each other in low voices. Something about the ease and fluidity with which Joan had expressed her concerns about revealing too much surprised me because it was quite in contrast with the safety concerns she had expressed earlier. But the conversation was ended before I had time to answer by the appearance of a man who was almost a twin of Sanjay.

"How may I help you, Mr. Wyeth? My name is Sunil Dandekar. Sanjay and I work...sorry...worked closely together. His death comes as a terrible shock to me. Would you please tell me exactly what happened?"

"Unfortunately, Mr. Dandekar, I don't have a lot of information. Sanjay and I had just exchanged our bona fides and were ready to start discussing what each of us knew about EMP technology and what we were doing about it when Sanjay was shot by a gunman who was standing behind me. I don't even know for sure if his target was Sanjay. It might have been me. At the precise moment of the shooting, I'd turned, and had perhaps ducked, to look at my friends, who were sitting at a table nearby. Meanwhile, Sanjay was texting someone here, possibly you. The shot was fired at close range. Sanjay never felt a thing, nor did he have any time to react. I'm devastated by the thought that I might have inadvertently caused his death. Naturally, I've told the police all of this, except for the text message. I might add that a shot was fired at Ms. Singer-Taylor, or at me, this morning as we were getting in a cab to come here. The bullet grazed her arm, but she was otherwise unhurt."

"That would seem to support the conclusion it is you they are after, Mr. Wyeth. Do you have any idea who they might be?"

"The only thing I know is that my employer, Franklin Pierce, and I are trying to develop information about the use of EMP as an instrument of terrorism, and perhaps more. We recently had a briefing in Frank's offices from a high-level Pentagon official on EMP technology. Now that I think of it, he was Indian, a Dr. Gangehar. Perhaps you know him?"

Either Sunil didn't know him or didn't choose to disclose that he knew him because he gave no reaction to my question.

"We have a friend, now living in Casablanca, who has dedicated his life to infiltrating cells of fanatical Muslims. He's picked up information about a possible EMP operation which he understands is targeted either against Western financial markets or against a number of cities in India, or perhaps against another target entirely. That's why my meeting with Sanjay was, or would have been, fortuitous."

"Perhaps your efforts have not been wasted, Mr. Wyeth. I am totally familiar with Sanjay's efforts. Please come into my office."

Joan and I followed Sunil into a brightly lit office overlooking the East River. Before we sat down I remarked on the view, to which Sunil gave a half wave of his hand.

"Yes, it is an incredible view, but one ceases to notice it after repeated exposure. It is not a good thing to become tired of something so magnificent, is it?" he asked rhetorically.

"Mr. Wyeth, Sanjay was pursuing a rumor in the financial markets about a possible use of an e-bomb, a device which would fracture the information systems of the financial markets in the United States. You may or may not be aware that the Indian government takes the threat of EMP technology very, very seriously. India has become a country completely wedded to high technology to shape its future prosperity. While we have worked closely with your government, and intend to do so in the future, we do have different views of the technology. Your government, probably because of your immense resources, has directed its interest toward high-power microwave sources—HPM—using a high-altitude launch platform, most probably a B-2 bomber. While we may or may not have the capability to defend against such a weapon, the more immediate threat is from a lower level of technology. The flux compression generator is such a technology. It is by its basic physics constrained to the frequency band below 1 MHz. We recognize that an HPM device is tightly focused and has a much better ability to couple energy into many target types. However, we believe that a lower-level threat promises similar damage. Ten flux compression generator devices, which would cost less than twenty thousand dollars, would pose a greater threat to India than a weaponized HPM device launched from high altitude simply because we do not see the latter as a reasonable expectation at this time. We see the major threat to India coming from Pakistan, whose level of knowledge of physics we highly respect, but whose ability to weaponize technology and deliver it is different from the capabilities of the enemies or potential enemies of the United States."

"So what is your government doing to counteract the threat from these low-cost, low-technology e-bombs? We have conflicting information from our source regarding the targets of the specific threat we're dealing with now. Initial information came through suggesting the terrorists were targeting five cities in India. There was no more information than that, no specific targets selected within those cities, not even the names of the cities themselves. We've also received information suggesting four targets in Western Europe and the United States, and only one in India, that one being Bangalore, presumably because of the software and hardware infrastructure in the area. This lack of decision leads us to believe there might be a struggle for influence either within the cell itself or between the cell and its superiors in Islamabad. What do you think?"

"Our information also leads us to believe that there is a substantial difference of opinion in the ISI. Let's not call it a power struggle. I like your use of the term 'struggle for influence'. The ISI is very effective, and we have been challenged by it for decades. We have had our successes and failures, and they have had theirs. Some in the ISI want their resources directed to Islam's challenge of the West. Others want their resources dedicated to their continuing struggle with us, India. You know, Mr. Wyeth, we have fought three major wars with Pakistan. We have won all of them, but we do not underestimate their military or their intelligence services. We have information that suggests their targets in India may have again changed. Given the catastrophic meltdown in fixed income and equity markets worldwide, it would not be surprising if the terrorists had decided to change their targets."

"How might they have changed?" I asked.

"I'm sorry, but I cannot discuss anything further. I am comfortable with your security background, Mr. Wyeth, but I only have your word about Ms. Singer-Taylor."

Joan hadn't offered anything to the conversation in Sunil's office. I was more than a little surprised by her earlier, private, reference to the Mossad, but I had tucked that away in the back of my mind to consider at a later date. Now she really stunned me!

"Sunil," she said. "Perhaps you will remember January 21, 2008, when an Indian space launch vehicle lifted off from the Sriharikota spaceport on Sriharikota Island in the Bay of Bengal. It carried Israel's most sophisticated spy satellite ever launched, the Polaris. It was carried on the Polar Satellite Launch Vehicle—PSLV—which also carried your country's first military reconnaissance spacecraft. The public press is aware of the launch and the payload, but no one in the public sector knows the degree of the information sharing which was a part of the project. The Polaris satellite is Israel's first satellite equipped with synthetic aperture radar that allows it to take high-resolution imagery in all weather conditions. The radar looks through clouds or fog to see objects on the ground. While the purpose of the launch is to offer new coverage of sites in Iran for Israeli defense planners, it does also provide coverage of events in Pakistan which are of critical importance to Indian military defense."

Both Sunil and I were speechless! Who was this unassuming person I had with me? Was it Erin? Or Joan? Or someone else entirely? She clearly had intimate access to secrets in the Israeli intelligence services. Sunil was the first to speak.

"Joan, you are privy to events that are not publicly known. I suppose there are a number of reasons why that would be. But the most obvious is that you are not who you say you are, but rather someone who is a part of, or closely connected to, the Israeli intelligence services. Now, I, and I suspect Mr. Wyeth, do not have a problem with your connection to Israeli intelligence, I do have a question about the nature of the connection. Who are you? And what do you do?" Sunil demanded.

"And what's your connection to Frank and to American intelligence?" I demanded in turn.

Joan was calm, but her voice had the timbre of someone unloading an enormous burden, one that had been bothering her for too long. Her calm was in contrast to Sunil and I; both of us grappling with her knowledge of things one would assume were beyond the reach of her awareness.

"Well, gentlemen, I do have ties to Israeli intelligence. I work for Israeli intelligence. We are friends here, kind of in the classic sense of he who is the enemy of my enemy is my friend, and maybe better than that, so I'll put my cards on the table, or at least some of them. I have joint citizenship, US and Israeli, and have had for many years now. I worked on a kibbutz while in high school and became sympathetic to Israel. I admire the people for their successes in a hostile land surrounded by hostile people. On the other hand, I am also sympathetic to the rights of the Palestinian people. Unfortunately, it is next to impossible to determine with any degree of fairness what the rights of the Israelis are versus the rights of the Palestinians. Do you start with historic rights? Holy rights, biblical rights, rights under the Koran? Rights determined by power? Demographic rights? Anyway, you know the problem.

"While on the kibbutz, I worked with an Israeli, a woman somewhat older than I. She was kind of a mentor to me. I later found out she worked for the Mossad and was sent to the kibbutz to recruit young Americans who were sympathetic to Israel, but I didn't know that at the time. I guess by definition we were all sympathetic to Israel, but her mission was to develop a sort of organic relationship between young Americans and Israel and through that to the Mossad. They took me to Jerusalem, where I talked to some people, all very vague and general, and then I returned to the states, to college, graduate school and law school. Yes, Anderson, I am a clinical psychologist as well as a lawyer. I practiced for several years in Ohio, then went back to law school.

"Toward the end of law school I was contacted again by my mentor, who by this time had ascended to a higher level position in the Mossad. She is now a public figure in Israel, a member of the Knesset, and if I told you her name, you would recognize it immediately. She asked me what I was going to do after graduation from law school and I said I didn't know. I should say I'd been contacted off and on all during the nine years of my education, but they never asked anything of me. My mentor had earlier suggested I take a minor in physics in undergraduate, which was no imposition since I loved physics.

"To make an already long story a bit shorter, my mentor said she could help me get a position with a lobbying firm in Washington. I jumped at the chance, and before I knew it, they were asking me for low-level information about Washington politics, information which I was sure they already knew. Then they invited me to Israel again, where I met some higher-level people, and before I could say boo, I was working for the Mossad. They asked me questions about science and math, as well as Washington politics, and I could tell they were really interested in EMP technology. I accompanied the Israeli military attaché on frequent briefings by the Pentagon, a Dr. Gangehar I believe his name was. They always asked me for my ID, but never for my bona fides, which always surprised me. I guess I was in the Pentagon's computer as 'okay'.

"In January, 2008 they asked me to attend the PSLV launch with our, Israel's, satellite onboard. Then, I went to the luncheon in New York where I talked with Andre about the EMP threat. Fortunately, or not, I ran into Anderson at a reception hosted by Frank Pierce, a longtime friend of Israel. Our interests coincide and here we are.

I might add that my contact in the Mossad gives high marks to Anderson, despite a few bungles here and there."

I winced at this, recalling two unfortunate kidnappings in my career, one in Jordan and one in Mexico, kidnappings which could have been avoided if I had been just a little more careful.

Joan continued. "I'm not privy to any information the Mossad has that an attack is planned, but they have led me to believe one is imminent. Where it is supposed to take place and against whom is uncertain, but if it's against financial markets, that would have major implications for the Israelis, given the interconnectedness of markets worldwide. If it's against missile defense communications, Israel really has even more of an interest because Israel is now the largest supplier of military equipment, dollar wise, to India. Israel of course wants to make sure that the equipment works, and does not want its interests in danger. Pakistan's hostility toward Israel has always been ideological rather than military. That might be changing! Have either of you heard of a group called 'The Spirit of our Fathers?'"

I immediately shook my head and looked at Sunil. The color drained from his face, but it was otherwise totally impassive as his heavily lidded eyes gazed at Joan like a cobra ready to strike. With a voice barely above a whisper, he said, "Just for conversation, let's say I have. What do you know about such a group, assuming it exists."

"I don't have any hard evidence that it exists. Rumor has it that there's a secret group of Pakistani military officers, who trace their lineage back not only to the Moguls who ruled the subcontinent in the middle of the last millennium, but much, much further back, to the Aryans, a fair complected, gray-eyed people who overran the ancient Mohenjo-daro civilization, which dates back to the earliest time when Homo sapiens formed civilizations in the Indus Valley. The Aryans are curious. It isn't known whether they had any relationship to the 'Super Race' Hitler chose to exalt, although he once referred to the Afghans as the 'pure race'.

"But anyway, back to the story! The senior statesmen of this group have met regularly for eons. Recently, they've been meeting more frequently. As a member dies, he's replaced by his eldest son, if he has one, or by a military officer selected by the group if he doesn't. No member has ever tried to leave the group, or so it's said. The power of the group, operating under the cloak of the 'Spirit of our Fathers' is absolute where its writ runs, which is said to include Pakistan, Pakistan controlled Kashmir, possibly parts of Afghanistan."

"This is a fascinating story, Joan," Sunil said, his face grim. "However, it contains some elements of a child's fairy tale."

"Yes, I understand, and perhaps it is fantasy, but some elements give us pause, even if sketchy and sometimes conflicting."

I had listened with rapt attention, never having heard anything about this. I did notice that Joan had said some elements had given 'us' pause. Who was 'us'? The Israeli intelligence? And, were they taking it seriously? Or, was it some other 'us' that Joan was affiliated with, someone else she hadn't told me about?

There was tension in the room, not because of our interactions, but because we felt like we were sitting on a powder keg, and we didn't know when it was going to go off, but we were pretty sure it was going to. We had talked for a long time. It was well after lunchtime, but no one was thinking of food. It was one of those 'aha!' moments. Each of us brought information to the table. Three different countries' intelligence had been laid on the table like a buffet. Each of us was sampling the fare, integrating it with what we already knew.

Whatever one tried to make of it, one central theme emerged. An attack with heretofore narrowly used technology was about to be waged on a broad front against Western or Indian institutions. Its goal was to cause confusion and chaos and perhaps more. The target or targets were in flux. It could be financial institutions, it could be airlines, or it could be India's defense program, with attacks at the ISRO in Bangalore or the space launch site at Sriharikota, the missile launch site at Balasore in Orissa, or all of the above.

One fact had emerged. It appeared that by pulling up the curtain of the EMP attack, we had opened the window to something far greater and far more sinister, a possible nuclear strike by Pakistan against India, and possibly Israel.

We were occupied with our own thoughts. I was pretty sure in my own mind that it was me the assailant was shooting at in Delmonico's, and also when Joan and I were getting into the cab. The only bright spot was his lousy aim. He ought to be spending more time on the firing range and less time dreaming of Islamic resurgence I thought sardonically.

I let the silence expand. The early afternoon March sunlight was weak and shadows were long over the East River before we all realized it was time to make decisions.

"I think I should visit my friend in Casablanca. He has a connection with the cell that is contemplating the EMP attack," I decided.

CHAPTER SIXTEEN
***
AMTRAK

After Joan's startling revelations, the conversation in the UN Secretariat Building had been strained. The three of us, representing three powerful countries, three countries with interests which sometimes joined, despite being in a sea of divergent interests, were struggling with the meaning of the tragedy which we had experienced.

The conflict we were experiencing, the West vs. Islam, brought to mind a favorite parable my father had told me about waves in the ocean. The West's conflict with Islam was like the eternal thrust of the waves on the beach, which build until the seventh wave releases the energy built up by the intervening waves. Waves relentlessly pound the beach, but the seventh wave, which gathers its strength from distant gravitational forces, pushes and pulls toward and away from the beach until it finally crashes in a torrent of foam. The intervening six smaller waves are cast off by the seventh wave before it reaches the beach, and those intermediate waves lend their strength to the power of the seventh wave.

The beach and the seventh wave have been in opposition throughout modern history. The beach is to the wave as Islam is to the West, the beach resisting the progress and changes the West hammers upon it. The seventh wave grinds slowly and inexorably on the rock and sands of the beach, which resists and obstructs the wave. Success is not predestined to either. In the ebb and flow of time, one is transcendent, then in turn the other.

In this, our vastly overpopulated world, the odds favor the disciplined, not the profligate. Both the beach and the wave have been at times disciplined and profligate. At this moment in time, the West was the less disciplined and the callous and desperate young men of

Islam the more disciplined. Could the West pull itself together to resume hammering Islam with change, or would Islam deflect the seventh wave in massive opposition? The answer was unknown to any of us in that room.

It was seven in the evening and Joan and I were on Amtrak's high-speed train to Washington. The Metroliner scarcely ranks with the high-speed trains of Europe and Asia, rarely reaching velocities in excess of 70 or 80 miles an hour, compared to their 125 to 150 mph, but it was comfortable and, we hoped, secure. Neither Joan nor I wanted to chance the air shuttles after our harrowing trip to New York.

Joan's head rested on my left shoulder, her hair redolent in the warm air of the train, but she was sleeping uneasily, with sudden moves and sounds that suggested a restless subconscious. After dozing off briefly, I was now wide awake, wishing Joan were awake to share my thoughts, thoughts which careened around my brain like bumper cars in a Midwest carnival. Impressions of the past few days were chaotic. Making sense of them was likely impossible, but I tried.

It now seemed certain meeting Joan at Frank's home was more than happenstance. Frank wanted to bring us together at the reception. The reception itself may have been arranged to make that possible, but to appear casual.

I wryly admitted to myself that I had been the beneficiary of our acquaintance; from the enjoyment of her company, the information about the proposed threat, our thoughtful discussions, her astonishing revelation that she worked for Israeli intelligence, and now, the warm feeling of her head on my shoulder as the train shot through the dark, chilly night toward Washington, all had all been to my advantage.

Joan would probably tally the scorecard the same way, the benefit going to me, the cost going to her. So far, since joining me, she had enjoyed a near air disaster, she had been involved in a brutal murder, she had been denied sleep, and she had been shot at. Not a really great experience!

She moaned, and her shoulder moved sharply against my arm, her head falling forward, but not off my shoulder. She caught herself reflexively, her head snapping back, her face taking on a deathly appearance, exacerbated by the subdued night light of the train. Her body stiffening and the moan transmogrifying into a sharp intake of breath, as if the effort of dealing with the image in her subconscious had taken her breath away.

What could be so disturbing in her subconscious to cause a physical response of that nature? What memories lay so deeply hidden and artfully covered that the disturbance would provoke such a forceful reaction, so distinct from what I knew as her warm and affectionate, uncomplicated self. I started to move my right arm across my body to comfort her, but before I could reach her, she shot up violently in her seat, her eyes open wide, and she distanced herself from me.

"It's okay, it's okay!" she said forcefully, as much to convince herself as anyone within the purview of her awareness. Then, to my amazement, she fell back against my shoulder and resumed sleeping just as she had been before.

What was the cause of this anxiety in a person who seemed so gathered together when she was conscious? Were the events of the past several days so contrary to her nature that the contrast between what I assumed to be her placid upbringing in Ohio and the extreme violence she was a part of, and perhaps a target of, last evening and this morning could not be reconciled in her dreams?

She continued her restlessness, rolling her head along my shoulder, and her body continued its jerky, spasmodic movements as if seized by images in her unconscious so real and threatening as to require escape or release from some imagined physical presence that didn't currently exist in her consciousness but represented a memory of a horrible event or place from her past.

I still thought of Joan as Erin. We had experienced events which would have been life-changing for people who lived unusual lives, not to mention normal ones, which I had once assumed Joan did even if I did not, that is, until the multiple personas she had revealed to me this past week.

We were just beyond the Philadelphia stop when Joan began to throw off her deep and restless sleep. She pushed violently against me and sat up straight in the leather chair. "What are you trying to do?" she demanded.

I was taken aback by the forcefulness of her remonstrance, remonstrance against what I didn't have a clue. Then her eyes fixed me with a stare so startling in its vacancy and intensity that I was completely unnerved. Her lips moved, but she said nothing. It was as if her body was possessed by another consciousness.

Gradually, her eyes began to gather focus and she became aware that I was there and that she was staring at me. "Anderson?" she said with a question in her voice, then, "Anderson," a statement, and she slumped casually against me again. She had engaged her cognition, and I was again registered as a friendly, not a hostile, presence.

Her face softened, the tightness around her eyes and mouth relaxing into the softness that was her normal countenance, and she lost the deathly pallor which had gripped her while she was sleeping. As recognition flowed over her, she allowed her eyes to drift from my face and take in the circumstances of our surroundings, with each object in her view, the window, the seat in front of her, lending reassurance to her recovery from her journey to that place where no one but she had been, or could go.

The viselike grips of her fingers on the muscle of my upper arm also relaxed, giving her entire body permission to let loose the rigid control she had forced on it. Her eyes drifted back to my face and the slightest shadow of a smile revealed itself at the left side of her mouth.

"Are you all right?" I asked lamely. "I'm afraid you had a bad dream." I recognized as I said it that to call her experience a bad dream was like comparing a monsoon to a spring shower.

She took her time before answering, as if to protect her thoughts before entrusting them to her voice. She had been leaning against my left side and now she straightened out, replacing the support of my shoulder with the back of her seat. Thus composed, she turned again toward me with an angelic face and said with a voice I will never forget, cool and remote, "I don't think so! I'm quite rested. Where are we?"

I was so taken aback by her complete denial it took a few seconds to focus my thoughts on her question. "Erin…Joan, aren't you even remotely aware of the violence that's had possession of your subconscious this past hour? Not one little bit?" I asked.

She looked at me kindly and said, "Anderson, I have no idea what you're talking about. What have you been thinking during my sleep that's disturbed you so?"

At this, I realized there was no way she was going to talk about her dream, whether because she chose not to or genuinely had no recall, I would probably never know—certainly not now. So I gave up trying to join her in her subconscious and to share with her something that I had been thinking about, something deeply troubling to me.

I've been thinking that Frank's office has been compromised and that Frank's trust and confidence in me is being eroded from within his inner circle. I sensed it when he was so defensive of both Khalida and of Gordon. I can't put my finger on it, but I sensed it again when he was unwilling to give me any time with al-Tabari, and again when he was so eager to see me off to New York with you to try to track down a rumor. He gave me the okay to talk to Sanjay, but it appeared to be grudgingly done. This evening, while you were sleeping, I tried to call him several times, but his receptionist, who was very friendly before, put me off with excuses why Frank wasn't available. Am I, are we, getting too close to something that someone in Frank's inner circle doesn't want found out?"

"I thought you had unshakable confidence in Frank."

"I do, but that doesn't mean he might not make a mistake in placing his confidence in someone who's unworthy. I'm deeply concerned, Joan. I think we must assume that Frank's office is not friendly territory for me."

CHAPTER SEVENTEEN

✷✷✷

MONTMARTRE

Shahid rushed into the central room of the house in Montmartre carrying a copy of the *International Herald Tribune*. He was excited! Ahmed, Salman and Taufig were in the room. Ibrahim wasn't there and no one knew where he had gone. "It worked! It worked! One small e-bomb in an FAA service center virtually brought the US air transport system to a halt. Traffic on the heavily traveled Washington to New York route was cut by 80%, and they still reported a near collision. Airplanes had to fly on visual flight rules over the entire eastern half of the country, including Chicago. It was a nightmare. That is a small measure of what we can accomplish, my brothers. If only we had more money and more people, think of what we could achieve."

"Let me see that paper!" Salman said urgently. He read the article word for word.

"You see what our problem is? And our opportunity?" he asked of no one in particular.

"It took them almost an hour, but they did get backup systems in place. The slowdown in the air traffic control system was caused by the backlog that built up during the one-hour period of time. What if we were able to detonate a series of e-bombs, one after the other in one-hour intervals? You see in most American service providers, backup systems for information technology systems are well maintained and backed up on a regular basis. But there is no backup system for backup systems, or if there is, it's extremely rare. If we could destroy or severely damage the main system, then wait until the backup system is operating and data files uploaded to the hardware, and a second e-bomb were to be exploded, it would destroy the backup operating files and data files as well. That assumes that the hardware would continue to function, which is unlikely. In many companies, the company employs what's called a 'hot site', where the entire system, hardware and software, is replicated.

"In the backup site, the hardware is not usually in continuous operation, but rather is updated daily or hourly, as the case may be, and the 'hot site' backup system is hard cabled to the primary system. So even if the company were to switch to the 'hot site', the EMP would be back-end coupled directly to the 'hot site' hardware by the cable, and the second explosion at the primary system would destroy the secondary site as well. The most desirable situation would be to have a third and redundant explosion which would ensure the failure of the entire system, requiring months to repair. That may be in excess of the resources the ISI is prepared to give us, but surely we can get two bombs for each target. After all, these things are really cheap."

"Excuse me, Salman, but my knowledge of explosives is not as extensive as yours," Taufig said. "What does 'coupling' mean?"

"Coupling is critical, Taufig, somehow the energy must go from the e-bomb to the target; the computer system, radar installation, telephone switching gear, whatever. In other words, the energy must couple from the e-bomb to the target. Generally speaking there are two ways the coupling takes place. In one case, the energy goes directly from the e-bomb to the antenna which is associated with radar or communications equipment, for example, because the antenna itself is designed to couple power into and out of the equipment. That is called 'front-end coupling'.

"'Back-end coupling' takes place when the energy from the e-bomb produces large transient currents on fixed electrical wiring and cables interconnecting equipment. That is the case we're talking about here. You see, with high volumes of data being required, 'hot sites' are almost always cabled to the primary system. So, the cables are actually our friends and carry the EMP effect directly to where we want it to go. If we can set our timers for a one-hour delay, that should be optimal. Most backup systems must be in place and operating within an hour.

"Shahid, you must get us additional money or material! We can literally increase our capabilities exponentially if we can set two or three e-bombs to go off an hour apart. The timers must be faultless, no cheap junk! Can you do it?"

"I can try, Salman, but you must help me. You are passionate about your knowledge and the effectiveness of the e-bombs. Such passion will be necessary to convince our superiors. They have many claims on their resources, and even though the amount of money is small, we do not have a very high priority. Unfortunately, my handler fell out of favor with the power center, and so my access is somewhat limited. With your passion, perhaps we can move the priority up somewhat.

"Unfortunately, we do have a deadline and we must have all preparations made by that deadline. If we are required to return to Islamabad in order to seek additional resources, it will make our deadline very difficult to meet. I would not want to be in a position of asking for more resources and at the same time explaining why we would be unable to meet our deadline. Rather than be in that position, I would rather sacrifice the second e-bomb per target and concentrate on making sure the first e-bomb functions properly."

Salman reacted angrily. His face reddened and he clenched and unclenched his fists. "It is your responsibility to get us the resources we need! It is our responsibility to ensure that we can make the greatest blow against our enemies. We are talking about very small sums of money and material. We are willing to serve Allah with our lives! It is not too much to ask that we get an extra ten thousand dollars in order to have the maximum impact when we carry out our mission. I insist that you approach our superiors and request, no, demand, the additional funds! If I must do your job for you, then I must conclude that you are not necessary for the effective execution of this operation!" Salman finished his statement with a steely voice, restoring his icy control just in time to see Ibrahim enter the room from the room where he had been sleeping. Salman quickly turned to Ibrahim and their eyes locked in a look of understanding.

Ibrahim saw and sensed the fear building in the room. He should. He had seen enough fear. In fact, fear followed him wherever he went, even when it wasn't his purpose to instill fear. His purpose was to bend people's wills to his own. Fear, he had found, was the most successful tool, always within reach, to accomplish his purpose. Greed was also useful, but one did not always have access to enough resources to use greed effectively, and more often than not, greed wasn't satisfied in a lasting manner. Fear lasted longer and could be reinforced quickly and effectively. Furthermore, fear could be generated subtlety and by implication. If the context were created properly, the individual in whom he wished to instill fear would draw his own conclusions and create the fear himself. It was, he thought, a very nice tool.

He broke his gaze from Salman and looked at Shahid. Now, Shahid was a perfect illustration. Shahid didn't know it was he, Ibrahim, who had killed his handler in Islamabad and left him to bleed to death in an alleyway, his throat slit from ear to ear, but Shahid suspected that it was, and the unknown is the strongest component of fear. One can fear the known as well, but with the known, fear can be defined and contained. With the unknown, fear feeds on itself and becomes boundless.

As he looked at Shahid, he let his hand move toward the inner layer of his jacket, where he kept the long stiletto he had used to kill Shahid's handler. Shahid willed his eyes to look toward Ibrahim, but he couldn't successfully engage Ibrahim's eyes. His eyes instead wandered over Ibrahim's cruel hawkish face, the thin lips not quite covering the misaligned teeth, the scraggly beard with large patches of open space where no hair would grow, as if it refused to complement such a face. Shahid's memories went back to the alley in Melody Park, and the sound of blood and air escaping from his handler's body was as if it were happening again and again, right next to him. It was true, he didn't know if it was Ibrahim who had committed the murder, but he knew that Ibrahim had been in Islamabad that day because his handler had told him so before their fateful meeting in the restaurant. Was this one of the two members of his team his handler had told him could not be trusted?

Ibrahim El Sharkawy was born in Cairo, in the wealthy Maadi section of the city, in 1973, three years after President Gamal Abdel Nasser died and Anwar Sadat succeeded him, and in the same year Al-Gama'a al-Islamiyya, the Islamic group, was organized in the upper Nile regions of the country. Ibrahim knew nothing of this. He was born to a sheltered life. His parents were both lawyers and property owners in the Cairo of the seventies. Nasser's strident nationalism and socialism had given way to Sadat's pragmatic bias toward the West, partially influenced by his British wife. During World War II, both Nasser and Sadat had been members of the 'Young Egypt' movement, which was modeled directly on the Nazi party of Germany, complete with paramilitary 'Green Shirts', Nazi salutes and Nazi slogans. Indeed, the smoothness and efficiency of Nasser's coup d'état in 1952 had been attributed by *Newsweek* magazine to be the direct result of involvement by Nazi officers who had taken refuge and had found a postwar home in Cairo.

That was ancient history to the teenage Ibrahim as he attended an exclusive high school in Maadi. He and his friends were concerned about a more contemporary issue. Although Egypt had acquitted itself reasonably well, or at least better than in prior campaigns against Israel, in the 1973 war, young Egyptians continued to be bitter over the failure of their country's leadership to dominate the conflict between Arab and Jew in the Middle East.

The older generation was less bitter. Ibrahim's parents were successful and content. The Sadat regime offered hope and stability after the social and economic instability of the Nasser period.

The future was promising for Ibrahim, and he should have been settled in his excellent prospects. He had decided on medical school and a career as a physician. There was little doubt he would be accepted to Cairo University and then to the medical faculty. His grades were excellent and with his family connections there were no serious impediments.

In his second year at medical school, he was approached by a bearded cleric only a few years older than himself. It was a hot humid day in the university library, and he found it difficult to concentrate on the text he was poring over. Most of his courses were in the sciences, but he was taking one class in the history of Islam and the West.

Egypt under Hosni Mubarak, who took power after Sadat's assassination, was secular, but the influence of the Al-Gama'a al-Islamiyya, an Egyptian Islamist movement considered a terrorist organization dedicated to the overthrow of the Egyptian government and its replacement with an Islamic state, was felt in the university, despite being carefully watched.

The university library was a dreary place and Ibrahim's attention wandered from the book *Ma'alim fi-l-Tariq* (Milestones), written by Sayyid Qutb. The text was difficult for a young man, and Ibrahim was more impressed by the manner of Qutb's death than he was by Qutb's commentaries, although the two were inseparable. Qutb was jailed after the attempt on Nasser's life in 1954, because of his membership in the Muslim Brotherhood, was released in 1965 then tried in 1966, condemned and hung. Much of the evidence in the trial was taken from the commentaries in the 'Milestones'.

"You appear tired from your reading, my brother," the young cleric said. "Accompany me outside and we can sit in the shade of the trees along the Nile and enjoy the breeze coming off the water. Perhaps I can breathe some life into Qutb's commentaries."

Ibrahim had no classes scheduled for the day and was intrigued by the young cleric's demeanor, so he collected his books and the two went out of the library and to the Corniche which paralleled the Nile. When they had seated themselves, the young cleric introduced himself only as Marwa.

"You are surely aware that Qutb is one of the greatest of the commentators on the Koran in modern times. He stands alongside Maulana Mawdudi, Hasan al-Banna and Ruhollah Khomeini in having the greatest influence. In his philosophy, he is a *Salafist*, believing that so-called Islamic culture after the first four caliphs is in reality un-Islamic and therefore worthless. In fact, he thought that the Muslim world had ceased to be and had reverted back to pre-Islamic ignorance known as *jahiliyya* because of the absence of *sharia* law."

"Are you a *Salafist*?"

"Yes, I am a *Salafist*, and I believe Qutb was correct. Qutb also believed that Islamic society should only be ruled by *sharia*, Islamic law, and that Muslims should resist any system where men are in servitude to other men."

"So is that a democracy then?"

"No, absolutely not because democracy implies that elected representatives pass laws which then bind men to law other than *sharia*."

"Then how does Islam reach the enlightened state ruled by *sharia*?"

"Qutb believed, and I believe, that there must be a revolutionary vanguard which will fight *jahiliyya* with a twofold approach: the first through preaching and the second through a *jihad* to forcibly tear down the institutions and authorities of the *jahil* state through physical violence."

"Are you a part of that revolutionary vanguard?"

"I am," said the young cleric, "and we need more bright young men such as you to join us!"

Ibrahim was impressed by the young cleric's knowledge and flattered that he had sought him out. He was also intrigued by the idea of a 'revolutionary vanguard'. Although he himself had no familiarity with *sharia* or how it would be implemented, it sounded very utopian and therefore appealing, especially as he was being asked to join this vanguard.

What was it that appealed to Ibrahim? In every culture, in every social order, there is in every young man's soul a longing to be a part of something greater than himself. In some, it is sublimated into individual pursuits, such as medicine or the pursuit of wealth; in others into social causes, politics or sports; in others into leadership of large organizations, military or business.

In the case of Ibrahim, all of these avenues were open to him. Perhaps there were too many options for him. Nothing was impossible. Perhaps it was the plethora of opportunities that left him receptive to a voice that said 'follow me'.

He didn't decide immediately. It was several weeks after his first meeting with Marwa before he took the initiative to seek him out. But when he did, his commitment was an accomplished fact. All doubts were suppressed. He was an eager, committed member of the vanguard, open to all opportunities for leadership.

At first, Marwa tried to encourage Ibrahim to stay in medical school, to finish his professional degree, but then, witnessing the intensity of his new young friend's conviction, he reversed himself and brought Ibrahim into plans for subversive activity against the Egyptian government. It was risky! The Egyptian government did not look kindly on dissent. Because of his zealous commitment to the revolutionary vanguard, Ibrahim was introduced to Sheikh Omar Abdel al-Rahman who had assumed the mantle of spiritual leadership of Egyptian Islam, especially with regard to Al-Gama'a al-Islamiyya.

Why did this gentle, privileged son of the wealthy classes, raised in relative luxury, become increasingly connected to violence, even to torture? Ibrahim himself could not have explained it. But every incident of violence left him emptier and angrier, until gradually he sought more and more extreme ways to release his anger and hurt the object of his cruelty. Each time he anticipated the violence more, but enjoyed it less, leaving him anxious for the next encounter, which perforce had to be more extreme. His reputation for violence grew in the movement, and even the hardest of the young Muslims began to fear him because his actions were unpredictable. He became, in the ultimate sense of the word, a terrorist, not only for the fear he inspired in the objects of his terror, but in his comrades in crime.

Because of his appetite for violence and cruelty, his comrades tended to avoid him, but they feared and respected him. His reputation grew. He became the favorite of Shaik Rahman and was considered for participation in the World Trade Center bombing in 1993, for which Shaik Rahman had moved to the US, but his importance to Al-Gama'a al-Islamiyya was already considered too important to lose his services, even for a short time. His most infamous activities were leadership roles in the murder of nine German tourists in Cairo in September 1997, and the murder of sixty-two people two months later at a tourist site in Luxor. When the Al-Gama'a al-Islamiyya split, he followed Rifa'i Taha Musa and went underground. He was widely assumed to be an active participant against the Americans in Iraq and even now boasted an ugly downward sloping scar on the left side of his face, presumably the result of an American sniper's bullet, which should have killed him but only cut deeply into his face, ripping the flesh from his cheekbone.

Sometime after the 1997 mass murder at Luxor, he used his scientific training to help him understand EMP technology, which he viewed as a useful weapon for disrupting all manner of communications in the electronics-dependent West, including financial markets, air traffic control communications, communications at missile launch platforms and satellite launch sites. But he was most valuable in his role in making operations secure by intimidating his comrades.

Shahid was no stranger to intrigue. For twenty years he had lived by his wits and he had done his share of scheming, indeed, he had used fear himself. However, he had used fear judiciously and sparingly to accomplish his ends, and he did not particularly enjoy doing it. He knew that Ibrahim enjoyed using fear and seeing its effects. He wondered what it was about their different backgrounds that would explain their different relationship to fear. Ibrahim was Egyptian. He had studied medicine. Was it his knowledge of the human body, and what the human body could stand and what it couldn't stand that was the basis for his use of fear? Or was it because he was from the moneyed class in Egypt and was accustomed to having whatever he wanted satisfied immediately and without question that was at the root of his callous attitude toward fellow human beings?

Instead of finishing medical school, despite being within months of completing the requirements, he joined with radical terrorists. It was a form of intellectual suicide. He no longer cared about serving others, only about controlling them, and he intended to exercise absolute control over the brothers in this room, Shahid knew.

One of Ibrahim's 'skills' was his ability to reverse his convictions instantaneously without warning and without apparent reason. The only constant in his set of beliefs was his hatred of 'Zionists' and the Jewish state, and Western culture itself. His quick reversals, the result of no moral compass, added to his aura of terror, as it eroded the self-confidence of his friends as well as his enemies. And he was never troubled by self-doubt or reflection about his own motivations for past actions. One of his disturbing reversals was about to take his brothers' breath away.

Ibrahim, despite, or because of, being Egyptian, had enormous credibility and influence with Islamic terrorists. The fact that he was currently working with a terrorist cell comprised totally of Pakistanis didn't affect his personal assertion of control and direction. His communications with the leadership in Pakistan was wider and deeper than any of the other members of the cell. And in fact, while his colleagues were discussing EMP technology, thinking he was napping in one of the bedrooms, he was in fact in communication with the leaders of the 'Senior Military Officers Group' in Islamabad discussing strategy.

Following the meltdown of financial markets in the West, Ibrahim himself had raised the question about the usefulness of attacks on financial markets in Western Europe and the US. What was the point? He argued. Western financial markets were reeling from the collapse of confidence. The US and Western Europe were already in recession, a recession which could very well deepen into a depression. "Why waste resources on beating a dead cow?" he asked.

The economy of India was increasingly free-market oriented, and therefore, just as bad as the West itself. Its defense establishment was tied to Israel through the supply of high-tech military equipment. Why not fuse the goals of Pakistan with the goals of Islamic terror to undermine the successes of India and weaken or destroy its defensive capability? The e-bombs they were making in Montmartre would be effective against Indian launch sites in Sriharikota and Balasore. All military communications could be compromised by strategic placement of e-bombs in Indian military headquarters in Delhi.

He knew he could count on the other members of the cell to redirect their efforts, this time toward India, with great enthusiasm. To strike against India, and possibly die, for both their homeland and their religion was more motivation than they would need.

CHAPTER EIGHTEEN

✳✳✳

UNION STATION

When the Metroliner pulled into Union Station in Washington D.C., Joan and I collected our coats and our briefcases and stepped out onto the dock. It was cold and dark as we walked into the cavernous station. The classical pillars and the enormous lobby greeted us coldly. Our heels clicked across the tiled floors on our way to the exits.

We stopped halfway across the lobby and Joan looked up at me and said, "What do we do now, Anderson? We've been involved in something, haven't? Something of major significance. A man has died. I don't think we can just walk away from it. Who do we tell? What do we tell? Am I going to be a part of your efforts? Are you going to include me?"

"I don't know right now, Joan. I should talk to Frank about Sanjay's death before I do anything. I'm not sure what our obligation is at this point. We have cooperated fully with the New York City police. Under whose jurisdiction does it now fall? Certainly not the Washington police. The CIA isn't involved because their jurisdiction stops at the border. They have no authority within the US. Does it fall within the jurisdiction of the FBI? Not unless a state line was crossed in the commission of the crime. But since an element of national security is involved, I suppose they will at least be notified. I'll let Frank decide. But, Erin…Joan…whoever, we have to talk! I've patiently acceded to your request to accept you as 'Joan', and I've accepted you as an agent of Israel, but enough is enough. We've known each other for a long time. We were lovers, for God's sake. You owe me an explanation. I thought we might talk on the train, but you were exhausted, and I understand why. Are you rested enough to talk? There's an out-of-the-way bar here in Union Station."

"Can't it wait until tomorrow, Anderson? I'm not sure I'm up to a complete unraveling tonight."

I was, myself, longing for bed, but I had to know who she was, or purported to be, know everything that is, before I talked to Frank. Besides, my world had been pretty badly shaken up by incidents in the last week, all taking place since I had seen Erin in Tubac a week before. I had assumed Erin to be above suspicion, but that was when I knew her as a practicing clinical psychologist in Dayton, Ohio. Now, she was someone else. She had called me in Tubac to ask if I wanted her to come there. Did she have ulterior motives?

"No, Erin, I don't think it can wait. I have to meet with Frank tomorrow, and I need to know who you are before that. Let's go have a drink and talk!" I had called her 'Erin', which I suppose was significant given that I had called her Joan earlier. Did 'Erin' mean a higher comfort level and 'Joan' a lower one for me? In fact, I really didn't know this 'Joan' person—not like I thought I knew Erin.

We entered the bar, which appeared to be empty except for the bartender, who was polishing a beer glass with a dishtowel. He studiously ignored us as we walked to one of the straight-backed hardwood bench type booths and sat down. There was a huge mirror behind the bar, framed on each end with faux classical half pillars painted deep black, like ebony. The bartender was mostly bald, and where he wasn't bald he had shaved his head, which was shaped like a huge bullet, much like a poor imitation of Mussolini.

He ignored my repeated attempts to catch his eye. Finally, he ambled to the end of the bar and slapped open the one working half of low batwing doors. Stepping into the customer area, he came over to our booth. Still he said nothing, placing a cocktail napkin in front of each of us, then he turned to me, raised one eyebrow and waited. I looked at Joan and she ordered Chardonnay, and I asked for a Bloody Mary. He turned without a word and walked back to the bar.

"This guy makes taciturn sound wild," I said to Erin, who by this time had shrugged out of her coat and was nervously fingering a strand of beads she had worn since yesterday. She ignored my comment. Erin looked far younger than her age, and very vulnerable, but I was determined not to be considerate but rather to insist on getting the whole story.

"Erin, the sooner we get started, the sooner I'll understand, and we can both go. You can start by telling me about Erin and Joan."

"What I've told you is true, most of it anyway." As she said the latter, she cast her eyes away so I couldn't evaluate the truthfulness of the phrase 'most of it anyway'. "You have to view my story sequentially. If you view it as a story of parallel tracks, some of it on one track may be at odds with something on the other track."

She sighed deeply, as if the prospect of revealing her life story was something dreadful to contemplate. "I was born..." she started to say, just as the bartender returned with our drinks, and she stopped quickly, welcoming the interruption and consequent delay. We waited silently while the bartender placed our drinks before us. He took his time, as if savoring his ability to delay our interaction, possibly his only enjoyment in the bleakest bar in Washington.

Finally, he turned to me, again raised one eyebrow and asked, "Tab?" Only one word, but in its terseness it expressed the whole tenor of the loneliness, the shabbiness, the inaptness, of a bar in an empty railway station when all of the incoming trains are in and all of the outgoing trains are out. It was in this hollow barn of a building that I was trying to wrest an explanation from Erin. The unrelenting starkness was more appropriate than the comfort of my home, or the pleasantness of a fine restaurant for such a task. I said no to the bartender and turned back to Erin, raising my eyebrows in question as the bartender retreated. "Go on!" I said.

"I was born Erin Singer-Murphy in Dayton, Ohio. Both of my parents taught at the university, as you know. My childhood was normal, as normal as one can expect with a German Jewish mother and an Irish Catholic father. After high school, I—"

"Stop!" I said. "You don't get off that easily with your childhood. I suspect something, or many somethings, occurred during your growing-up years which determined your later choices. You have a wonderfully rich, though unconventional, adult life. I do suspect that isn't the product of a 'normal' childhood."

Erin's penetrating hazel eyes never left mine. She scarcely blinked. Her face was taut, but not harsh. Her stare spelled defiance, written large! Finally, she said, "God! Do we have to do this here? It's like a tryst in a cheap hotel room. I feel like I'm being assaulted. Couldn't we go someplace a little less barren than a bar in an empty train station, with the hunchback of Notre Dame over there to serve us?"

"We could, but we won't! I don't think comfort is what we need. I want harsh unvarnished truth from you, and a harsh unvarnished bar is just the place for it, I think."

Erin's composure had grown more stressed, as she glanced from side to side, first eyeing the bartender, then the door into the gloomy lobby of Union Station, then me, her look becoming more malevolent as she did so. I knew she had scarcely heard me, or if she had, she wasn't in a frame of mind that receptive to my opinion. "I suppose there might have been something," she said, haltingly, "but I'm not sure why I should bare my soul to you."

"Because you've misled me, misinformed me if not lied to me, because my recent association with you has been accompanied by several acts of violence against me, because your disturbance on the train this evening was, to say the least, violent, but most of all, because I care for you and I want to understand what's driving you."

Erin let out a huge breath, and I realized she had been in iron control of her body as well as her emotions. "I was an only child. My parents married late. My mother was forty-four when I was born. My birth wasn't an easy one, something about the cord becoming wrapped around my neck, which prevented me from passing through the birth canal with ease. My mother was in hard labor for thirty-three hours and nearly died.

"She and my father mutually agreed that another child was unthinkable, but that disturbed my father greatly. Despite being a highly educated scientist, he had never been able to shake his Catholic roots, and all methods of birth control were anathema to him. They had met in graduate school and assumed religion would not be an issue, but his Catholicism kept rising up between them.

"He tried and failed many times to convert my mother, and it led to angry conflict. College professors didn't make as much then as they do now, and our house was small. My bedroom was next to theirs, and the walls were thin. There were violent arguments at night after I went to bed.

"I would awaken in terror as their angry words flew through the walls and into my room. Apparently my father hadn't known everything about my mother's history. She was born in 1929 in Hamburg, Germany. Her parents were wealthy importers, but were virtually wiped out in the 1929 crash. They rebuilt their wealth, only to see it confiscated by the Nazis. They died in the Holocaust, but my mother, who was a teenage girl, was appealing to the Nazis. I don't know what transpired, I don't want to know what transpired, but she was accused after the war of collaborating with them. An American soldier adopted her and brought her to the US. Her collaboration shamed her, and her guilt affected her personality. Despite my father's consolations, it polluted their relationship, and they divorced when I was seventeen."

During this discourse, Erin was openly becoming more agitated, and I could tell she was either going to lash out at me, or she was going to break down in total release. She did the former. She abruptly lurched to her feet, and with the slightest of a grimace she said, "Anderson, you are a very dear person, but I don't have to tell you this shit! I don't owe you anything, and you're being presumptuous to say I do! I'll take a cab home!"

I stood and reached out to stop her, but she had already thrown a bill on the table, and before she turned to the door I saw the tears welling up in her eyes. "Here's for my drink," she said.

It was useless to go after her, so I paid the bill and followed her to the door just in time to see her step into a cab. If I was lonely before, now I was bereft.

I hailed a cab and settled into the back seat for my short trip to Alexandria. As I rode through the darkened streets of Washington and across the Potomac River, I tried to make sense of the last forty-eight hours. I had made some progress. I had furthered my understanding of EMP technology and had developed an important contact with the Indian intelligence services. And, quite by accident, learned that I already had another important contact with Israeli intelligence. I had also learned there was significant high-level cooperation between Indian intelligence and Israeli intelligence, and in the area of defense, enough to provoke enemies of India to also consider Israel an enemy.

I still didn't know much more about Joan/Erin than I had before. Our intimacy in New York was real. It was precious to me, but it didn't explain anything. Who was she? Indeed, what defined who she was, or for that matter, who any of us were? Was she defined by the tumultuous years of her youth? By her studies to become a clinical psychologist? By her studies to become an attorney? Or by her activities as an agent of Israel?

It was easy to say she was all of the above, but it was more accurate to say she was any one of the above at any given moment in time. Perhaps that was what she meant when she said one could understand who she was only by looking at her life sequentially, not by comparing different personas as if they were on two, or three, or four, or more, parallel tracks. Looking at parallel personalities at a point in time made it impossible to integrate them into one person because in such a paradigm, the personality fractured. In Joan's case, such a view caused her personality to disintegrate into broken pieces and shards. But that was exactly what I had been trying to do.

Looked at sequentially, her multiple personas made sense and were an integrated whole. She studied psychology in order to understand her mother and herself and to deal with the traumas of her youth. That was who she was when I knew her in New York and Dayton. She studied law and was an attorney and lobbyist. I could only assume that, as Joan, she had gone directly to law school from Ohio State.

Looked at sequentially, it meant that the only relevant person was the last in the line of development. The last person I knew was an Israeli spy. That was the person I knew. Acknowledgment of that reality was like ice water. It was a jolt, and it conveyed an immense degree of finality, but it was also liberating because I could accept the Joan I now knew.

CHAPTER NINETEEN
***
ALEXANDRIA–FOGGY BOTTOM

When I got home, I checked my answering machine for messages. I have an unlisted phone number, so I don't get many. There was only one, and it was from Frank.

"Anderson," he said. "News of your activities in New York has reached me through Khalida. I'm assuming you're okay, from what I have been told, so I'll skip expressions of concern for your health. The concern I must express is for the breakdown in security and the manner in which you breached it, not to mention your night in the hotel with the Singer-Taylor woman and your unauthorized contact with an Indian intelligence official at the Indian delegation to the UN. I'm surprised and... and feel somewhat let down. I would never have expected this of you. I must leave Washington early tomorrow morning, which is why I'm leaving you this message. I'll be out of touch for several days. Please call Khalida first thing in the morning and make an appointment to meet with her to explain your activities in New York. I'll talk to you soon!"

I collapsed on the sofa by the phone and the air went out of my lungs with a whoosh! I couldn't have been more shocked if Frank himself had emerged from the phone and spoken to me personally. My first reaction was painful shock. What could possibly have been told to Frank that had shaken his trust in me? I thought of him as a father. I would do nothing to violate his trust. I thought back over the last forty-eight hours. What had I done to provoke this response? Surely the night in the hotel with Joan wouldn't prompt it. Frank was no prude.

I had called Frank last night to vet Sanjay before I told him anything, which wouldn't have mattered anyway given the circumstances of his sudden death. So was it the meeting with Sunil, which I didn't even think he knew about? Or, and this was the big one, did he know that Joan was an Israeli agent and was it the fact of her meeting with a representative of Indian intelligence, which happened because of my intervention, the cause of his dismay? And, if it was a problem, for whom was it a problem? Was it a problem for Frank or for someone else in his office? Since Gordon was out of the office, that someone would likely be Khalida! And now Frank was asking me to call her for an appointment, during which, supposedly, I would spill my guts to her.

It just didn't smell right! Frank had never acted this way toward me before, and I truly didn't believe I had done anything to trigger his distrust now. I leaned back in the sofa in a state of confusion. In the space of a few hours, I had lost the trust of the two people whose confidence was most important to me, and what was even worse, I couldn't fathom what I had done to either of them to warrant such a loss.

I spent a restless night tossing and turning until dawn. With a heavy heart, I called Frank's office the next morning and asked for Khalida. She was pleasant on the phone, but totally noncommittal. She would be free about one p.m., she said, and I prepared to go meet with her.

The morning hours passed slowly, but it gave me time to go online and catch up on some e-mail correspondence. I deleted some mass marketing e-mails and was about to delete one from a sender named 'Ivan'.

I hesitated. 'Ivan' was al-Tabari's code name in his communications with Frank whenever he was functioning in their unusual relationship. He had chosen that because he identified with the character Ivan in Dostoevsky's *Brothers Karamazov*. And, indeed, he was like Ivan—severe, emotionless and intelligent to the nth degree. I opened the e-mail with eager anticipation. It was brief, as I expected it to be, and its content was obscure, also as I expected it to be. He said simply: 'Don't trust the Aryans. Ivan'.

Okay, what Aryans? I had spoken to Gordon within the past week about Aryans. And, Joan had spoken of the Aryan legend in Pakistan. Gordon was rightly proud of his heritage. Was there a reason not to trust him? And al-Tabari referred to Aryans, plural. Was there another in Frank's office, or more? Were they involved somehow with foreign intelligence? What caution with reference to Aryans could he have intended? One of those nagging little half thoughts kept dancing in the back of my mind but refused to come forward. I couldn't focus it, so I put al-Tabari's message out of my mind, closed the connection to the Internet and, putting on a sports coat, went out to catch the Metro into Washington and Foggy Bottom.

I arrived in Frank's offices fifteen minutes early and asked the receptionist, the same receptionist, Angelina Markey, who had greeted me so warmly only days before, for directions to Khalida's office. In a distinctly reserved voice, she suggested I take a seat and she would let Ms. Azmat know I was here. I sat and selected a magazine to thumb through while I waited. Forty-five minutes later, I was still waiting. I am not a patient man and my impatience was beginning to take on a menacing character. The receptionist studiously ignored me.

Finally, I rose to my feet and approached the reception desk in two strides. Angelina jerked her eyes away from her computer terminal and skidded her chair several inches before the casters swiveled, enabling her to retreat to the furthest corner of her cubicle in a stunned reaction. I clamped my jaw shut, clenched my teeth and said, as levelly as I could, "I had a one o'clock appointment. I was here before one o'clock. I expect the courtesy of a meeting. Where is Ms. Azmat's office?" She started to reply, but I cut her off, saying, "Never mind! I will find it myself."

I wheeled around; leaving reception by a door that I recalled had led to Frank's office. I suspected Khalida's office was near Frank's, and I was right. The executive offices had full glass walls front and back and Khalida's drapes were open, as was her door. She sat at her desk, coolly watching me approach. I careened through her door, catching my shoulder on the jamb as I passed through. I reached her desk in one giant stride and without asking took a seat in one of the two chairs that sat in front of her desk. I conspicuously looked at my watch and said flatly, "I'm here for my one o'clock meeting."

I had just enough time to exhale before two burly security guards, one on either side, grabbed my arms and twisted them around the back of the chair. I was immobilized in an instant. Khalida still hadn't said a word. We stared at one another and I had to admit, to myself, that she was cooler than I was.

"I think Mr. Wyeth is harmless, at least for the moment. You may release him." They released my arms, and I involuntarily began to rise up from my chair, only to feel four meaty fists slam me back down.

"Are you ready to talk, Mr. Wyeth? Or do you want to play some more games with Eric and William?" It wasn't a promising thought, and I nodded my submission without saying anything. "You may go, gentlemen."

"Who on earth do you think you are, and what do you think you're doing? I work for this firm. I am not threatening it!" I was positively fuming.

"I'm sorry, Mr. Wyeth, but your behavior in the reception area alarmed Ms. Markey, and she triggered a concealed alarm. Mr. Pierce had the alarm installed last year after a particularly nasty threat. Come to think of it, the threat may have coincided with some of your improper behavior with Layla Abboud. Some Muslim men are not very open-minded toward nonbelievers who they feel are consorting with Muslim women. If you were a little more knowledgeable about Islam, you might be a little more sensitive."

"I have studied Islam extensively, Ms. Azmat, and I suspect you would not find my views on Islam, or any other religion for that matter, to be very sensitive at all. Common superstition is not a sound basis on which to build a rational understanding of life."

I tried to keep my voice as polite as possible, but failed. "What's going on here? And, what's the meaning of Frank's message to me. I'm accustomed to speaking directly with Frank and with Frank alone, and especially when I'm engaged on an assignment in which one man has already died and attempts have been made on my own life. We are confronting a palpable threat and I expect help, not hindrance from this office. Where is Frank anyway?"

"Mr. Pierce was asked by the national security advisor to go out of the country on an assignment. He will not be back for several days, or perhaps longer. I spoke to the NSA yesterday, and he assured me that I could reach Mr. Pierce through him. Is there any particular reason you want to see Fran... Mr. Pierce?"

I hesitated before answering. So Khalida was now talking directly with the ANSA, and Mr. Pierce had become 'Frank'. Her star was rising fast, and I could tell I was being marginalized.

"No, nothing I want to talk about. I'll call the ANSA and have him put me in touch with Frank." For the first time, I saw her lose a little control, but just for an instant.

"I don't think you need to do that. I can get information to Mr. Pierce very quickly and easily. What is it you want to talk to him about?"

"I need to get in touch with al-Tabari. He has some information I need, and I need to give him some information. Do you have a secure e-mail address for him?"

"Yes, I do. Why don't you just give me the information, and I will send it to him? In fact, you can dictate it to me. I'm quite fast on the keyboard." She actually batted her long lashes across the desk at me.

I had had enough. I had tested her, and she had failed. She was attempting to intercept my communications, not only with Frank, but with al-Tabari as well. It was apparent that she was playing a game, and that her position in the office was strong.

"Where are the other senior officers? It seems rather quiet around here."

"I think you know Gordon is in Canada. Oleg is here. Giovanni is here. Andreas is on assignment in Brazil, and Chou Li is no longer with us."

"What do you mean Chou Li is no longer with us?" I had developed an immediate rapport with Chou Li. He had been with Frank the longest and had seemed very knowledgeable. According to Frank, he had developed a unique understanding of India, with very strong and deep contacts in the Indian intelligence services.

"Chou Li," Khalida said very slowly, "developed some serious differences of opinion with the strategic direction of Pierce Consulting Services. We mutually agreed that an amicable separation would be best all around."

I simply sat and stared at her. I couldn't think of anything polite to say under the circumstances. She stared back at me, and I couldn't help but be struck by her fair skin and gray eyes. She looked Pakistani, but then she didn't look Pakistani. What the blazes was her ethnic background? Who else had I seen recently who had the same facial structure and characteristics? Then it hit me! Gordon! We had been talking the first day I arrived and were discussing ancient Pakistani history... Mohenjo-daro, before the Aryans invaded and settled there. That was it, Khalida and Gordon were both Aryan, both Pakistani. There was something else about Aryans. Al-Tabari's e-mail! What had he said? He had said 'Don't trust the Aryans'. Did he mean I should not trust Gordon and Khalida?

"What is it, Anderson?" Khalida asked, with some genuine concern, the concern stemming from concern over what I was thinking rather than concern about the state of my mental health.

"It's nothing, really, Khalida. Just some random thoughts. I really should be going."

"But what about your message to al-Tabari? Can we at least send it? I would hate for your visit to be unsuccessful."

"My visit has been very productive, Khalida. The information I needed from al-Tabari now seems less important—trivial, almost. I don't want to bother you with it."

Her eyes betrayed her realization that she had overreached, and that I was beyond her range of control. "At least I can reach Frank for you." She was now losing control.

"No, again, thanks. What I need to say to Frank can wait. Please excuse me and I'll be going."

I stood up and held her eyes with my own. The transformation in her was shocking. Where she had previously shown some concern, if not caring, her face was now hardening and her lips drew back as her voice came out very nearly in a hiss. "Don't do something you will regret, Anderson. Frank is not as enamored with your talents as he once was."

"I assure you I'll keep your admonition in mind."

As I turned to leave her office, I was confronted by the two beefy security guards who had manhandled me previously. They stood side by side just outside Khalida's door, effectively blocking my passage.

"He can go! But remember his face. I don't want him back here again." She said this in a voice as cold as a winter wind, completely devoid of any human warmth. "You are off the payroll here, Wyeth. Don't bother to collect your things. If there's anything of value, I'll have it sent to you." She was speaking to my back as I stood staring at the two guards. I wasn't even weighing my chances of forcing my way past them because there were none, so I was relieved when they stood aside to let me pass, which I did without saying another word. I had been in her office for about ten minutes.

Outside, the March air was sharp and the sky was clear. I felt I had emerged from an ominous presence, kind of a gray cloud of answered questions, threats and real dangers. The easy, uncomplicated relationship I had with Frank was now completely gone, replaced by a web of complexity and by threads of uncertainty. I could not imagine how Khalida had insinuated herself into Frank's organization so deftly, but it seemed she had. And now, even Frank himself was missing from his own firm.

I drew the clean sharp air deeply into my lungs and expelled it in a whoosh, as if by this process I might cleanse myself of the contamination I felt in the offices of Pierce Consulting Services. Khalida's ability to terminate my relationship to Frank's firm was in itself astounding. Where was the man I had come to think of as a father figure? He was strong and powerful, not a wimp to be knocked about at the whim of a wisp of a young woman, no matter what her political connections. It was deeply disconcerting.

CHAPTER TWENTY
✳✳✳
FOGGY BOTTOM

Khalida drummed her fingers furiously on her desk, her light gray eyes brimming with anger. After her exchange with Anderson Wyeth and despite the intervention of her two bodyguards, she felt that Wyeth had gotten the best of her. There had been moments during the course of the meeting where she felt out of control, and even during the tensest parts of the meeting he never lost his composure. She had sought to impress him with evidence of her connections to the national security advisor and her dominance over Frank, but it did not seem to her that she had been successful.

He had refused to entrust a message to her for transmission to al-Tabari or to Frank. Although he hadn't said anything specific, it seemed Wyeth had become more cautious when she had told him about the departure of Chou Li.

Other events were contributing to a higher anxiety level for her as well. Operation Broken Spark was not coming together as planned. In fact, it was at a very critical juncture. Khalida received and communicated information on the operation in two different ways. Salman Rahman informed her about developments within the cell itself. These communications were carried out by e-mails, or prepaid cell phones, which had to be heavily masked to avoid communicating sensitive information to anyone who might accidentally intercept them. While it would have been convenient to communicate in Urdu, a language both she and Salman were fluent in, that would have been an invitation to suspicion.

Her other channel was directly with the ISI. These communications from the ISI were carried out via encrypted messages to the Pakistani Embassy in Washington, then by letter drop in the National Zoo in Rock Creek Park. When a message arrived in the Pakistani Embassy, it was encrypted, translated into Urdu, placed in a small cylinder, much like Kodak film canisters used to be, then placed in a dead drop in the Zoo. The dead drop in a rotted out crevice in an old tree just to the right of the main entrance. Once the drop was made, a white mark in the form of a triangle was made amongst other graffiti on the fence adjacent to the main entrance. A nondescript call would then be made to Khalida in Frank's office, and she would retrieve the canister. If she needed to communicate back to the ISI, the procedure was reversed. She never knew exactly who her contact in the ISI was. She was well acquainted with a number of high-level officials, but her contact never signed his real name to a communication.

Just before Anderson Wyeth's visit, she had received communications from both of her contacts. Salman had informed her of the condition of the cell, and he had indicated that the cell was leaderless and drifting until someone clearly took charge. The nominal leader, Shahid, had just returned from Islamabad with confusing instructions. Ibrahim was like a sphinx and had dissembled information, which added to the confusion. Shahid was wary of Ibrahim's reputation and feared making a decision which might be disapproved or countermanded by him. In effect, the cell was in disarray.

Her contact in the ISI had informed her that operation Broken Spark had been reevaluated and had new goals. Her instructions were to dissemble information in the interim to Frank and to the national security advisor.

He had also said that the objective of Broken Spark was conclusively set to prepare for war with India and that Ibrahim was now in charge of the cell. Meanwhile, ISI had become aware that Anderson Wyeth was communicating directly with al-Tabari in Casablanca, and that both of them were getting too close to learning the membership and capabilities of Broken Spark. Khalida was to take all measures necessary to deflect Wyeth from his activities.

So her meeting with Wyeth had achieved exactly the opposite of what she was supposed to have achieved. If anything, his dedication to pursuing Broken Spark was intensified. She did not appreciate the irony.

The more she thought about Wyeth, the angrier she became. She had isolated him from Frank and the ANSA. He was effectively persona non grata in the office. The only other person in the office who might have become an ally for him was Chou Li, and he was gone. His only ally left was al-Tabari, but he was one of the most dangerous. What perplexed Khalida was her inability to understand what al-Tabari's motives were. He was a Muslim, a scholar of the Koran, a Palestinian who had every reason to hate the West, but instead he appeared to assist the West. He was an enigma. She was sure he wasn't doing it for money. She was also certain he was not an apostate. He hadn't departed from the path of Islam. He had been discussed in Islamic circles and was thought of as a 'decent' man who objected to the 'ends justify the means' philosophy of extreme Islam. What was it that caused him to risk his life and endanger the plans of extreme Islam? Was it his bourgeois decency?

After he had relocated to Istanbul from Ramallah, he had secreted his wife and 'adoptive' son in the old city where they could not be found. Without being able to seize them as hostages, Khalida could think of no way to apply pressure on him. Her thoughts turned to Wyeth. Sex and money, the two principal tools of influence over undercover agents who lived in the gray areas of secret information and operations, were not available to her. Or, she thought, were they? Who was the woman Wyeth had spent the night with in New York? Frank had mentioned her frequently. Her name was Joan Singer-Taylor, she was sure. Could she be used against Wyeth?

Khalida sat at Frank's desk without physically moving for a long time. Her thoughts were so focused she lost track of time and space. If she had been asked, she couldn't have said where she was or what date and time she occupied. Her mind worked relentlessly, overwhelmed by one central question: how could she defeat Wyeth's interest in Broken Spark by persuasion if possible, or by force if necessary? Gradually, an idea began stirring slowly, collecting information from all of the secret storage cells in her mind. Public embarrassment would not be effective, she thought. She had no evidence that anything untoward had happened between the Jewish woman and Wyeth in the New York hotel room. Besides, in this country, sex was hardly something that could be used for blackmail, except in extreme circumstances.

How unlike my culture, she thought, where even a lustful look could invite the stoning of a female and possibly a ritual killing of the offending male. More evidence of the West's decadence! I *must think like someone from the West, not like myself. The Western male, if one can believe their literature and their abominable TV, is motivated to care for and protect the female. Granted, it has been dramatically watered down since women's liberation started in the sixties, but it is still there, at least a shadow of its former value.* Wyeth had demonstrated his affection for Layla, to Khalida's surprise. Layla hadn't expected gallantry, coming from the culture of Saudi Arabia and Pakistan.

So it was possible Wyeth might be manipulated by threatening the Jewess, but what about al-Tabari? He had such a curious value system for a Muslim scholar. His dedication to his wife, Hana, and his ward, Saeed—Layla's brother—was unusual, more secular than religious. Could he be manipulated by threats to either of them, assuming they could be found? He had run to Istanbul when they were threatened in Ramallah. That was a good indication! She would see if it was possible to manipulate both of them by the use of one woman, and a Jewess at that!

Khalida selected one of her four prepaid cell phones, which lay in her personal locked cabinet, always charged, always ready, and pressed in the number of another prepaid cell phone in Montmartre. The phone rang twice, then a quiet voice said, "Broken Spark."

Khalida relaxed. If Gordon had answered with his clerical name, Salman Rahman, they couldn't have spoken openly, but Gordon was apparently in a secure or isolated location.

"Are your preparations complete?" she asked.

"Not really," was the answer. "Ahmed is making good progress assembling the devices. We still have to design and create nondescript exterior shells for them so they can be placed without arousing suspicion. We're thinking about using table lamps with the device in the lampshade. They can even be placed in a waiting room, then plugged into the wall socket. This will couple the EMP directly into the electric power grid, scorching all electronic components attached to the grid. If we can get them into the control or communications rooms in the Indian launch sites of Sriharikota or Balasore, or both, we should be able to seriously damage the Indian military's ability to respond to our launch, at least temporarily.

"We cannot eliminate all potential response, but we can reduce it substantially. It's a straightforward calculation. What casualties can we inflict on the Indians in return for what level of casualties we're prepared to accept ourselves. If we can get our priorities in focus in Islamabad, we should be able to move forward rapidly. We can corrupt the Indians' data analysis and guidance systems to the extent that they themselves recognize it is unreliable by causing their computers to malfunction. As their computers malfunction, they will struggle with the issue of whether and how to respond, giving us a dramatic edge. Our homeland is now fighting against time. The Indians are advancing their military preparedness dramatically. We must be prepared to act quickly. How are you doing with the Americans? Surely they wouldn't be foolish enough to intervene!"

"No, I think we can be certain they will not intervene militarily. I have developed a comfortable personal acquaintanceship with America's national security advisor, and I will, I think, convince him in the next several days of the rightness of our position. There is no use arguing our position on Kashmir anymore. Westerners are tired of Kashmir. What I am trying to do is create a new picture for him to consider, a picture of a confident, resurgent India flexing its muscles and threatening its neighbors, especially those it does not control. He will ask for our restraint and urge us to think of all the human casualties, not to mention the precedent that would be set by a regional nuclear war. I will say we are cognizant of our responsibilities as a nuclear power, but point out to him that our armed forces, which have the responsibility of protecting the Republic, cannot stand idly by as India's aggressive, out-of-control military edges closer to upsetting the balance of power and possessing a devastating first strike capability against us. It's a persuasive argument, I think, and one which will freeze American decision makers like deer in the headlights. I will point out that India just recently launched a surface-to-surface missile from its launch facilities at Balasore."

"And what of this tiresome Don Quixote, Anderson Wyeth? Is there anything we should be doing to neutralize him? Doesn't he have access to Frank and to the ANSA? And speaking of Frank, where is he and is he a potential problem?"

"Both Frank and Wyeth have significant influence with the ANSA. Frank is off on a wild goose chase to Israel. You know how the Americans jump when Israel snaps its fingers. He'll be out of touch for a few days. Wyeth is another matter. Dealing with Wyeth is a multifaceted challenge because of his relationship with Frank, the ANSA, and now this Joan Singer-Taylor woman. My information indicates that Singer-Taylor has connections with Israeli intelligence, which could have major implications for our targeting. The other part of the Wyeth problem is his friendship for and relationship with al-Tabari. I continue to be angered by al-Tabari's near apostasy. For a Muslim, he is far too secular and undependable. If you meet up with him, treat him like a leper. He must not learn of our plans."

"What are you going to do about Wyeth?"

"I'll arrange to kidnap the Jewess here in Washington and have her sent under guard to Casablanca to use as leverage on both Wyeth and al-Tabari. If successful, we will neutralize their influence in Washington, and be able to use them as a bargaining chip in the event Washington tries to get involved in the execution of our plan before it is fully underway. Ibrahim will be absent from your cell for a while. I need his skills to carry out this operation. He will return as soon as the operation is complete."

CHAPTER TWENTY-ONE
***
|CASABLANCA

After leaving Khalida's office I fairly jogged to the Metro station, catching the first train to Alexandria. My goal was on talking to al-Tabari. He ought to be able to shed some light on what was happening at Pierce Consulting. After all, he had known Frank far longer than I, and the EMP conspiracy was picking up steam. Frank had first been alerted to it by al-Tabari, so he should be able to help me find its source. It seemed to me that we were getting closer to understanding the goals of the operation, and because of that, I was getting more threats and more actual physical violence. I burst through the door of my townhouse and flew up the steps three at a time.

I turned on my computer and paced the floor as it loaded its operating system and hooked on to the Internet. 'Ivan's' e-mail was still in my e-mail account. I opened it and stared again at the words: 'Don't trust the Aryans'. I knew now that I was right. The Aryans were Gordon and Khalida, and their takeover of Frank's operation, his reputation, his connections and his contacts meant the EMP operation was moving into high gear. It also meant a foreign state had its agents very close to the levers of national security power in the US. That was not good!

I typed out a response to al-Tabari's e-mail: "I understand! Would love to visit you and Hana. Are you still staying near the White House? I am planning to visit the White House tomorrow, but I don't know how to get in. Can you help? 1605851." It was 2:45 in the afternoon.

I didn't know if my crude code would communicate discreetly, or if it was so simplistic anyone could figure it out. Worst case, 'Ivan' couldn't figure it out and my enemies could, but I didn't have time to worry about that. The reference to the White House, Casablanca, would only be transparent to someone who knew al-Tabari was in Casablanca. All airlines have unique flight numbers, but 1605851 might not have meaning if you didn't know someone was coming to Casablanca.

There was an Air Maroc flight, number 851, arriving in Casablanca at 4:05 the following afternoon, and I would be on it. I had just enough time to get to Dulles an hour before the 4:20 p.m. departure of a KLM flight that flew to Amsterdam with connections on Air Maroc to Casablanca. It seemed like a long way to go to get from Washington to Casablanca, but who can figure airline schedules? I was lucky! My cab got me from Alexandria to Dulles in forty-five minutes. That put me a little behind schedule for the security requirements, but the customer service agent was efficient and I was through security and ready to board in plenty of time. Nineteen hours later, plus five hours for time zones, I was in Casablanca.

It was a feeling I had had many times, deplaning in a strange city, knowing no one, or at least no one well. I didn't expect al-Tabari to meet me at the airport. That would have been too risky. Assuming he got, and deciphered, my e-mail, he would make contact with me in the next twenty-four hours.

I took the first cab from the ten or so lined up at the terminal exit. I thought I felt eyes on me as I stood at the cabstand, but it was hard to say. I was a little paranoid to say the least. Sometimes, those six senses are right and sometimes they aren't. When they're right, you tend to think they're awesome. When they're wrong, you shrug them off. Inside the cab, I tried very hard to convince myself my sixth sense was wrong. Or maybe it was the eyes of al-Tabari I was sensing. I could only hope so.

The ride from Mohammed V airport north into Casablanca took twenty-five minutes, and because of traffic on Boulevard D'Anfa another fifteen minutes to reach the Hyatt. As I paid the bill and got out of the cab, I could hear the Atlantic Ocean pounding the shore less than a kilometer away. I entered the plush lobby, decorated with furniture of fine Moroccan leather, and turned left to the front desk. The smell of the Moroccan leather overrode the fragrance of the cut flowers placed in a profusion of vases scattered throughout the lobby like petals scattered before high dignitaries on parade. I still felt I wasn't alone, that someone was watching me. Was it al-Tabari or a less benign pair of eyes that accompanied me as I took the elevator to my floor?

I had no sooner entered my room than a soft knock sounded on the just-closed door. I quickly stepped to the door and looked through the peephole, and, seeing nothing, stepped back, looked down and saw that a piece of paper had been slipped under the door. I studied it carefully before picking it up. I could see no traces of powder or other smudges to indicate it was anything other than what it appeared to be. I opened the door and looked right and left, but saw no one, so I picked up the paper, unfolded it carefully and read the words: "Dar Beida Restaurant 7:00 p.m. tomorrow. Take a table in a discreet location. a/T."

So, I wasn't paranoid. Al-Tabari had been watching me. I felt good and uneasy at the same time. I was glad he was here, but I was more than a little upset at myself for not spotting him. If he could observe me without detection, were there others? On the other hand, I hadn't taken any special measures to avoid detection. Sometimes you need to be a sitting duck. I had to find people and find them fast. Letting them find me was one way. But with al-Tabari's note, I had short-circuited the process.

I spent the next day in a frustrating attempt to contact Frank. All communications seemed to run through Khalida, and even an innocuous message sent to Frank's e-mail address went unanswered. Achieving nothing, it was six p.m. before I knew it. I had time to shower and find my way to the Dar Beida, which was off the lobby.

I arrived well before seven p.m. and found the perfect table in a protected nook where both al-Tabari and I could watch the room for any unusual activity. We would be able to have a serious conversation and still enjoy our meal. I ordered a martini, shaken, and perused the menu while I waited. I found the expected Moroccan dishes, couscous, lamb tagine, stewed in olives, dates and raisins, and others. There was also French cuisine. My martini came, but still no al-Tabari. I looked at my watch. It was 7:15.

I began to worry that something might have happened but then the waiter arrived, supposedly to take my order. Instead, he leaned toward me and said in a low voice, "A Mr. Khalid is waiting for you at the table near the far wall," and nodded his head toward a table for two where a clean-shaven, well-dressed man sat, wearing an expensive blue pinstripe suit and a fashionable colored shirt with a white collar. His tie was conservative and perfectly tied in a Windsor.

My face was blank and I said, "I do not recognize the gentleman. Perhaps there is some mistake?"

"He said you might recall him as al-Tabari?"

I looked again and saw what I had missed at first glance. Without his keffiyeh and his robe, and without his Vandyke, his hair slicked back, al-Tabari looked every bit the part of a Middle Eastern businessman ready to do business with his Western counterpart.

As I looked for a third time, I could recognize the sharp chin and high cheekbones I had first feared in Ramallah when Layla and I had been given over to al-Tabari's care after being seized in Mexico and sent by sea to the West Bank for interrogation and punishment. As I looked, he dipped his head in the slightest nod of recognition. I reciprocated the gesture, and turning to the waiter, ordered a lamb tagine and asked him to deliver it to me at al-Tabari's table. I didn't expect a warm greeting, and I got what I expected. Al-Tabari, whose given name was Khalid, I now recalled, rose slightly and extended his hand. I took it in acknowledgment, then let it drop. He waved me to the other chair and I sat.

I looked at him curiously and said, "I'm not sure which is the disguise and which is the real person, but it is effective. On casual observation, I would never recognize you. Have you worn this appearance since you came to Casablanca? What has it been, two or three months?"

"Yes, Anderson, I felt my public appearance should change with Casablanca. When I meet with a member of the cell, however, I do revert to my true identity as a scholar of the Koran. I am more effective seen that way, I think."

"You're effective in any guise, I would say. Is Hana with you here in Casablanca? And Saeed?" naming his wife and Layla's brother in turn. "No, alas, Hana remains in Istanbul and Saeed stays with her while attending university. I return as often as I can. Why are you in Casablanca?"

"Why am I here? I'm here primarily because you made Frank aware that an EMP operation was in the process of being developed by a cell comprised primarily of Pakistani Islamic terrorists. I'm here because the closer I get to knowing more about that EMP operation, the more dangerous it becomes for me and others around me. One man has died because I got too close to the source. I'm here to talk to you because the New York and world financial markets have turned to mush and are full of rumors. I don't know if there's a connection with the EMP operation or not. US economic, financial and security interests are seriously threatened. I'm here talking with you because extreme Islam is having too many successes: success in Iraq, success in Gaza, success in Lebanon, success in Mumbai, and success in the elevated price of oil which is indirectly funding their operations. I'm here because the locus of activity seems to be shifting to Asia, Pakistan, China and India. And if that isn't enough, I'm here because of your e-mail message to me about the Aryans, because you, al-Tabari, warned Frank about the development of a terrorist threat involving EMP and because Frank's office appears to me to be compromised. I'm here simply because you are the best! And, I'm increasingly feeling that I'm being alienated and shut out in the cold. I want help and I want to know what's going on!"

"This is a very difficult and fluid time, Anderson. Some of what you say is still accurate and some things have changed. There is an EMP plot being developed. When I talked to Frank, I had been informed it was designed to attack Western financial markets, including New York and Chicago. However, since the time the plot was beginning to be formed, Western financial markets have self-destructed on their own. My source indicates to me that the feeling is: why waste resources on something that is already in its death throes? This is combined with the feeling, as you rightly observe, that extreme Islam has been realizing some significant successes. You mentioned several of them, but you did not mention one of the most important, and that is the success of Al-Qaeda and the Taliban in reestablishing their influence in Afghanistan, and now Pakistan. They would agree with you that Iraq is a success for them.

"While extreme Islam has not achieved a resounding success in Iraq, it has been successful in keeping the US military and its so-called allies bogged down for almost six years. That is no small achievement. Extreme Islam was successful in Mumbai, Guantánamo has blackened the image of the US, and the price of oil, while off its highs, is still elevated and is providing a steady cash flow to extreme Islamic militants.

"There are, Anderson, many winds sweeping through Islam today. That Islam is resurgent there can be no doubt. There are over a billion and a half Muslims in the world. There are many different strains of Islam, some of them reasonably moderate, and some of them absolutely fanatic. That is true of other religions as well. The Jews have their Orthodox Hasidic sect, which insists to the death their right to settle in Palestinian territories. The Christians have the extreme right wing, which has a whole agenda of demands, many of which do not even relate to religion.

"Back to Islam. Among the many crosscurrents, there are those who believe the war against the nonbelievers, you, should be fought with swords and bombs and steel, simple hack and burn. There are those who think the war should be fought with words and philosophy. There are those who believe the war should be fought on a technological level, disabling the technological superiority the West possesses. Among the latter there are those who believe the ruination of the West's technological superiority is sufficient, and those who believe that technology should be used to destroy and kill people.

"I believe the sect engaged in the EMP plot are among those who believe that harming the West's technology will further its decline more dramatically than bombing individual targets in order to kill people. They are not opposed to killing people, mind you; it is just that killing is simply not their primary goal. However, I also believe the sect we are dealing with has deep divisions. There are some in the cell, at least one, who believe that the use of technology should be directed toward the initiation or stimulation of violence using higher orders of technology, specifically, nuclear weapons. Such a goal would involve the initiation of nuclear war between...say...India and Pakistan."

"Is that why Sanjay Singh and Sunil Dandekar were so interested in and involved in the rumors going around the New York financial markets?"

"Yes, I suspect that is a part of it. As you may or may not know, the Indian intelligence services, RAW, have an advanced appreciation of the impact an EMP bomb could have on their sophisticated electronic infrastructure. India is a highly bifurcated society, disposing extraordinary sophistication at the upper levels and extraordinary poverty and illiteracy at the lower levels. Pakistan is similar, although to a lesser degree of sophistication. Although Pakistan's nuclear capability is real, it was largely developed with the assistance of the Chinese, who saw Pakistan as a valuable counterweight to the growing military power of India. The friendship between the old Soviet Union and India posed a serious potential threat to China, creating a real possibility of a two-front war in the event of hostilities between either China and the Soviet Union or China and India.

"Therefore, they extended their assistance to Pakistan so that India would be faced with a two-front war in the event of hostilities with China. It worked for a period of time. At the same time, during the Cold War, the US was a major supporter of Pakistan, again as a counterweight to India, who was then a friend of the Soviets, and particularly during the Soviet occupation of Afghanistan.

"Everything has changed. Now there are, at least presently, no serious issues between China and India, and the US is trying to use Pakistan as a club against Al-Qaeda and the Taliban. Pakistan is left friendless, unstable, economically distraught, and under poor leadership. That is a recipe for a soup of unpleasant ingredients, and likely to cause indigestion in the region."

"Tell me what you know about the composition of the cell you have discussed. How is it composed? Who are the members? What are their individual motivations?"

"As you can appreciate, I don't have a complete understanding of the cell. It's not like they write out their own charter and send me updates on their progress. I get bits and pieces of information from surreptitious communications with only one of the members and from other sources. From what I can understand, my source is one of the more gentle and highly principled members of the cell. His name is Taufig, which I feel free to tell you because it is probably not his real name, and it may or may not have been changed by now, anyway.

"Taufig himself is Pakistani. He views himself as heir to the brilliant Mogul rulers who gave India a golden civilization in the 16th and 17th centuries. He appears to be motivated by the more lofty ideals of Islam. He believes that Islam has produced higher civilizations with greater levels of learning, as well as higher artistic achievements and greater generalship then civilizations in the West. He attributes the decline in Muslim influence throughout the world to the decadent practices and lifestyles of contemporary Muslim leaders, particularly the Ottomans until WWI, and the Arab kings and princes now. Their self-indulgent lifestyles and softness enabled a more dedicated and committed, though, in his view inferior and non-believing Western culture to overwhelm the leadership of Islamic countries.

"He is a Shiite. He believes in total commitment to Islam and is willing to sacrifice his and everyone else's lives to the cause of resurgent Islam. He was sent to Morocco, here in Casablanca in fact, to recruit foot soldiers who would be willing to die in suicide missions to either advance the rise of Islam or promote the decline of the secular West. He has recruited and trained two such individuals from the slums of Casablanca, the most notorious slum being Al Massira. These two are simple individuals whose minds are filled with hate and desire for revenge. One of them had a brother who was killed by the Moroccan police in the May, 2003 suicide bombings in the Casablanca financial district. They now believe that all of their problems have been caused by the secular West and by Zionists."

"Is Taufig the leader of the cell?"

"No, not even close. In fact, of the five members of the cell, Taufig may be the furthest from a leadership role. The nominal leader appears to be a Pakistani with close ties to the ISI. His name, I think, is Shahid. He is a professional intelligence operative and, again, my information is sketchy, I believe he has just returned to Montmartre from Islamabad. No doubt he has the most recent instructions from the ISI. He has extensive experience in intelligence operations abroad, including 'black' operations, that is, operations involving the license to kill.

"A third Pakistani in the cell is Ahmed. Ahmed is the technician. He knows how to make bombs and how to make them work. It is not clear to me how much he knows about EMP bombs. However, he has studied physics in the US and the construction of a flux compression generator to produce the EMP burst would not be beyond his capabilities I would think. The final two members of the cell are murky. One of them you know. His name is Salman Rahman. Does that ring a bell?"

"Not in the slightest! I have never heard that name before."

"Salman Rahman you may know under his American/Canadian name, Gordon Rhoads. Gordon was born in the United States, and so is a US citizen, Pakistani parents. His parents emigrated from Sindh state in Pakistan, first to England, then to the United States, where he was born. They subsequently moved to Calgary, and he acquired Canadian citizenship there."

"So Gordon is of Pakistani origin and his lineage is from the ancient Aryans. As I recall, he's very fair-skinned and has light gray eyes. Ah, wait! We discussed that briefly when I first went to Frank's offices. He said he was fair-skinned because of his Aryan ethnic background. We talked about the ancient Indus Valley civilizations and how traditional historians have assumed the Aryans overran the Indus Valley around fifteen hundred B.C. Incredible! So Gordon Rhoads is a member of a Pakistani cell and goes by the name of Salman Rahman?"

Not only was Gordon one of the Aryans al-Tabari had warned me about, he was also part of a terrorist cell. If Khalida was the other Aryan, was she a member of the terrorist cell as well?

"How does Khalida fit in? Is she an active member of the cell?"

"No, she is not an active member, if you mean by that does she meet regularly with the cell members. She is, however, an active member of the cell in the sense that she relays information from the cell, in the form they wish to distribute it, to Frank and to the national security advisor, and she in turn feeds information back to the cell members through Gordon, and I believe she also has direct communication with the ISI. So, while she is not an active member of the cell, she may be one of the leaders of it."

By this time, we had finished our meal and darkness had descended over Casablanca.

"Shall we go for a walk outside?" al-Tabari asked. "It is pleasantly cool this time of year, especially here with the breezes off the ocean."

I paid the check and we exited the hotel through the front entrance. "You've told me about four members of the cell, plus Khalida. Who's the fifth member?"

"The fifth member of the cell is the de facto leader. I hope it is never your misfortune to meet him. He is a killer without conscience, skilled in the arts, if one can call them that, of torture and murder. He is an Egyptian by birth, growing up in the wealthy Maadi district of

Cairo. His parents owned property and he had every privilege during his youth. He entered medical school but withdrew in favor of underground political activism."

"That sounds very much like al-Zawahiri, the number two man in Al-Qaeda. Some say he has the brains and is the de facto leader of Al-Qaeda."

"Yes, there are strong parallels, although Ibrahim is considerably younger than al-Zawahiri, and though he entered medical school, he did not become a physician, as did al-Zawahiri. Ibrahim has direct links to, and direct communications with, the darker side of ISI. He can be, and has been, involved in internal politics in the ISI, and has been known to completely change the direction of foreign operations that have already been set on a course, in response to his private directives from the dark side of ISI. It is at least possible that he is engaged in doing that very thing even as we speak. The man is completely lacking a moral compass, which is why he is so effective in the business of terror."

"How do you know these people? Have you met them?"

"I have met Taufig and Salman Rahman. Almost all of what I know about the cell I have learned through Taufig. Salman Rahman I have met only as Gordon Rhoads, and he is not aware that I know he is Rahman. The others, I have not seen. Taufig's descriptions of them, however, have been complete, and he is terrified of Ibrahim. He literally shakes when he talks about him. You should know that all of them, with the exception of Ibrahim, have a background in physics. Pakistan's high school and undergraduate education maintains a high priority for physics in its curriculum. In addition, many young Pakistanis have studied abroad, in Britain and the United States. This capability should not be underestimated."

"Is Taufig here in Casablanca?"

"No, he left several days ago to join the cell, meeting in Paris. Unfortunately, I don't know where in Paris, but I have the sense it is somewhere near Montmartre."

"Do you think the cell is aware of your extensive relationship with Taufig?"

"I honestly don't know. If they are aware, they have not manifested it, but I doubt it. Otherwise Taufig would be dead."

"Do you intend to maintain contact with Taufig in any way?"

"Yes, even now I am preparing to leave for Paris. I would have left earlier were it not for your arrival in Casablanca."

"Why do you think Taufig has opened up to you so much?"

"Who knows? Perhaps it is the loneliness. Perhaps it is because he is intelligent and can see that radical Islam's way of confronting the West is not necessarily the only or the best way. Perhaps he doesn't like violence."

"But he was here to recruit two suicide bombers. Isn't that inconsistent with what you say?"

"Perhaps, but aren't we all a package of inconsistencies? I myself, you recall, recruited Istishhadiyas, female suicide bombers. And while I recruited them, I carefully selected them to find those who had a propensity to terminate their commitment as suicide bombers, like Layla. I don't really know why Taufig is willing to talk to me. I do know he is taking enormous risks, especially given what I know about Ibrahim. Those risks extend on to me, and now to you."

"As if I didn't have enough threats to deal with," I said with an ironic smile. "I'm intrigued, you said 'loneliness' first. Loneliness is powerful. It takes a strong, or an emotionless, person to live a life where accomplishments must remain unknown, unrecognized, silent to the outside world. There's no way to take pride in your achievements, or to seek solace from others when you've failed. If you love someone, the best protection for them is to know nothing about what you do.

"It's a sorry existence, living a life of lies, rootless, seeking warmth and comfort in an ideology of lies and violence. Yes, I suspect loneliness is a major motivator for all people operating under cover, causing them to seek a friend, a contact, someone they can talk to even if they doubt they can implicitly trust that someone.

"In fact, they tend to seek someone with a position which to them seems non-threatening, like you being an Islamic scholar of Palestinian origin. You would appear to be involved in work tangential to Taufig's cause, and therefore anything he might say to you wouldn't be a breach of security in his mind because you'd have no use for the information."

We had reached the end of the lighted street, and the pounding surf was only seconds ahead of us. It drowned out most other sounds, and the bright lights of Casablanca were behind us. Ahead of us was only darkness and surf. Low-hanging clouds had accumulated over the Atlantic and drifted toward the coast. They obliterated whatever chance there was of light from the stars and the moon, leaving the darkest of darkness. They absorbed whatever light there was from the streets of the city. It was a night made for deeds which could not survive the light of day.

I was having difficulty focusing on philosophical thoughts and found myself thinking more and more about action. I experienced the nervous thrill that arises when the body and mind sense danger, and my senses went to high alert. Al-Tabari had ceased talking minutes earlier and was silent while I spoke aloud of my meandering theory on loneliness.

Now, both of us were quiet, straining to hear the slightest sound. I had had enough threats over the last week and a half to make me continuously edgy, but my concern was nothing compared to what al-Tabari must have been experiencing. If the cell members were to become aware of the extent of his relationship with Taufig, Taufig's and al-Tabari's lives were meaningless.

I started to say, "Al-Tabari," but he cut me off with a "ssh!"

I stopped and listened, but I could hear nothing but the silence of the impenetrable darkness of night. The restlessness of the surf struck a corresponding chord in the restlessness in my body and was an echo of the stillness of the night. I strained to hear any sound other than the surf, but I could hear none. I could not contain my anxiety and turned to begin the walk back to the hotel. Al-Tabari placed his hand on my arm and squeezed lightly. It seemed he had heard something I had not.

Finally, I heard the strained breathing of someone laboring to keep his or her presence quiet. I sensed rather than saw the movement of a large physical presence gain momentum toward us. I expected the worst! But the huge form, just as it reached us, dropped a large bundle on the ground and turned away, racing toward the lights of the city.

Al-Tabari flicked a cigarette lighter into flame and by its weak illumination we saw that the bundle was a body. We assumed the worst and wondered why a dead body would be thrown before us. But as al-Tabari's flame went out, we heard a low moan emerge from the bundle. We knelt down, and in the darkness of night, our hands tried to discern the form of the body within the wrappings. I could not see, so, later, when I thought about it, it had to be a paranormal sense which caused me to say to al-Tabari, "My God, this is Erin!"

CHAPTER TWENTY-TWO
✻✻✻
WASHINGTON, D.C.

Only a day earlier, halfway around the world, Joan and Chou Li had sat across from one another in one of the many obscure cafés that dot Wisconsin Avenue north of Georgetown. It was eight p.m. and every table in the establishment was occupied. They had been there for half an hour and were finishing light salads and glasses of wine.

Joan had been a little surprised when Chou had called. She had known him through Frank and had seen him at several receptions. His responsibility for Asian affairs for Frank, including India, matched her own area of interest, so it was natural that their patterns of activity interacted from time to time. What did surprise her was his request that she meet him in this small café and his subsequently telling her that he had been forced out of Pierce Consulting by Khalida.

"What's her agenda, Li? She has sent Frank off to parts unknown, ingratiated herself with the ANSA and fired you. She has herself become Pierce Consulting, but to what purpose? What is she trying to accomplish?"

"Don't forget, Joan, she has also sent her co-ethnic friend Gordon off to… where? I don't know where! But there is no mistaking the fact that the two of them are very close, and what Gordon is doing is directly related to what Khalida is doing, and what Khalida is doing is not aimed at improving the international security position of the US. I personally think her purpose is to neutralize the US in the event of another Indo- Pakistani war, which, I think, is coming.

"Keep in mind that US relations with India have changed dramatically since the dark days of the Cold War. India and the Soviet Union were at that time very close. The Indian Air Force flew MIG and Sukhoi fighters and, diplomatically, India was aligned with the

Soviets. Pakistan was aligned with the US. US involvement, through the CIA, with Pakistan's ISI, in the Mujahedin Jihad against the Soviet Union was extensive.

"The cooperation and joint efforts against the Soviets carried out by the ISI and the CIA were unusual in their scope and extent. During that time, the Pakistani government went from Ali Bhutto to Zia al Huq to Benazir Bhutto to Nawaz Sharif to Musharraf in uncertain jerks and stops, but the US-Pakistan relationship remained strong, despite the lack of common principles of culture and governance. They were united by the common enemy, the Soviet Union.

"Since the collapse of the Soviet Union, US relations with India, cultural, business and military, have blossomed, and the US's client state in the Middle East, Israel, has become the largest supplier of military hardware to India, and US relations with Pakistan have withered. The US attitude has gone from hostility to Pakistan's nuclear weapons and its brazen marketing of their expertise to other countries to toleration because of the critical support of Pakistan in the struggle against Al-Qaeda and the Taliban.

"The US has borne a series of terrorist attacks carried out by Pakistani individuals in the US, and now has to sort through the murky interaction between the Pakistani military and the Taliban and Al-Qaeda. This is particularly apparent in the North-West Frontier, where the rule of law does not run from the Pakistani government but from whatever tribe is dominant in the particular geography.

"So, Pakistan is nearly isolated now. It can no longer count on China or the US as a great and powerful friend; it is threatened by India, indirectly by the US, it has no friend in Russia, and who can it count on in the Muslim world for support?"

"But how can Khalida's activities neutralize the US, then? That seems like a tall order."

"She will do it by feeding false information to the national security advisor. With Frank and particularly Anderson out of the way, and with the relationship she has established with the ANSA, she can feed crafted information to the inner circles of foreign policy decision-makers.

"They already have sensory overload from all of the foreign crises they are currently dealing with. The idea is to feed conflicting and ambiguous information in such a way that decision-makers are paralyzed. She doesn't need to cause them to act, only not to act.

"The US has agents on the ground, of course, presumably to verify information, but the key to decisive action is one consistent set of facts which make policy decisions clear and supportable. It is not difficult to present an alternative set of facts to confuse and mislead the decision-makers. And agents on the ground are not perfect. Their information is often wrong, so it is not hard to raise questions about their veracity.

"A well thought-out plan, which we must assume Khalida's to be, has great chances for success. What concerns me is that I believe the evidence suggests some kind of action between Pakistan and India is about to take place. Remember, Khalida came from the ISI, or was recommended to Frank by a high-ranking member of the ISI, possibly a family member."

"Li, one of the things that puzzles me is Khalida's apparent position of authority. Pakistan is one of the centers of radical Islam. Women are stoned there for committing the offense of being raped. It's barbaric. Yet she seems to have significant stature. What's with that?"

"All cultures are diverse, Joan, and Pakistan is no exception. Don't forget, Benazir Bhutto was prime minister. She was from a prominent family in Sindh Province, and Khalida's family prominence goes a long way toward providing her with authority, even in the male-dominated culture of Pakistani Islam."

"Assuming I buy all of this, Li, and I think I do, what does it mean for me, and I guess for Anderson and for you? Why did you call me?"

"I may be wrong, Joan, but I suspect you have a way to communicate with Anderson. It is urgent that he be aware of Khalida's plans. I want you to contact him."

Joan's heart sank. She had had a communication link with Anderson, but after her blow up with him at Union Station, she had, in a fit of anger, reprogrammed her cell phone and in the process had deleted Anderson's number. She had, in fact, no way to contact him! She couldn't look directly at Li. She almost choked when she said, in a very low voice, "I'm sorry, Li, I don't have any way of contacting him. I think he might be in Casablanca by now talking with al-Tabari, but I don't have his cell phone number, and he isn't likely to be calling me." She said this in a mournful tone which was not lost on Chou Li, but he said nothing about it.

"Do you have any idea how we might contact al-Tabari, Joan?"

"No, I'm really sorry, but I know al-Tabari only through Anderson. I don't know him well enough to contact him directly, even if I could. I doubt he would reveal Anderson's whereabouts to me in any case. What do we do now?"

"I don't know what we do now, Joan. You are my last hope. I have tried to get in touch with Frank directly, but he won't take my calls. He is poisoned against me, I suppose by Khalida. Despite Khalida's ongoing smear campaign against all of us, I think Frank still thinks highly enough of Anderson to at least talk to him. Failing that, I don't think there is anyone else from Frank's organization, other than Khalida, the national security advisor will listen to. I fear that time is running short. I don't have any hard evidence about the timing, or about the nature of the Pakistani operation, 'Broken Spark', but I know it is operational.

"However, with three lost wars behind them, the Pakistanis are not likely to use conventional weapons in a fourth conflict. What would be the purpose? No! They will almost certainly use nuclear weapons in a desperate gambit to produce quick and dramatic results, without regard to the human cost.

"The EMP weapons they have developed, if properly placed, just might tip the balance in their favor for a first strike by impairing the Indian military's defensive launch capability. They cannot do more than reduce its effectiveness, but all they need is a slight edge. The Pakistanis must know that their own nuclear arsenal grows more inferior by the day, week and month. Abdul Qadeer Khan was, until recently, under house arrest; the Pakistani economy is in tatters compared to the Indian economy, and their political will weakens by the hour. They risk becoming irrelevant, absent some dramatic strike."

"It would be a terrible event on the subcontinent, Li, but, assuming we could get to the ANSA, is there really anything the US government could, or should, do? Beyond helping with the casualties, of course. What's the real deterrent effect of non-proliferation treaties and statements of outrage on the actions of rogue nations anyway?

How could the US intervene to prevent the initiation of nuclear war by either side? Short of intervening militarily, which I'm certain the US will not do, what can prevent Pakistan from launching a first strike against India? If the Pakistani military is prepared to step over the line, verbal persuasion will not deter them."

"You are possibly right, Joan, but I don't think that to be ignorant of the threat of a regional nuclear war is a good place to be right now. Sadly, the US image in the world is not what it used to be. For a long time, a call from the US president might very well have stopped a military action, or at least given rise to second thoughts. But now, US moral suasion is pretty weak. We have lost the effectiveness of 'soft' diplomacy.

"Who does carry the torch of moral righteousness now that the US has dropped it? Europe is exhausted! Russia's corruption taints the very thought of moral leadership; China's modified capitalism, while effective, does not carry with it any moral leadership or force for restraint; India doesn't exhibit qualities of moral leadership yet. We are, I fear, living in a world without a moral sense, for the first time in a very long time. Moral leadership, unfortunately, requires big power status behind it, and after you identify the obvious current big powers and you don't find moral leadership, one gets a sense of how aimlessly, hopelessly, we are adrift.

"It is an unusual time, when America's free market capitalism pollutes the world financial markets through its exports of toxic assets to a world greedy for financial returns and for the privilege of selling to America's insatiable consumers, who have been willing to borrow and spend without restraint to provide markets for the exports of the world. Think about it, the world applauds the American consumers' gluttony and feeds it with glee. But now, the American consumer is tapped out and can no longer buy; the world's exporters' product shipments collapse and America is blamed. Perhaps we deserve it. We certainly owe the world nothing, but we have been propping up export economies since we started with the Germans and the Japanese in the fifties until the collapse of 2008. We were doing it for everyone, from Australia to Zambia."

Joan and Chou Li said goodbye, and Joan was soon in her apartment on Wisconsin Avenue sorting through the events of the past week. It had not gone well, she thought, certainly not what she had expected. In addition to Chou's alarming conversation, she had had a tumultuous week. She had begun the week after culminating an abbreviated visit to Anderson in Arizona. At that point, her life was more or less in order. She had been Erin Cohen to Anderson, they had had a pleasant day and a half in Tubac, and they had parted friends, respectful and sensitive toward one another. Anderson had accepted the difficult situation at the reception in Washington when they were introduced as unknowns.

But then came New York, the shocking murder of Sanjay, the exquisite lovemaking, the meeting with Sanjay's superior at the Indian mission to the United Nations, her own revelation that she was an Israeli agent, and the train ride back to Washington and the disastrous confrontation in the bar in Union Station. She hadn't intended to terminate their tete a tete so abruptly or angrily. It just came out, probably as a result of the extreme stress of the previous few days.

In any case, that succession of events had exposed her life to her for what it really was, a tattered collection of lies that neither gave her psychological nor physical comfort. She was satisfied, even thrilled at times, being two people with different challenges, different goals and responsibilities, as long as no one got hurt. But when people died, were threatened and abused, the charm and thrill left the game. She felt especially bad about her relationship with Anderson. He had been a friend, true and loyal, in the face of his personal and professional challenges. She wondered to what extent she was culpable for his failures.

The next day, as she reviewed a position paper for a client, her thoughts were interrupted by the doorbell. She went to the door, looking first through the peephole, as she always did, but seeing nothing she opened the door to two of the most ferocious appearing figures, faces hooded, she had ever seen. They slammed open the door with a crash and immediately seized her arms, twisting them behind her back in a painful wrench.

She was immobilized immediately, and in a deft motion one of her assailants strapped a bulky belt around her waist and cinched it tight, fastening it with a tiny key lock. He lifted her sweater and pulled it over the belt, effectively concealing it and giving Joan the appearance of only a slightly thicker waist.

"What are you doing?" she implored. "Who are you?" But she heard only unintelligible grunts coming from beneath the masks. "What do you want?" she begged.

Finally, from under one of the masks a guttural voice said, "You are going on a trip, lady!"

No matter how hard she tried, Joan could get no more details from her abductors. As they marched her out of her apartment and down the corridor, she looked forlornly at her cell phone resting on the kitchen counter. Just like that, her access to the outside world had been cut off, and she was alone.

When they reached the street, Joan was forced into the back seat of a late model Mercedes and one of her assailants squeezed in beside her. Her companion in the backseat wasted no time in forcing a packet of documents into her limp hands.

"Listen up, lady! I don't know who you are or who you were, but for today and tomorrow you are 'Virginia White'. That's what your passport says, and that's what your picture says. We are putting you on a plane to Casablanca. I will be sitting right behind you on the trip all the way, so don't try anything unusual."

"What do I do when we get to Casablanca?"

"I'll tell you what to do when we get there, so don't worry about it!" Joan could tell they were going toward Dulles, but whenever she tried to get her bearings by looking around, her gruff seatmate punched her with his elbow and forced her to look straight ahead.

They arrived at Dulles a little before two and went directly to executive aviation. She fervently hoped the ungainly belt about her waist would be picked up by security procedures, but she was to be disappointed. Security procedures for private jets were almost nonexistent, and her flimsy identity passed inspection easily. Her assailant was never more than two feet away from her. Whenever she moved from the most rigid of positions, he forced her to return to an upright and uncomfortable position. All of the time they were airborne Joan was terrified, thinking the plane might be struck down at any moment by the terrorist sitting behind her.

She wondered how she had gotten involved in this. There were many Islamic terrorist groups, she knew, who might be offended by her presence and by her activities as a spy for Israel, assuming they knew. The thought jarred her consciousness—a spy! She didn't think of herself as a spy. She thought of herself as helping Israel, and that didn't bother her one bit, but a 'spy'! That was beyond her frame of reference. She was not a spy, she thought. She didn't do cloak and dagger things. Everything she did was above board, or so she viewed what she did.

Twice during the trip, Joan needed to use the ladies' room, and both times her guard accompanied her to the door and waited outside. Each time he admonished her, "You got three minutes, lady, and then I push a button on this remote and that little belt you're wearing will cut you in half, so don't try anything strange. If you behave, you'll live. If you don't, you won't. Is that simple enough for you?"

Joan nodded wordlessly, intimidated by the brazen nature of the harsh threat. After what seemed like an eternity to her, the plane started its descent into Casablanca's Mohammed V Airport. This was less than three hours before Anderson was scheduled to meet al-Tabari in the Dar Beida Restaurant in the Hyatt hotel.

Joan departed the jet's folding stairs with dread, dread made all the worse because she had no idea what kind of harm was to befall her, though harm she felt sure she would experience. She stood on the curb in front of the executive jet terminal, suddenly alone as her 'babysitter' melted away. Her assailants had had plenty of opportunities to maim or even kill her and had not, they had only terrorized and frightened her. Their objective obviously included something less than murder, or they would already have carried that out.

So what were their goals? Why go to all the trouble to seize her and put her on a plane to Casablanca? She must be of some importance for a purpose of which she was not aware, but it couldn't be good.

Her companions for the past twelve hours had disappeared, and she was momentarily alone. Was that good or bad? She didn't have time to think about it as a black sedan raced to a stop in front of her and two men sprang from the right side doors. They immediately grabbed her and stuffed her into the back seat.

The sedan pulled away from the curb, drove for a few minutes, stopped briefly at what she supposed to be a security checkpoint and then merged into heavy traffic, heading, according to the signs Joan could see intermittently as they flashed by, toward Casablanca. Her heart beat rapidly and her mind struggled with possible outcomes. She shuddered involuntarily as she felt the shoulder of the man on her right push heavily into her right breast. She tried to shift her body to gain relief but was unable.

She wasn't typically claustrophobic, but she felt stifled, and uncontrolled panic, like an unwanted memory, welled up in her. She forced it down and tried to look outside the speeding car for landmarks, signs, tree formations, anything to help identify where she was or had been, assuming she might live, but it was futile. What signs she saw were in French and Arabic, and the speed of the car caused her to doubt even the most recognizable of the images.

She was unmoored, adrift on a black sea, shifting and churning with anxiety. She tried to calm herself, but to no avail. She wanted to cry out, but she knew it would be counterproductive, so she swallowed her terror and tried to control her thoughts.

The lights of Casablanca surged toward them and the big sedan slowed and succumbed to the demands of urban traffic. There was a bewildering series of right and left turns, and then finally a garage door opened and the car glided into a darkened space, made even darker by the door closing behind them. Joan's terror increased, despite her extreme efforts to control it. Alone! People who have never experienced being without a single person in the world who knows where they are, where no one cares where they are, cannot appreciate the alienation Joan felt.

She was at the end of time, with no way back. Two car doors opened and Joan could hear two of the occupants get out of the car, including the one on her right, whose last act before leaving had been to tie a black blindfold over her eyes and a tight cord around her wrists, which he surprisingly left in front of her, lying on her lap. The interior light had not come on when the doors were opened; either a malfunction or they had been disabled, leaving the intense blackness intact.

Joan knew there had been three people in the car. Obviously the driver and the two men who had jumped out of the car to seize her. Now she was sure that only two had gotten out. She stilled her breathing and listened for any sound. Was it her imagination, or did she hear shallow breathing from the driver's seat? But there was no other sound to confirm it, and her senses were so weakened by the past day's assault on them that she had no confidence in what they were telling her. She raised her hands, which were bound as one, and lifted the blindfold from her eyes. Total, absolute, blackness!

She moved very slowly to lift the latch on the door beside her. Her bound hands searched for the lever as her heart pounded in her chest and she forced her breathing to be quiet. When she felt the outline of the latch, she slowly lifted it, jerking involuntarily when the latch clicked, sounding like a rifle shot in the black quiet of the garage. She stopped, certain that the driver would make some move to intercept her but still she sensed nothing.

She pushed against the door, mouthing a silent invocation 'please don't let it squeak!' But it did! She stopped it in mid-swing, but the squeak, which sounded to her like a scream, seemed to echo against the walls, the door and even the ceiling of the garage before fleeing into the darkness of the night.

Finally, after an eternity, she heard the left front door of the sedan click and a soft movement of air accompanied, she was sure, the opening of the door. She heard a soft rustle of clothing slide out of the seat and the slightest sound of a heel striking the concrete floor of the garage. She was paralyzed with fear and stopped moving, her right leg extended with her shoe nearing the garage floor, now dangling and trembling as it hung in midair, attached to her body, but nearly out of control.

She heard a step and she knew it was from the driver, and another, and another as the driver walked around the back of the car from the left side to the right and approached where she sat, half out of the car. She knew she should jump from the car, run screaming to... where? She didn't know where; she didn't know where she was or where she should run to if she should reach freedom.

She was frozen by the twin instincts of fight or flight, but for this moment at least flight lost. She pulled her leg into the car and slammed the door, feeling she was ready for conflict but knowing she was not. She sat, trembling, waiting for her assailant to open the door. She turned toward the door, bound hands held high, prepared to slam them down on her attacker when he opened the door.

When the door finally opened, Joan was shocked to hear the soft, heavily accented English of a woman, who said, "Please relax, Ms.

Singer. I am not going to strike you." The tension drained from Joan's body like excess water drains from a swimmer. She knew she should be furious, but her relief was so great she was devoid of any emotion—save relief.

"What am I doing here? Why have you kidnapped me? Where am I?"

The fear of being seized at Mohammed V Airport and driven wildly into Casablanca had caused Joan to forget her primary source of terror, the belt around her waist. She wondered if it was in fact an explosive. Perhaps it was only used to induce fear and control her on the long flight from Washington. Maybe that's why she was able to pass security. Maybe it was a fake! All this flashed through her mind while waiting for the young woman, at least she had sounded young, to answer her.

"I know you have many questions, Ms. Singer. Unfortunately, I would not be permitted to answer them even if I knew the answers, and I don't."

Joan found comfort in the young woman's soft voice and non-threatening demeanor and was emboldened to ask, "What about this belt locked around my waist? Is it real? Is it explosive? Who has the remote control now? Am I in danger?"

"I have already told you, Ms. Singer, that I can't answer all of your questions. However, I can answer several. Yes, the belt is an explosive. I do not know who has the remote. My instructions were to deliver you to this address. I will keep you here until eight o'clock, about an hour from now, and then you will be picked up by a colleague of mine. After that I don't know what is to befall you. Your death is not our goal, but it might be a collateral result if you do not do as we say."

"Could we at least have some light? This total blackness is unnerving."

"Yes, of course! However, we cannot leave this garage. If you try to do so, I will shoot you, and I would not like to have to do that." The softness of her voice was offset by the revolver in her hand.

Joan shuddered involuntarily. "What's your name?" she asked.

"You really don't expect me answer that, do you? In fact, you really don't want me to tell you my real name. It would increase your already considerable danger. Why don't you just call me 'Hana'."

As the minutes ticked away, Joan's anxiety grew. She hadn't reset her watch to adjust for time changes during the flights to Casablanca. So when she occasionally looked at her watch the Washington time was meaningless and her chaotic mind was unable to recalculate to Casablanca time.

She tried to remember how long it had been since Hana had told her a colleague would come to collect her so she could calculate how close her next trauma would be, but the time became longer and shorter as she tried to focus on it, and it contributed to the sense of being unmoored and adrift, almost to the point of nausea. Time for Joan was incredibly elastic and relative.

She tried to organize her thoughts. Why would they possibly want to kidnap her? Yes, she thought, she was technically an Israeli agent, but would they know that? Her most recent contact with any intelligence significance was her relationship with Anderson and the meeting with Sunil, the Indian intelligence official.

Then it struck her with a flash of light! Anderson might be in Casablanca by now, or at least he said he needed to see his contact in Casablanca. There were so many missing pieces the gaps made her head hurt. She dropped her face into her hands and sobbed. Not only was she not helping Anderson, could she now be in a position to possibly harm him? Could her abductors use her in some way as leverage over Anderson? She very much regretted the way in which she had terminated their last moments together.

After what seemed like hours, Hana put her finger to her lips to keep Joan quiet and turned off the interior light in the sedan. "My friend is coming," she said as she raised the revolver to a ready position, cautioning Joan against any unusual movement. Images raced through Joan's mind, heightening her fear, fear about what might happen to her and fear that she might be used against Anderson.

One slightly calming thought was the recognition that they had not been physically violent to her, either when she was abducted in Washington or when she was brought to the garage. She had no doubt they were capable of it, but either they weren't personally inclined to violence, or they had been directed to avoid it. It was only slightly reassuring because a myriad of other possibilities flooded over her.

The small access door to the garage opened slightly, and Joan could see just the slightest difference the outside darkness revealed. She couldn't see any lights, but the black was grayer than the absolute black she had experienced inside the garage. She sensed a slight movement as a black robed figure slipped into the interior of the building.

A few words were exchanged with Hana, in Arabic she supposed, and the black figure approached her, dimly outlined by the slightly lighter darkness from outside the door. He spoke in heavily accented English, so thick Joan could scarcely understand him.

"I'm going to have to hurt you," he said, "but only a little bit. I'm sorry, but to send the right message it has to look real."

Joan tensed, fully expecting to be permanently disfigured or injured by whatever was to come. She was surprised more than hurt by the full-hand slap that struck her on the left cheek. Her head was jerked to the right by the force of the blow, but the pain felt like a sting more than an injury.

She returned her gaze to the front, only to receive another jarring full-hand slap on the right cheek. Again, her head jerked in the direction of the force of the slap. She returned her gaze to the darkened figure in front of her. She could feel the blood rush to the nerve endings on both sides of her face, her body prepared for more serious assaults, but none came.

"Now, Madame, I must place this bag over your head. Please do not cry out, or I shall have to strike you again."

Joan nearly smiled at the stilted, yet oddly formal speech, but she merely nodded, and he placed a large coarse bag over her head. It fell to her knees and obliterated any light that remained.

CHAPTER TWENTY-THREE
✳✳✳
CASABLANCA TO ???

I tore at the sack covering Joan like a madman, pulling and scraping and tearing at the fabric until my nails were broken and my fingers bled. I was able to make a small opening in the bottom of the stack, which was at the top of Joan's head.

"Joan, do you have any serious injuries, knife wounds, broken bones?"

With a faint voice she said, "No, I don't think so, but…"

She was interrupted by al-Tabari, who had been working at the other end of the sack, around Joan's legs. "Anderson, stop what you're doing, there is some kind of device around her waist. Ask her if she knows what it is."

Joan's muffled voice came out of the sack. "I…I think it's some kind of explosive. The man who put it on me threatened he would cut me in half with it if I didn't obey. I don't know if it's real or fake."

"Did he say how he would set it off?"

"He said he would punch a button on a remote, and it would cut me in half. That's all I know."

"I think it is safe to assume, Anderson, that the bag itself is not wired, just the device. I have a knife and will cut it from the bottom up. Ms. Singer, please remain perfectly still. Can you do that?"

"Yes!"

Al-Tabari cut and tore the rough burlap as gently as he could with the knife until Joan's body finally emerged in the pale light.

I reached out and Joan fell into my arms, exhausted by the tension and weak from fear. Our unpleasant evening at Union Station in Washington became a faded memory as we embraced each other, my heart pounding with joy, relief and wonder.

"Anderson, this is not something you and I can fix. We need to get the Casablanca Police Bomb Squad. I can probably secure their cooperation better than you. If you concur, you stay here with Ms. Singer, and I will be back as soon as I can."

Al-Tabari rose to his feet and turned to walk back to the hotel, but as he turned, a powerful floodlight made night into day and all three of us were blinded by its brilliant glare. The 'pfft' sound of a silenced revolver echoed twice and sand puffed up between al-Tabari's and my feet.

"Stop exactly where you are and face the light! The three of you are meddling in matters that are none of your concern. It is not our goal to kill any one of you, but if you persist in interfering, we will. Ms. Singer is wearing an explosive belt which I can detonate with one press of a button."

"What's with the theatrics?" I demanded. "Who are you and what do you want?"

"You will know soon enough! For now, stay where you are! My associates will be here momentarily."

He hadn't answered any of my three questions, and he didn't sound like he was in the mood to chat, but I persisted. "What are you going to do with us?" I demanded.

This time he answered me with another round from the silenced revolver. This one came within a yard of my feet, which suddenly felt very heavy in the sand. Not much of a conversationalist, I guessed.

A black van, its lights off, pulled up to the end of the street where the street abutted the beach. It stopped, turned around, and its two batwing doors flew open, forced from within. Two black-robed figures leapt out and raced to Joan, one on either side. They picked her up by her arms and dragged and carried her to the van.

Both al-Tabari and I started after her but were stopped by another silenced round that sliced into the sand between.

"You will do as I say, or Madame will die, either by a bullet between the eyes, or by the explosive. I can assure you, the explosive would be a horrible death, and while my associates might be slightly injured, they are wearing protection. The two of you, however, would not enjoy such protection and would most likely be blown to bits. Now, go to the van and follow my associates' instructions."

"At least tell us who you are," I asked, rather more subdued.

"My name is Ibrahim, and that is all you need to know."

We were shoved into seats in the van, forced to lean forward while our wrists were tied behind our backs and the doors closed. The windows were painted black and a partition had been fashioned to shield the driver's compartment from the interior of the van. The intensity of the darkness was palpable. I started to turn to al-Tabari, who was seated on my left, Joan was in the backseat, the two black-robed figures on either side of her. In the midst of my turn, I was struck on the head by what seemed to be a police baton, hard, but not hard enough to lose consciousness. I got the message!

The van was in stop-and-go traffic for ten or fifteen minutes, then picked up speed on what must have been a divided highway, but there was no way of judging time or direction. The van stopped and the driver spoke to someone outside, but he spoke so quietly I doubt if even al-Tabari could have recognized the Arabic. What I could hear were jet engines warming up. So, we were at a civilian airport or a military air base.

The van started to move again and the driver rolled up the window, but I could still hear the muffled sound of aircraft engines and the rise and fall I associated with the departures of civilian passenger jets from an airline terminal and the odor of jet fuel seeped into the van. Again, the van slowed to a stop and the high-pitched whine of smaller jet engines penetrated the interior.

Our captors tied hoods over our heads, and the blackness was again complete. I could hear the doors of the van open, and I was grabbed roughly by the right arm while another figure grabbed my left arm, and I was pulled out of the van. I stumbled to the ground and was half-dragged forward until my feet sensed some steps.

A hand lifted my right foot upward to the first step of a ladder, which was, evident to me now, the stairs leading into the cabin of an executive style jet. A hand reached up and bent my head forward, and I could immediately smell the unique aromas of the interior of an aircraft. I was guided to the rear of the cabin and shoved into a seat. Efficient hands buckled me in as I heard two more bodies shuffle into the aircraft. So they were taking all three of us somewhere, and fast.

"Joan," I asked as loudly as I thought I could. "Are you okay?" I could barely hear a muffled response, but it sounded like a yes. "Al-Tabari?" I asked and he said yes, firmly.

"Shut up!" came from a fourth voice, which I identified with the one who said he was Ibrahim.

After a short taxi, the plane started its roll on takeoff. We were immediately airborne and after a twenty-minute climb we leveled off in smooth air. I felt fingers about my neck and reacted instinctively, but whoever it was, was only untying the cord securing the hood to my head. I looked around in the dim light of the cabin and saw the hoods being removed from Joan and al-Tabari. We looked at one another in turn, then at our captors.

There were two young men, most likely in their twenties, heavily armed and brandishing knives. They certainly hadn't had to go through security, I thought, with more than a trace of irony. The man who identified himself as Ibrahim was not in evidence, so he must have been up front in the cockpit. Three of us, the two journeymen kidnappers, Ibrahim, and the pilot and copilot, six passengers and two crew.

I recognized the cabin as belonging to a French built Dassault Falcon. I didn't know what model, but popular models have a range of 4000 miles and a speed of about 600 mph. We had probably left Casablanca about midnight. Al-Tabari and I had met for dinner at seven. We were on the beach by nine or ten by the time we were seized. Add another hour for the drive to the airport and putting us on the plane. It was no later than midnight.

With a six-hour, 4000-mile range, we could be anywhere in Europe before we needed to refuel, or anywhere in the Middle East. My bet was on the Middle East. It wasn't rocket science. Our captors had spoken Arabic, not French, and they had to have some 'out of the ordinary' approvals from air traffic control officials in Casablanca.

But where in the Middle East? The terrorist cell we were tracking was primarily Pakistani. Could our plane reach Pakistan? I didn't know, but I didn't think so. I heard al-Tabari speaking quietly in

Arabic to one of the young men, who muttered something in reply, walked forward to the cockpit and knocked twice on the door. The door opened a crack and a man's face appeared—Ibrahim's I supposed. They exchanged a few words, the door closed with a click, and I could hear, just barely, the sound of a lock falling into place.

The young man turned around and all I could see were his eyes. He wore a ski mask which covered his face, head and neck. He nodded to his associate and the two of them untied Joan and al-Tabari's wrists. They also pulled the window shades down and with hand and head gestures made it clear that we were not to raise them, even though it was dark outside, and that we were not to talk to each other.

What was it about the Pakistani terrorist cell in Paris with EMP technology and the skills to use it that our very inquiry into it should provoke such an extreme reaction? Was the cell's activation symbolic of a larger more serious national security action being planned somewhere by someone? Was al-Tabari right? If so, who was doing the planning for what country and against whom was the attack directed? Was it Pakistan against India? How did the EMP technology fit in? It was demanding trying to think of all of the possibilities, and even more demanding trying to isolate the ones that made sense.

What role would EMP technology play? What was its unique characteristic? It didn't kill or maim except indirectly. It didn't destroy. It was the reverse of the neutron bomb, which killed people but not physical property, but only with regard to electronics. It didn't kill people but destroyed electronic equipment. Its military use had not been documented publicly, but its most effective use would be to destroy electronic systems for defense in such a way as to disable missile launch capabilities to prevent a first strike or the launch of a retaliatory strike. Disruption of missile launch programs would be an effective use of EMP.

Some observers have suggested that Iraq's inability to strike even one US plane with its surface-to-air missiles during the entire period from the end of the first Gulf War until the beginning of the second Gulf War, despite thousands of sorties, might have been due to the corruption of the SAM's software-driven guidance systems by American e-bombs dropped from fighter planes.

What was the implication of this line of reasoning? There was no 'hot war' going on in which Pakistan was an active belligerent. The country was deeply involved with the Taliban and Al-Qaeda, militarily and culturally, but e-bombs would be of limited utility in that struggle. They would be most effective in preventing a large-scale missile launch... either a first strike or a retaliatory strike.

So, was India contemplating a nuclear missile strike, and was Pakistan aware of it and planning on neutralizing India's first strike capability, or... was Pakistan actually planning a first strike with nuclear tipped missiles and before it did so, it wanted to neutralize or at least cripple India's retaliatory capability? My mind boggled at the prospect! *Was al-Tabari's speculation on the money?*

Surely the government of Pakistan would not be so reckless! But there were many powerful forces in Pakistan, in and out of the government. Then it hit me! When we were at the UN, Joan was talking about some 'Sacred Covenant' that had involved senior military officers for thousands of years. 'The Spirit of Our Fathers' she had called it. The current group was now comprised of a limited number of military officers of high rank, all of whom had served or were serving in the ISI and the military, all from ancient families tracing their lineage back to the Aryans.

I looked at Joan and al-Tabari. Joan knew of the covenant, of course, but what about al-Tabari? I didn't mention it to him because I thought it was a fairy tale, but he might already be aware of it. Right now, it seemed surreal but plausible. I felt like I was entering the 'Twilight Zone'. But why else would our probing of the cell be so sensitive that we were kidnapped? Our kidnapping would play a dual role, making it possible to blackmail Frank in some way.

I must have dozed off because a sudden change in the angle of flight of the Falcon woke me up. We were apparently going to land. Were we at our destination, or were we going to refuel? The two journeyman kidnappers came through the cabin, motioned for us to lean forward and retied our wrists behind our backs. It was a refueling stop, and it lasted less than twenty minutes.

The pilot and Ibrahim deplaned but re-boarded almost instantly, and soon we were back at 40,000 feet. There was no way to know where we were, but I had managed to sneak a look out a crack between the window shade and the window, and the two men refueling the plane were definitely Middle Eastern. And when the cabin door was opened for Ibrahim and the two pilots, a hot blast of dry air whooshed into the cabin. It was most likely Yemen. With full tanks, the Falcon's range would now take us anywhere in the Middle East or the subcontinent, including Pakistan.

I must have dozed off again because the next thing I knew the plane was descending. We were motioned to lean forward as our hands were tied behind our backs, and this time the hoods were placed over our heads. The Falcon landed smoothly and we were soon taxiing toward… where? I was totally disoriented, but I was guessing we were in Pakistan. It appeared to be daylight, although it was hard to tell with the hoods, but just the slightest light seeped in, enough to make it seem to be daylight.

The plane eased to a stop and I could hear the cabin door open with a high-pitched buzz as the motorized gears and cables lowered folding stairs. Two new voices entered the plane. They spoke in English and Ibrahim, I was sure it was he, responded in English. Then the two voices communicated with each other in another language, which I believe was Urdu. If so, it would confirm my suspicions that we were in Pakistan, but nothing else.

A sharp command was given in the same language, and I sensed someone begin to untie Joan and al-Tabari's hoods. Then my hood was removed, and I could see the interior of the aircraft. A military officer of high rank stood at the front of the cabin, and a subaltern was gathering up the hoods and returning to take a place beside the brigadier, for that was what he was. His uniform was crisp and sharply pressed and pleated. He stood erect and his face was adorned with a pencil thin mustache, and his light-colored hair was slicked back under his tautly framed cap. His eyes were an astonishing gray.

When he spoke, his voice was as youthful as his appearance, and it was in crisp, British-accented English. "You are our prisoners and will be treated with the courtesy accorded enemy officers. If you try to escape, you will be shot! Do you understand?"

We nodded reflexively. Our hands remained tied and a guard with a machine pistol watched us like a hawk.

We were taken in a military vehicle onto a military base and then into a military barracks. I caught Joan's eye as we parted. She was very pale and there were dark circles under her eyes. Her hair was disheveled and her mouth was drawn, but she gave me a brief smile, which lit up her drawn face. She had never looked more appealing to me. She still had the belt fastened about her waist, but her posture was erect and her step was confident.

I looked at al-Tabari, and he gave me a dignified nod, signifying that he was okay. I nodded in return just as my arm was seized roughly from behind. Ibrahim was my 'escort', and he wore a scowl which suggested he did not accord with the idea of treating us with military courtesy but was forced to do so. When we reached a door, he opened it and shoved me inside what I presumed would be my room.

With my hands still tied I was slightly off-balance, and I stumbled forward, nearly sprawling on the floor. When I regained my feet, he shoved me into the one chair that sat in the unadorned room, which seemed to serve as a cell as well as a room. Its single bed, with a single sheet and blanket stretched tautly across its thin mattress, stood out from the wall. One window, small and dull, was set deeply into the thick wall. The walls were painted an antiseptic white and everything was impeccably clean. The bathroom was down the hall, I was told, and was shared by all of the occupants, short and long-term. I could call for assistance if I needed to use it. Ibrahim untied my wrists and left the room with a snarl, slamming the door behind him. I could hear the lock click firmly into position.

I went to the window, which I could barely reach, and looked out on a military base brimming with activity. This could not be a normal day, I thought. Personnel carriers filled with troops in helmets and camouflage snaked through the base in long lines. Tanks formed their own lines. Helicopters landed and took off in great fanfares of whirling dust. Something was about to happen. These were not normal military maneuvers. While the terrorist cell with the EMP technology might be a part of the plan, whatever it was, it was not the main part.

Like peeling an onion, our pursuit of the truth about the EMP cell uncovered only the outer layer of something much bigger, and much more sinister. But what? Conventional military doctrine would not be helpful in a more aggressive engagement with the Taliban and Al-Qaeda. Nor did it make sense for Pakistan, which I was convinced it was by the view of the Margalla Hills, a view fixed in my mind by Layla's description of it. We must be outside of Islamabad. Military maneuvers on this scale are carried out either for a serious purpose such as preparation for actual war, they are meant to intimidate, or they are a mask, a feint, a diversion while other more sinister plans are underway.

CHAPTER TWENTY-FOUR
✴✴✴
A MILITARY BARRACKS

Joan, al-Tabari and I were taken separately to the bathroom and allowed to shower, and we were given clean military fatigues, which we were instructed to change into. After we had all returned to our rooms, we were advised that the brigadier wished to see us in ten minutes. We were escorted into a small conference room with a table and chairs for about ten people. We expected a team of interrogators, but none came. After about ten minutes, the brigadier entered the room alone.

He was dressed in the same uniform, which was adorned with many medals and ribbons. His posture was as straight as an arrow. He spoke with the same clipped British accent. He was very young for a brigadier.

"My name is Brigadier Zardari. My family is of ancient lineage, tracing our bloodlines back into the mists of time, to the Aryans who brought civilization to India and who remain the superior race in Pakistan. Our blood was enhanced by the Mogul emperors who brought Empire to the ragtag feudal tribes of India. My family is distantly related to the one-time prime minister of Pakistan, the widower of the late Benazir Bhutto. My cousins from that branch of the family do not measure up to the achievements and distinctions of my branch of the family.

"But let's talk about you. Mr. Wyeth, you are a fast-rising star in your country's national security establishment. This is primarily because of your relationship with Franklin Pierce. However, you have also had distinguished achievements during your time with the US Foreign Service. Your area of expertise is the Middle East. You have demonstrated a somewhat balanced, for an American, view of Islam and the Muslim world.

"Your last attempt at influencing American policy toward the Middle East was at one and the same time defeated by and helped by the Israelis. You had a, may I say, love relationship with a Muslim woman of Palestinian descent which was terminated by her unfortunate death.

"You failed, unfortunately, in your attempt to change your country's policy toward the Muslim world. Since that time, following weeks of recovery in southern Arizona, you have been engaged, with your friend al-Tabari, in an attempt to penetrate and suborn a cell of young Pakistani men who are loyal to their country and are engaged on a mission of the utmost importance to the state. They are the vanguard of a plan that will bring huge and deserved international recognition to Pakistan. That is unworthy of you."

"Perhaps that's because the mission your young Pakistanis are on is unworthy of the affairs of an honorable state," I said.

The young brigadier's face flushed and his anger was evident, but he chose not to retaliate, and instead he ignored my comment and turned to al-Tabari.

"Al-Tabari! You are an enigma. You are a Muslim, a scholar, whose commentaries on the Koran are widely respected in the Nation of Islam. Your lineage includes one of the most distinguished commentators in our history. You are a Palestinian, and yet you have done intelligence work for both the Iranians and the Israelis, and even now you are working with a representative of the national security interests of the United States. You are a valued friend of Franklin Pierce, whose relationship with the American national security advisor affords him significant influence on American policy matters.

"In family matters, you appear to be more secular than religious. You appear to have all of the tools appropriate for the grand struggle of Islam against the pernicious influence of the West, yet you conduct yourself more as a Westerner than as a Muslim. That paradox could produce unpleasant consequences for you. You are not the only Muslim who has important relationships with Franklin Pierce. As we speak, our sister, Khalida, and our brother, Gordon, each have more control over Franklin Pierce than do you and Mr. Wyeth combined. In fact, I myself enjoy a warm acquaintanceship with the US national security advisor."

There it was again, I thought, this connection between the Aryans. This time it was Khalida and Gordon and this brigadier. It was evident that the three had significant points of contact with very high levels of national security in the US and were therefore in a position to influence US policy.

Zardari turned to Joan. "Ms. Singer, you have cast your lot with an unfortunate group of international predators. The actions of the Israeli government in the Middle East border on criminal, with regard to the Palestinians especially, but also in its relationships with countries on the subcontinent. Israel is the largest supplier of military equipment to India and is involved in extensive collaboration with India's missile and space program, cooperating on highly advanced technology, most of which is undeniably directed at Pakistan. You seem like a pleasant woman. You should have stuck to being a psychologist, or a lawyer, and stayed away from the intelligence business.

"Well, well! What are we to do with you? It is unfortunate Mr. Pierce is not with you. In our plans, it was intended he would be here. Unfortunately, random events sometimes outrank carefully laid plans. Mr. Pierce, at the last minute, decided to visit Israel, and his old friend Nathan Pearlstein. He is due back in Washington soon. I believe the three of you will satisfy our needs, and it will be much easier conversing with Frank Pierce than with the national security advisor."

"Why did you kidnap us?" Joan asked. "You know the US government will not negotiate with hostage takers. Ultimately, you will have to release us or kill us. There is no benefit in holding us, and asking for ransom would fall on deaf ears. Even if one of us were the secretary of state, there would be no ransom."

"My dear Ms. Singer, we are not going to negotiate with the United States, nor are we going to ask for ransom payments in return for your release. All we expect from the government of the United States is that it remain neutral in what is in fact a purely regional matter. We cannot have the United States dashing in like an ill-informed modern-day Don Quixote, which it has a tendency to do, and roiling the waters. Unfortunately, the United States, through its CIA, has a history of meddling in our affairs. Prior Pakistani officials, military and ISI, have encouraged or permitted such activities. Our current leaders are made of sterner stuff, but even they need assistance sometimes."

"If you are capable of such awesome power, is there any reason why you must continue to have an explosive belt around my waist? I have learned to live with the knowledge that I can be blown up at the whim of whoever possesses the remote at any given time, but it does complicate showering, and it is somewhat distracting."

"But of course, Ms. Singer, the belt's function has been satisfied. You are here and there is no way to escape." He withdrew a cell phone from his uniform pocket and pressed a speed dial. He spoke rapidly in Urdu, and in less than a minute a uniformed soldier entered the room brandishing a key. Zardari nodded in Joan's direction and within seconds Joan was free of the explosive.

"Mr. Zardari…" Joan began, but was interrupted by Zardari.

"Brigadier," he said severely.

"Sorry, Brigadier Zardari, may I ask you a question?"

"Yes, of course."

"I have heard of a 'Senior Military Officers Group', active in Pakistan, the name of which escapes me, perhaps that's it, SMOG, which purports to act pursuant to the authority given to it by an ancient covenant which is secret and obscure. The philosophy of the group is known only to a group of military men, who believe their philosophy confers on them extraordinary powers and responsibilities. Could you enlighten us?"

"Why, Ms. Singer, what a strange tale. I have not heard of such a group." Zardari spoke without hesitation, but as I carefully watched his face, a hint of a smile tugged at the corners of his mouth, and his pride was evident.

"There is a legend, a fairy tale perhaps, which is passed down from father to son. It was told to me by my father when I was a small boy. Let's see if I can remember it. It goes something like this: In the mountains of Kashmir there is a cave at an altitude of 3000 meters. It is sumptuously appointed with rich and beautiful carpets, hand-woven by the mothers and grandmothers of an ancient military order. Three times a year the members of the group meet in a retreat in the mountains of Kashmir and seek the wisdom of their elders and the elders before them. It is said that the members of the group have formed an unbroken chain extending back beyond the Moguls to the very root and soul of Pakistan, the Aryans. It is a touching fairy tale, is it not? And now, I have important matters to attend to."

CHAPTER TWENTY-FIVE
✳✳✳
KASHMIR

The darkness enveloped the mountain peaks like a shroud. He stumbled every few steps as he misjudged the depth and smoothness of the track, but he couldn't stop, even though his lungs screamed for oxygen and his heart beat so strongly in his chest he thought it would advertise his location like a GPS spotter. It was after midnight. He knew he was being pursued! To think otherwise was out of the question.

He had been unable to conceal his horror at the purported deliberations and conclusions of the group to which he had just been elected. As a military man of high rank, he was not unacquainted with bloodshed, nor did he shrink from possible warfare with his country's hated adversary. No! He told himself. He had fought in the 1971-2 war, and he had been at Kargil in 1999 when the subcontinent looked into the abyss of a possible nuclear war. He was anything but a coward.

It was the act of barbarism being casually discussed at the meeting as if it was tomorrow's dinner plans that totally undid him. Then a vote was taken by secret ballot to confirm the decision, the decision which was all too evident from the discussion. Eleven in favor, one against. And no one was under any illusions about the identity of the one dissenting vote.

He had endured the remaining discussion, which had pointedly avoided him, until the group broke up for the night. As he made for the exit, he was confronted by one of the oldest members, an Aryan of ancient lineage. "You have disappointed us deeply in your very first meeting!"

He was an imposing figure, well over six feet, with a crown of blond hair creeping out from under his starched military cover. His handlebar mustache was waxed and tightly wound. He could well have been a British general, or Prussian for that matter, instead of the Pakistani he was. The new inductee was no less impressive, except younger, but his lineage was as long as the elder general, and he was himself a Brigadier.

He was intimidated nonetheless, knowing that his every word was being measured and weighed for its merit or lack thereof, and that he was watched as if a spotlight followed his every move. "I spoke my convictions, General," he said, "as I was led to believe we were expected to do. Where is the error in that?"

"Animated debate is welcome," the general intoned. "However, when decisions of great moment are taken, unanimity is expected by the members of the group."

"I would rather think the greater the decision, the greater the range of debate. In truth, we had little."

"Your claim to be a member of the group is very sound," the general said. "Your lineage is as long and strong as any of us, but do not believe this to be a place of anarchy. We are a collegium which makes decisions, not a debating society. You must remember that in the future."

With that, the ancient general turned abruptly on his heel and left the dining room, followed by ten other ancients of the highest military rank. The exit to the retreat was carved through thick stone, and the elders had to step carefully to avoid the brilliant carpets of every traditional Pakistani pattern, and they had to stoop to manage the stone exit.

He was left alone in the mountains of Kashmir. Even in battle he had never felt so alone. He left the retreat through the single entrance and felt better in the clean cold air of Kashmir, but he knew he would be watched, was being watched even then. As he turned to walk to his quarters, which were in a barracks bounded on three sides by the stone of the mountain, fronted by heavy timbers, he heard the poorly concealed step of a follower.

He assessed his situation. A defector would be dealt with quickly and harshly. He knew the other members personally and by reputation.

They were accustomed to having their orders obeyed and carried out without question. Each one had achieved the highest rank in the Army or the Air Force of Pakistan. There were eight from the Army, three from the Air Force and he himself was a brigadier, although yet only a brigadier in the Army, on detail to the Air Force. His last interview before being accepted into the group was conducted by two of the longest-serving generals in the Army.

He had passed the last hurdle. Along with the rite of passage came the admonition that no member of the group had ever left the group while living. The only acceptable resignation was death. He hadn't thought deeply about the statement because he hadn't intended to resign. He had thought the group was like an honorary society which he would attend willingly until his old age and natural death, unless he died in battle, which didn't appear likely. More likely, he would be killed in a terrorist bombing. But that was before the retreat in the mountains of Kashmir.

Tonight he had seen the faces of all of the members, and it was terrifying! If he had handpicked the people most able to lead Pakistan into a nuclear war, he could not have chosen a more appropriate group.

In Pakistan, the decision to use nuclear weapons was lodged in the National Command Authority, the NCA. The NCA consisted of the Employment Control Committee, the Development Control Committee and the Strategic Plans Division, which acted as Secretariat to the NCA. The Employment, or 'Launch' Committee, was the key committee. The NCA itself was comprised of the ministers of Finance, Interior and Defense; the chairman of the Joint Chiefs of Staff; the director general of the Strategic Plans Division; and the commanders of the Army, Air Force and Navy, the president and the prime minister, a total of ten. The president had the final vote, but given the military composition of the 'Launch' Committee, there was no doubt which way the president would vote.

And here was what almost stopped his heart from beating! Eight of the ten members of the 'Launch' Committee were in the room this night, and all eight, plus three others who occupied key positions in the ISI, voted in favor of a surprise nuclear strike against India!

His mind floated back to the military base in Rawalpindi. After he had left the barracks in which he held the two Americans and al-Tabari, Brigadier Zardari had talked to his line commander and had given explicit instructions about the guard on the barracks. There were to be no slip ups. Security had to be ironclad. Any military police guard who failed in his responsibility would be court-martialed with immediate sentencing, probably summary execution.

He was taking no chances. Tonight was to be his first meeting as a member of the group; a group of twelve of the greatest, the most ancient, the most distinguished and honored men of Pakistani history. To think that he, at the mere age of fifty-three would be asked to become a member of the group was unprecedented. Nothing could go wrong! It must not! It was almost as if a test had been given, and he must pass. He had left the military base at Rawalpindi feeling centered, at ease with himself. He had confidence in his line commander. He was a good man. Nothing would go wrong! But it had!

He had gone to the control tower on the airbase, where he was politely directed to a small two-person utility helicopter which took him to the tiny village of Murree. There, a US-built Cobra awaited him. He had strapped into the Cobra, which even now he was in training to fly, and the pilot had lifted off to take him into the mountains of Kashmir to an elaborate retreat, to an exclusive world of Pakistani ancients with whom he could discuss and debate the issues of the world. He was exhilarated! Unfortunately, he had had no clue what awaited him.

No sooner had the Cobra lifted off than an emergency transmission had broken through his headset. The prisoners had escaped! His line commander was distraught. Nothing like this had ever happened to him. The brigadier was devastated! Never in his military command had he or his people failed! The timing was unbelievable! That it should happen on this, his most special day, was beyond comprehension.

He had replied to his commander in terse orders. The prisoners must be caught and constrained. Under no circumstance was word of their escape to be spread across the base. As soon as they were recaptured, he was to be informed by code and no one else was to know.

Brigadier Zardari's world had just been turned upside down!

Zardari struggled to retain his mental composure as he clambered down the mountain. He knew that he was mortally wounded in his professional career, both by the incident tonight and by the escape of the Wyeth group in Rawalpindi, and he may be soon mortally wounded physically as well. He had supposed that a conventional strike of limited scope was being planned, as witnessed by the maneuvers at his command in Rawalpindi. How had his comrades in arms, his ancestral brothers, become capable of contemplating the mass murder of millions of Indians as well as their own Pakistani compatriots? He couldn't fathom it, nor could he do nothing and let it take place.

He had raced in the dark for an Army command car and started down the mountain on a rough track, scarcely deserving the name of road. He hoped, prayed, that he could evade his expected pursuers long enough to reach Murree, where the helicopter used to ferry the members of the group to their mountain redoubt was based, before the group sounded the alarm. The car gave out not five miles from Murree, and he had been walking for the last hour, constantly looking over his shoulder.

His military issue dress shoes were not made for hiking, and he felt them disintegrating on his feet as he walked. Fortunately, the rest of his uniform, which identified him as a brigadier in Pakistan's Army was more or less intact, which was more than could be said for Brigadier Zardari. He was fast losing composure, but was urged, compelled on by the sheer desperation of his plight.

He reached the gate to the small landing area where the helicopter sat at two a.m. and shocked the sleeping corporal technician on duty. Before he was awake and in possession of his faculties, Zardari compelled him by verbal and threatened physical abuse, to give him the controls to the helicopter. His preflight check consisted of no more than making sure the fuel tank was full. He powered up the US-made Cobra and pointed its nose toward Islamabad.

En route he had to decide what he was going to do when he reached the city. He knew he was finished, but he had brought all of the documents he had been given in Kashmir. He had studied them only cursorily. One was a plan for the targets of nuclear missiles and for the targeting of electromagnetic pulse bombs in crucial Indian launch sites.

Somehow, he had to get these documents to authorities who could prevent the holocaust contemplated. How ironic, he thought, that the Cobra gunships just delivered by the US, the first ones ever, were being used to ferry the members of the group to a meeting in a retreat where a decision was made which would probably result in the initiation of nuclear war.

He auto-rotated the Cobra down to the tarmac of the Islamabad airport. He was out of the helicopter and running before the rotors stopped turning. The tower was half asleep at three a.m. and didn't file a report on this strange landing of the Cobra. Zardari raced to the terminal and exited at the taxi stand, finding one single taxi, its driver asleep. He woke him, urging him to take him to a bed and breakfast near the UN building on Jinnah Avenue.

Finally, at the bed and breakfast he was greeted by a sleepy proprietor. By this time, Zardari had been up for almost twenty-four hours. He was totally exhausted, and his mind/muscle coordination was giving out. He gave the proprietor a fistful of cash and followed him to a room. He collapsed on the bed, hoping he was safe, but beyond caring at the moment.

He awoke at nine a.m., stiff and sore, but still alive, for which he was only moderately satisfied, knowing it was a temporary condition. He had a wound behind his left ear which suggested a bullet from a silenced revolver had grazed his head, but he was otherwise all right. He was immediately awake albeit disoriented. He looked around at his surroundings and began to calculate his next moves. Who could he contact? He knew he only had a few hours.

He had spoken with the American, whom he supposed to be CIA, but he didn't feel comfortable with him. He had also spoken with the Israeli, whom he knew was Mossad. It was really pretty simple. Given his short life span, he would talk to whichever was most quickly available. It was the Israeli. They had met before, he and the Israeli, on several occasions, and he had revealed the existence of the members of the group to him. It had seemed innocent at the time. He still then thought of the group as a policy debating society. Now he was glad he had described it to the agent. They set up a meeting for ten a.m. at an Internet café on Jinnah Avenue, close to a park that ran along a stream leading into the Lei Nala River.

He carefully laid the documents on top of one another in the order he thought most edifying.

CHAPTER TWENTY-SIX

✳✳✳

RAWALPINDI

After our meeting with Zardari, we were politely but firmly escorted back to our rooms. Whatever was going to happen was going to happen soon. The massive military maneuvers being carried out just outside my window, if related to an impending operation, could not be sustained for a very long period of time. Our own kidnapping must be a part of a larger plan.

Once in the room, I canvassed it over and over again. Because of its simplicity and lack of adornment, it offered few possibilities for escape. I had watched my guard carefully the few times he entered my room. He was a young peasant soldier, heavily armed but slight of build. He looked more friendly than ferocious. His routine was precise. He slid open the peephole, which was about two inches square, he then unlocked the key activated bolt and opened the door. He turned just for an instant while he relocked the door.

It wasn't much of an opportunity for escape, but if I could fashion a plausible figure on the bed, covered with a blanket, in the dim light of evening, I might have the element of surprise just for a second. It was the only chance I had as far as I could see. Assuming I was successful, I had to ask myself why I should escape? I didn't know! There was no reason to believe I could ever get away even if I did escape the room. Maybe some primal urge seized me and I simply knew that escape from the room was a first step.

I waited until late afternoon then stripped to my shorts. I rolled all of my clothing into something my wildest imagination might see as a human figure and put it on the bed under the blanket. In the darkness I might have a chance if I waited by the door, where I would be concealed when the door opened. Time crept by and I wondered if my guard had suspected something. But finally, I heard light scraping outside my door.

The peephole slid open and remained open for an agonizingly long time. Finally, he was apparently satisfied, and I heard the key slide into the lock. The door latch clicked and the door slowly opened. My muscles tensed, waiting for him to come into view.

"Hey! Wake up!" he said as he stepped further into the room.

As his full body emerged from behind the door, I moved. I had only my hands, and I had to make the most of them. I approached him from his left side with as much momentum as I could muster, fitting my right arm around his neck in a match with my left arm to make a headlock. He immediately went for his gun, but the headlock smashed his windpipe, and he dropped his gun to use both his hands to claw at my arms to try to break the headlock.

I was half a foot taller and at least twenty pounds heavier, and he didn't stand a chance. Gradually, he stopped struggling and his head fell forward. I released the pressure immediately, hoping I hadn't done any permanent damage. I let him fall to the floor and grabbed his handgun, a Colt 45, and his MP5 9 mm machine pistol and stripped his bag of clips for the MP5 from him. He had two clips for the 45. I pulled on the camouflage and the combat boots in a flash.

I raced down the hallway, stopping briefly to slam open the peephole on each door. I came to al-Tabari's room first. I grabbed the key I had taken from my guard and tried to insert it in the lock. It wouldn't go! My next option was the Colt 45, and it handled the lock perfectly. Regrettably, wood splinters flew everywhere and the roar of the 45 was deafening. I pushed the door open and stepped in. Al-Tabari moved to greet me and we left the room. Inanely I said, "We haven't much time," as if that thought would never occur to al-Tabari.

Al-Tabari was already four steps ahead of me. He looked in one room while I leapfrogged him to check the next one. Joan was four doors down from al-Tabari. I had to use the 45 again, and after the dust settled, the three of us were running down the hall toward an exit sign. It was a little late for a plan, but nonetheless I was beginning to formulate one on the fly.

We were most likely at a Pakistani Air Force base in Rawalpindi about ten miles from Islamabad. As the gateway to the capital, it would be heavily guarded, and in fact I could already hear sirens and alarm bells sounding ahead of us. They were not going to stop chasing us until they were reasonably certain we were dead. We burst through the exit door into a glare of lights focused on the door from four jeeps. The three of us turned around as one and dove back onto the floor of the barracks as a hail of bullets riddled the exit door above our heads.

Al-Tabari was the first to speak. "They will not stop until they believe we are dead or we are captured. We have given Brigadier Zardari and enormous black eye. He will not soon forget it. Any ideas?"

"I might have one," I said. "But first we have to get out of here alive. This building is heated by steam registers. I saw them in the rooms. It's unlikely that each barracks has its own steam plant. If there's a central steam plant, the pipes from it will run through an underground tunnel to each of the barracks, including this one. Let's look for stairs to the basement." My heart was pounding in my chest and my feet felt like lead.

"Staircases are usually placed at opposite ends of the building for ease of construction. Let's try the other end of the hall." The barracks was about a hundred feet long, but it seemed like a mile to the other end. I urged Joan to go first, al-Tabari second and me last. Even though the firing had stopped, we ran bent over in the hope they would be firing at chest height if they started again. As Joan passed me, I caught a glimpse of her face, and it was taut and determined. How far we were from that night of ecstasy in New York!

It was pitch black in the hall, but I didn't want to turn on the torch I had taken from the soldier in my room. As we passed the door to my room, I wondered if the soldier was dead. That hadn't been the plan, but stuff happens. I made a quick detour into the room and saw his body still lying there. I knelt and felt for a pulse, but there was none. I scooped him up and slung his slight body over my shoulder and pounded down the hall after the others.

We reached the end of the hall and found the stairs to the basement. Miraculously, the access door was unlocked. We dropped down the stairs as fast as we could in the dark, the lifeless body on my shoulder accentuating my unstable steps. When we reached the bottom, I thought it couldn't be any darker, but it was. Despite the risk, I turned on the torch. The basement hallway was overgrown with spider webs and mold. The dust and dirt on the floor was thick and undisturbed. Either the steam heat worked perfectly in this barracks or it didn't and the powers that be ignored it.

As I had hoped, the basement hallway led to a distribution point where the pipes from a central steam plant were routed by a manifold, sending steam to every room. The main pipe came to the distribution point through a tunnel insufficiently high to stand erect but high enough to traverse in a high crouch. We walked beyond the main tunnel entrance, backtracked, then covered our tracks in the dust as we went down the main tunnel.

It wasn't very good, but we hoped it was good enough to slow our pursuers a little. We could hear the sound of boots thumping in the hallway above us. Neither of my colleagues asked me why I was carrying the body of the Pakistani soldier. I didn't want to ask myself! What I was going to do was not something I wanted to talk to anyone about, least of all the two people who were closest to me, and whom I trusted with my life.

CHAPTER TWENTY-SEVEN

✱✱✱

KASHMIR

The orderly tapped gently on the door to the general's quarters. Hearing no sound, he increased the force of his blows. Finally, the general swung the door open with a flourish. The orderly found himself staring into the muzzle of a Colt 45 held by the general in a nightdress.

"What is it boy?" the general demanded.

The orderly, overwhelmed by the circumstances could only stammer an answer. "I'm t...terribly sorry to b...bother you, s...sir, I... we thought you should know that Brigadier Zardari has left the premises."

"What's that? What's that, you say? Zardari's gone? That's not possible!"

"I am afraid it is, s...sir. The duty NCO checked all of the sleeping quarters of all of the officers, sir, just to make sure they didn't need anything before they went to sleep. Well, sir, Brigadier Zardari didn't answer the knock on his door, so we were concerned, sir, so we broke the lock. When we entered the room, no one was there. We immediately called the duty officer and he said we should advise you."

"Where is he?"

"He didn't come with us, sir. He said he needed to review some security forms."

"He's a coward! Review some forms! That just means he didn't want to tell me himself, so he sent you. Well, okay. I will deal with him later! For now, we need to apprehend Brigadier Zardari. He must not leave this compound alive! Search the entire compound!"

"I…I'm afraid we have already done that, sir. The compound is a difficult place to hide, and we have searched all of the possible locations. There is an Army command car missing. We believe it is logical to believe Brigadier Zardari has taken the command car and has left the compound. He was last seen by us over an hour ago. Even though the track down the mountain is steep and unimproved, it should not take him more than two hours to get to Murree, where one of the command helicopters is based."

"All right! All right! I will call the members together for an emergency meeting. Make sure the conference room is prepared. We will be meeting there in ten minutes."

"It will be done, sir."

It took very little time for the members to assemble in the conference room. Some of the members were less fully dressed than others, but eleven members of the group were in attendance. Although the members sat at a circular conference table, the general was clearly the focus of everyone's attention. It was clear to everyone who was in charge.

"Esteemed members, it is with deep chagrin that I advise you our most newly elected member is missing. We thought, we all thought, that our selection process was thorough and complete. We were all pleased about selecting Brigadier Zardari to be our newest and youngest member of the group. His ancestral claim was impeccable. Despite his relative youth, he has achieved much, he has demonstrated great heroism and skill in battle in support of our ancestral homeland, and his lineage is as long as any of ours.

"Unfortunately, I must advise you that our judgment was in error and that Brigadier Zardari has betrayed our faith and trust in him. He is missing! Our mountain retreat is quite circumscribed. Our security detail has searched every possible hiding place. The conclusion is inescapable. Brigadier Zardari has abandoned us, and all that we believe in. This is not a trivial event! In the history of this group, no member has ever defected and lived! This is, possibly, the most serious event in our existence. Naturally, I have reached my own conclusion, but I do wish to hear the opinions of all of you as to how we deal with this matter."

The general paused and looked around the conference table, fixing his eyes on each and every member. His steely glare penetrated their souls. All of the members of the group shared the general's view of their burden as inheritors of their historic mission. By the time the general had finished speaking, each and every one had made his decision. Death! There was no alternative!

"Esteemed friends and colleagues. you are no doubt aware of the critical stakes in the political game now playing. The Taliban has moved into the Swat Valley and is imposing sharia law in all territories under their control. The civilian government is in over their heads, and we must decide when, and at what point, we publicly ally ourselves with the Taliban. We carry our tradition proudly, and our traditional beliefs do not align perfectly with the Taliban. However, we must be realists! The public opinion is disturbed and unsettled. Someone must exercise leadership in thought and action. It is our glorious responsibility to provide the vision required to lead us forward. We must not shirk our responsibilities!" General Rashid was from the ISI.

Another senior member of the group spoke. "General, I agree completely with your statements and with the statements of our esteemed colleague. We must eliminate the cancer of our recently selected member! There can be no question about that. At the same time, the remarks of our esteemed colleague must be recognized. We are at a critical point in the history of our homeland. Brigadier Zardari has heard our plans and is even now descending the mountain to try to make contact, we can only suppose, with persons or countries who do not agree with our view of the world. Therefore, in my opinion, no, it must be the opinion of this group, we must act immediately to eliminate the threat Zardari poses, and at the same time, accelerate our plans. The advances of the Taliban can be used in our favor by advancing the schedule of our attack against our ancient enemy, India."

A fourth general spoke. "Gentlemen, there is scarcely reason to discuss this issue any longer. We know what must be done. The only question remaining is how we are to terminate Zardari. We must recognize that he is very popular with the military, and with the public. He must be executed with a minimum of public notice. He must simply disappear! How are we to accomplish that?"

A fifth general, also from the ISI, heretofore quiet, spoke quietly but menacingly. "I have been responsible for an operation we have called 'Broken Spark', whose purpose is to neutralize, or at least minimize, the capability of the Indian military to launch a retaliatory strike against us if we launch a first strike against her. The importance of this operation can hardly be overstated. We have an underground cell responsible for the placement of advanced technology which will render ineffective the launch control software of the Indian military. An advance team has been working with brothers in India for some weeks now to pave the way for the actual placement of the devices. The members of the cell are highly skilled, highly educated, experts, who will execute our plan.

"One member of the cell, who is responsible for security, and who is, in fact, not Pakistani, is highly skilled in the arts of torture and execution. He is Egyptian. He has close relationships with Al-Qaeda, and through them, with the Taliban. He is in Paris, having just returned there from a mission to Casablanca and Islamabad for the purpose of securing three hostages in order to neutralize the American government at the moment of our launch against India. He is particularly good at methods of persuasion which might be important with Brigadier Zardari in order to find out whom he has discussed our plans with, if anybody. I could arrange to have Ibrahim in Islamabad within hours."

The other members of the group nodded their heads in affirmation, recognizing the wisdom of the general's words. "Do it!" said the old general to whom the others deferred.

The meeting broke up, and the members of the group rose to their feet, but instead of returning to their quarters, they coalesced into groups of two, three and four to discuss the implications of the defection. To a man, they concluded that it was catastrophic.

CHAPTER TWENTY-EIGHT
***
PARIS – ISLAMABAD

The call originated in Kashmir, went to Washington, then Khalida called Gordon in Montmartre, who then spoke urgently to Ibrahim. "You must return to Islamabad. There is more work to do. While you get ready, I will arrange transportation from Charles de Gaulle Airport. I will ride with you to the airport and brief you on what I know." It was one a.m. in Kashmir, three p.m. the previous day in Washington and nine p.m. in Paris.

Ibrahim did not say a word, but a menacing smile tugged at his lips. Within minutes he was ready, and Gordon had arranged for an executive Falcon jet as well as a taxi to take them to the airport. As they stood in the doorway waiting for the taxi, Ibrahim finally spoke.

"What is the nature of the work I'm supposed to do?"

"Details are very sketchy. However, the target of your skills it is a brigadier in the Pakistani Army. Brigadier Zardari is a member of the inner power structure in the military, and therefore in the country. He was recently elected to one of the most secret organizations in the country. He apparently defected in the middle of the night and is even now proceeding to Islamabad to effect whatever damage he can with the knowledge he obtained from the group. He is to be stopped at all costs and with any methods conceivable. When you land in Islamabad, you will be met by a trusted senior military official who will brief you on the last known whereabouts of Zardari. He will also provide you with the tools you need to carry out your mission. That is about everything I know. Failure is not an option!"

"Does this mission have significance relative to the mission of Broken Spark? And how am I to recognize this individual and how is he to recognize me?"

"He will say 'Qutb was a patriot' and you will respond by saying 'Al-Gama'a al-Islamiyya' showed the way."

"Will this Pakistani understand who Qutb was and the importance of Al-Gama'a al-Islamiyya?"

"You forget, my brother, that although Egypt was the early leader in Islamic thought, Islamic studies and Islamic scholarship has spread to other countries, and Pakistan is now one of the leaders in Islamic scholarship. Yes, he will understand very well. We all do."

"I have arranged for a private jet very much like the one that took you from Casablanca to Islamabad. It belongs to a very wealthy individual from an oil-rich country whose views are similar to ours. Its range is approximately 6000 km and at the cruising speed of this particular aircraft, you should reach there in approximately seven hours.

"It is my understanding that Zardari defected approximately two hours ago. His route will take him down very difficult mountainous terrain, and then he has to reach Islamabad. Airport Control has been alerted, as have the military police at the military base near Islamabad. They have been instructed to watch for him and to follow him, but not to apprehend him. That is to be left to you. It goes without saying that it should not be possible to trace your movements or identify you, certainly to apprehend you."

"It never is."

The taxi took them to the private aviation terminal, and Ibrahim was able to board with a minimum of security checks. Gordon watched as the Falcon streaked down the runway and into the night sky over Paris. Within minutes it disappeared.

As the Falcon touched down in Islamabad in the early morning and taxied toward the tower, a military vehicle swung in front and escorted the plane to a parking and tie down area. A man in his early fifties, recognizable as military by his erect bearing although he was wearing civilian clothes, left the car and strode to the front of the plane. As the engines whined to a stop, the main cabin door opened and the folding stairs reached for the tarmac. No sooner had they touched than the ISI representative took the stairs two at a time and entered the cabin. Turning right, he walked down the aisle, where he found Ibrahim. Neither man expressed any warmth or recognition.

The configuration of seating in the cabin enabled the two men to sit facing each other. The ISI representative said without prelude, "Qutb was a patriot."

Ibrahim, without emotion, said, "Al-Gama'a al-Islamiyya showed the way." The ISI representative reached into his pocket and pulled out a photo of Brigadier Zardari.

"This is your target. He stole a helicopter in a small town about thirty minutes from here and arrived about three a.m. We picked him up immediately and followed him to a bed and breakfast, where he apparently felt he could get some sleep. We posted a watch on the building and put a tap on the phone lines. He made two calls, one to an American we know as CIA, and another to an Israeli under deep cover with the Mossad. There was no conversation, so we assume that one or both will be calling him back. If he moves, we will follow him. If he doesn't, we will watch and wait. We are at your disposal."

"I need some tools. What have you brought for me?"

"I brought you a Colt 45 with a silencer, a folding knife, and a garrote. What more do you need?"

"I need something to tie him down. I assume you want his death to be memorable from his point of view."

"I brought these leather thongs."

"That will suffice."

At that moment, the ISI representative's cell phone chirped, and he answered it with a brisk 'yes?'

"Colonel, he was called back by the Israeli. They are going to meet at an Internet café on Jinnah Avenue. It is on the opposite side of the UN building from the bed and breakfast where he is staying, but it isn't a long walk. We could pick him up now or we could pick him up as he's walking to the meeting, or we could pick him up with the Israeli during the meeting. What are your instructions?"

"I think we have an opportunity to wrap up several strands of foreign intelligence that have been giving us a problem. Let him meet with the Israeli. I assume you have sufficient time to get listening devices in place in the Internet café?"

"Yes, Colonel, we do."

"Do you have enough men to form two surveillance teams?" the colonel asked.

"I have four men plus myself. We could make teams of three and two. Which one of them do you want the three-man surveillance team assigned to?"

"I think Zardari will have completed his dirty work by the end of the meeting with the Israeli. The Israeli will then meet with someone else in order to pass the information on. Let's put the three-man team on the Israeli and stop him from meeting with his next contact. I have someone with me now who will join the two-man team on Zardari. His instructions are explicit. Zardari will not see the end of the day. You are to give Ibrahim all of the support he needs in order to accomplish his mission. Is that clear?"

"Very clear, sir."

CHAPTER TWENTY-NINE
***
JERUSALEM – ISRAELI NATIONAL SECURITY ADVISOR-I

Frank was bewildered! He was standing in his elegant suite in the King David Hotel looking out the east window in the direction of the Old City, but his eyes were seeing nothing. He had arrived in Jerusalem two days ago prepared to meet with the principal assistant to the head of the National Security Council, the NSC. His meeting was set for eleven a.m. the previous day, but when he had arrived, the receptionist said she was not aware of any meeting.

In fact, she said the Israeli National Security Advisor to the NSC, the INSA, was in Tel Aviv for an all-day meeting there. Given Frank's stature, the administrative assistant to the INSA said he would squeeze Frank in today at five p.m. for thirty minutes, but, even more surprising, the meeting was with the INSA himself, not his assistant.

What is going on? Frank asked himself. He was unsettled because he normally called to verify his appointments before leaving his office, especially when he was traveling out of the country. But Khalida was such a perfectionist, and she had developed such an admirable track record that he hadn't bothered this time. Now he wondered what they would be discussing.

The INSA's office had been quite specific, according to Khalida. They were supposed to exchange information regarding an unusual secret organization in Pakistan. 'Exchange' information was not quite the proper description because Frank didn't have any information to exchange. That's another reason why the NSA's absence was so strange. The INSA's office had called Frank, not the other way around, according to Khalida.

Khalida had been quite detailed about the arrangements, so tightly did she schedule, in fact, he had to make a special trip to his townhouse in Georgetown to get a suitcase with a change of clothes. When Khalida found out he planned to make a side trip home before going to the airport, she was beside herself, alternately pleading, then demanding he go straight to the airport. He had tried to explain, but gave up and left the office.

As he sat in his Town Car, he had reflected on Khalida's behavior. It seemed inconsistent with her demonstrated professionalism and competence. On the other hand, she was demanding of herself as well as those around her, so maybe she got a little rattled when he didn't follow her schedule to a 'T'. He wouldn't know until much later that the reason for her chagrin was that his unpredictable behavior had foiled her plan to seize him along with Joan Singer.

Frank was at the INSA's office ten minutes early. He was sitting in the anteroom when a familiar voice said, "Frank, I thought you were going to hang it up." It was Nathan Pearlstein, his old friend and colleague, a cerebral Israeli spy who had spent many years in the Mossad at home and abroad. Frank and Nathan were at the same time wary but comfortable with one another. Each knew where the other's loyalties lay, which was a comfort, but both knew that the other was calculating at least three steps ahead, and that put each of them on high alert.

"Nathan, my friend, are you going to participate with me in this most puzzling meeting?"

"Yes, I am, Frank. I'm afraid we again find ourselves at the brink and must again try to find a way to help people climb down off the precipice. When we last met in Washington, we talked about the growing number of religious fanatics who have power and authority in their respective countries, and who stand with their fingers on the triggers of nuclear weapons. This time it involves perhaps the most dangerous country of them all. It's a politically unstable country, driven by different military, intelligence and civilian factions which also, unfortunately, possesses nuclear weapons and the ability to deliver them effectively far from their homeland. They are so fanatical, they are willing to subject their own people to the risk of retaliation, regardless of the cost in lives lost and economic destruction."

"The only country which fits that description would be Pakistan. But what's the condition that would cause them to take such an insane step at this time?"

Nathan started to answer Frank, but just then the receptionist indicated they were to follow her into the INSA's inner office.

As Frank and Nathan entered the office, the INSA hung up the phone and swiveled his chair so he could face them. He was silent for a moment while he studied them, which gave Frank time to improve on his first impression. The INSA was old enough to have fought for independence prior to 1947. His steely gray eyes reflected the pain and joys of his experiences. He had seen the worst and the best of Israel's sixty-plus years of existence.

Like almost all senior Israeli politicians, he had served with heroism and distinction in the Israeli Army. He had seen the dark days of the Six-Day War in 1967, when all of the Arab states had been arrayed against Israel and then the joy when Israeli forces seized the Golan Heights and drove the Egyptian and Syrian Armies back.

He was in command of a division during the war, and his spirits were lifted as reports of the seizure of East Jerusalem were received. He was thrilled by the performance of the Israeli Air Force, the IAF, as it dominated the skies and destroyed enemy air forces on the ground.

He was likewise deeply disturbed by the Israeli invasions of Lebanon in 1978, 1982 and 2006. He was proud of his service and retired a highly decorated general of the IDF.

He joined the Kadima Party and successfully ran for Parliament. He liked the title Member of Knesset, MK, and still preferred to be called 'Mr. Member'. He was picked to head the Mossad for a short period of time and was then chosen as head of the NSC. At one time he thought about seeking the position of prime minister, but his thoughts, actions and speech were then too lacking in the subterfuge of politics, and now he was too old. He and Nathan Pearlstein had been friends through thick and thin since 1947.

"Mr. Pierce, please sit down. I apologize for the confusion, but my movements are tracked carefully, both by the press and by enemies of Israel, and meetings with people associated with national security in the US are not exactly advertised. Do you have any idea, Mr. Pierce, what I wish to talk with you about?"

"Very little, sir. Your office told my office that the subject had something to do with a secret organization in Pakistan. My friend, Nathan, said it had something to do with a country, probably Pakistan, which was getting trigger-happy with its nuclear arsenal. Other than that, I'm in the dark."

The INSA settled back into his chair and made a steeple of his fingers, with his elbows resting on his desk. "Mr. Pierce, just to clear the air, we are, of course, fully aware of your government's deep involvement with the Pakistani intelligence service, the ISI. Your past involvement is fully understandable. The ISI was helpful as a channel for your support of the Mujahedin in their war against the Soviet occupation. What we don't believe you fully appreciate is the extent to which the ISI has embraced the culture of the Taliban. They continue to take your money and your support, but you must appreciate that any action the Pakistani military, or the ISI, they are one and the same, takes against the Taliban or Al-Qaeda is considered an action against their brothers for the benefit of their inconstant ally, the United States. There are no cultural ties of any breadth or depth with the United States. They respect your power and your money, and little else. I don't believe you fully understand that.

"Also, I'm not sure you fully understand the extent to which the ISI has become a destabilizing force in Pakistani politics. The civilian government is mildly pro-Western, but it is fighting a losing battle against the influence of the military, which in turn is heavily influenced by the ISI. I said before they are one and the same. That is a slight overstatement, but not much. The leadership of the ISI is always drawn from the military. Historically, the head of the ISI has always been a general of the army. I suppose that could change in the future.

"In any case, the top leaders of both organizations form a kind of collegium. They socialize together, they play golf together, they hunt together, and during these informal relationships, they unify the policies of the two organizations. And of course, since the head of the ISI is a military officer, he is responsible to the senior officer above him in the military chain of command.

"The only time the director general of the ISI was more loyal to the civilian government than to the military was when Prime Minister Nawaz Sharif appointed General Khwaja Ziauddin to be director general of the ISI. That hapless individual was disgraced and thrown out with the military coup that put Pervez Musharraf in power. Suffice it to say that the role of the ISI in domestic politics is extensive, and is currently destabilizing.

"The military and the ISI will only permit the civilian government in Pakistan to follow a certain path. If the government strays outside of the parameters of the path, it will either be nudged back in, or will be displaced by another coup, adding to the…how many are there…three overt military interventions in government.

"There are several 'third rail' issues which cannot be altered by the civilian government. The first and foremost is India. The Pakistani military view India as the permanent enemy of Pakistan. There are senior officers who have publicly stated that Pakistan can never befriend India as long as they live. It is an emotional issue of infinite depth and ideological appeal.

"The second issue is the readiness of Pakistan's nuclear arsenal. The doctrine of the Pakistan military is one of strategic defense, which is interpreted to mean that Pakistan will not constrain itself from initiating a first strike, but will rather take the offensive in order to protect Pakistan's territorial integrity. As applied to the use of nuclear weapons, it means Pakistan could rationalize a first strike with nuclear weapons, assuming real or imagined provocation. There are other issues as well. All of that is by way of background and the general threat to stability in Pakistan.

"What I want to talk to you about, Mr. Pierce, Frank, is a very strange development which suggests there is a fourth element in Pakistan's governance structure. There is the military, the ISI, and the civilian government. There is also, apparently, a secret organization, referred to only as the Senior Military Officers Group, which has enormous power and influence over all three other branches of government. How do we know this? Not long ago, a high-ranking military officer, a brigadier, approached our man in Islamabad. He said he was a member of the group and described its goals and hinted at major military activity in the near future.

"The story he told, Frank, requires you to suspend judgment for a time and to open your mind to truly out of the box thinking. If you are not willing to do that, his story will make no sense whatsoever and we will be wasting your time and mine. Do you think you can do that, Frank?"

"I feel like I'm beginning a ritual, like taking orders in some satanic cult, Mr. Member. But, yes, I can do that! What do I need to do?"

"Just listen!"

"The origin of this group began in the mists of Pakistani history. It is a rich and glorious history. We shouldn't forget that. It seems a group of twelve leaders emerged who represented the most powerful tribes in the Mohenjo-daro civilization. This ancient civilization was anchored along the banks of the Indus River, and was one of the earliest civilizations in human history. The power of the group of twelve waxed and waned but continued its thread of presumed authority in mysticism and ritual until the Aryan period when its membership was infiltrated by the Aryans in the 18th to 14th centuries B.C.

"The Aryans were not content to let such a revered organization, with atrophied powers, continue underutilized. The Aryans provided great new energy to the group. It is important to recognize that the group has always been a shadow organization, never operating as a visible branch of government, always existing in the background, manipulating public figures to achieve its goals.

"Its goals were expressed as enhancement of the Aryans, then the Moguls; the spread of Islam after the Mogul emperors conquered what is now Pakistan, Afghanistan and most of India, as well as the expansion of the personal power and glory of the Moguls themselves, and now the perpetuation of permanent enmity toward India following the partition. This brigadier has been talking with us in Islamabad and now it appears that this group is planning some sort of military action against India in the near future."

"Mr. Member, based on what you say, and I'm certain your evidence is sound, you will appreciate that I must get in touch with my government as soon as possible. I believe we still have some leverage remaining with the military in Pakistan. I will call the national security advisor, and he will take it up with the State Department and the Defense Department.

"Unfortunately, as you know, Pakistan is in a serious tilt toward radical Islam. The military and the civilian leadership both seem to be out of touch with the shift in the broad base of public opinion. We have been concerned for some time about the growth and influence of the Taliban and Al-Qaeda in the North-West Frontier Territories.

"The Taliban especially is consolidating its control over the population, even to the point of imposing sharia law in the areas under their control. It is a short distance from Taliban strongholds to the capital in Islamabad and control over Pakistan's potent nuclear arsenal. Now with these fanatics who do control Pakistan's nuclear weapons, we have a vile mixture. So, if you'll excuse me, I will take my leave, but remain at your disposal should you wish."

"I understand, Frank."

Frank left the Israeli national security advisor's office and took a taxi directly to the US Embassy in Jerusalem, where he was assured of getting secure communications with the American national security advisor in Washington. He was able to get an immediate meeting with the US ambassador. Frank explained the situation in Islamabad in great detail call the ANSA in Washington.

At the end of his explanation, the ANSA said, "That's an incredible story, Frank. Do you have any sources on the ground in Islamabad who can verify its accuracy? Didn't I see a wire from the State Department to our embassy in Islamabad indicating that your man Wyeth had been taken to Islamabad? Is that true? What's his status? It's very strange. I also received a call from your personal assistant, Khalida. She sounded very tense and her message was quite confusing. She invoked your name and said 'Frank is on top of the situation in Islamabad and Washington need have no concern about developments there.' I thought she was somewhat taking advantage of her personal situation with you so I said something noncommittal and hung up."

Frank was speechless! "I don't know what she was talking about, sir. Not two days ago, Wyeth was in Washington. I left for Jerusalem the morning after he arrived in Washington from New York, and so I didn't have a chance to talk with him. Quite honestly, sir, I do not know where Wyeth is right now, and I certainly don't know what Khalida is up to."

"Hold the line while I call the CIA and see if they can shed any light on this." The secure line went dead while the ANSA conducted another call with the director of the CIA. Apparently the director had to contact his resources because it was a full ten minutes before the ANSA came back on the line with Frank. "It seems developments are taking on a very serious cast, Frank. The CIA says that a private executive jet landed in Islamabad in the early yesterday morning with six passengers and two crew. Three of the passengers were clearly under restraints and the CIA man in Islamabad has been burning his sources trying to find out who they were. One was an American male, one was an American female, and one appeared to be of an Arabic nationality. Does that fit with your Wyeth group?"

"My God! That is probably Wyeth, Joan Singer and al-Tabari. All three of them were investigating a terrorist cell in Paris which was engaged in, we think, the utilization of electromagnetic pulse technology which they intended to weaponize. With this, they would damage or destroy Western computer systems either in financial markets or in defense facilities. All of the members of the cell except one were Pakistani. It would make sense for these individuals to be an advance team in India if an attack of the kind we are talking about were to be launched. It would also make sense for Wyeth to be pursuing the cell. Perhaps he was abducted and taken to Islamabad to keep him on ice until after the launch."

The ANSA told Frank to keep in touch, and Frank hung up the phone with trembling fingers.

"Mr. Ambassador, would the CIA people in Islamabad have any way of contacting Wyeth? These are critical developments taking place in Islamabad. If Wyeth is free, he could be very helpful working with the CIA. If he is not free, I strongly suspect that he will be soon. He is not the type to experience captivity without a fight."

"I can only try, Frank. Although our communications are rapid, I still have to go through Washington in order to get in communication with the CIA in Islamabad. Let's start with what you want to say to him." The two men reached for the yellow pads, ubiquitous in all US government offices, which had been placed on the table in the secure communications room.

Frank's draft read: "To whom it may concern: If you can locate Anderson Wyeth, will you please deliver to him the following message: 'Anderson, it is critically important that you contact Brigadier Zardari, who we believe has defected, or will, from the inner circle of the Pakistani military. He has personal information which is of utmost importance to us, parts of which have been forwarded by one of our friends from Jerusalem to his national security head. Sorry I can't give you more details, but this is all I have. Regards, Frank.'"

"Is there anything you'd like to add, Mr. Ambassador?"

"No, I don't think so, Frank, it's brief and to the point. I believe the most important thing is speed. Let's get this on the wire." The ambassador gave the draft to a senior Foreign Service officer in the political section and asked her to transmit it to the CIA with a copy to the State Department.

"May I use an outside line to call my room in the King David Hotel and see if I have any messages?"

"Of course, follow me."

Frank called the hotel and asked for his room. He entered the answering machine security code and found he had two messages. The first was from Khalida, and she said simply, although there was a sense of urgency in her voice, "You must call me as soon as possible," and she gave him her cell phone number. The second caller didn't identify herself, but Frank could tell from her voice that it was Khalida again. This time, she didn't mince any words and the tone of her voice was different from anything he had ever heard.

"My colleagues have taken Wyeth, Singer and al-Tabari into protective custody as a result of their combined actions which resulted in a breach of security in Pakistan. There are events about to take place which do not infringe on the national interests of the United States of America. I urge you to exercise your influence in assuring that the US maintains a posture of neutrality with respect to these events. The military exchange is a regional matter of no direct significance to the US. No harm will befall your colleagues if you follow my instructions. If you do not follow my instructions, the most terrible consequences will occur to them. I strongly suggest you acknowledge my call and your willingness to accede to these instructions. Should you not do so, the danger your colleagues find themselves in will only be greater."

Frank sat back in the government-issue chair in the US Embassy in Jerusalem. He suddenly felt defeated and lonely. He had, foolishly, placed confidence in a young woman with deep ties to a foreign intelligence service. Because of his confidence in his assessment of her, he had betrayed a man whom he had considered a son. He had ignored warnings from Anderson himself, and from Chou Li. Was he an old man mesmerized by her icy beauty, with an intelligence matching his, to the point where he believed her, overriding all others?

He reflected on his relationship with her. He had never allowed himself to be influenced by the wiles of young women, foreign or domestic, beautiful or not. He lived an austere and childless life with his wife of forty years. He was not inclined to stray, but now, in reflection, he knew he had been seduced by the light touch of her fingers on the back of his hand as she gazed into his eyes. Her eyes were striking, an opaque gray that defied description.

He remembered now how he had felt young again, with stirrings of affection for a beautiful young woman who exuded confidence and skill, and hinted ever so deftly at the possibility of an intimacy much more intense than he had ever imagined. Her very remoteness and exoticism only added to her desirability. She was, he knew, as a conservative Muslim woman, beyond the understanding of a Western male, but that had only enhanced her attraction.

Frank shook himself out of his reverie and forced himself to assess the current situation. He had to call the national security advisor again and warn him now of the perfidy of a senior-level foreign intelligence official with whom he, the ANSA, had confidence in only because of Frank's own recommendation.

With great difficulty, he forced himself back to the present. He knew that action was what he needed, not reflection. Indecision was not one of his long-term companions. He knew he had to call the ANSA and resolve the Khalida problem. Then, he would be free to go where he needed. His Gulfstream 550 sat at the Ben Gurion International Airport fueled and ready to go. But there was no real question where he would go—Islamabad! He had no idea how he would contact Anderson, or even if he could contact him, but he knew he had to try, and Islamabad was where he had to be. Khalida's clumsy attempt to influence US policy would be laughable were it not so threatening, and if he were not himself culpable.

He again prevailed on the ambassador for the use of the secure phone. It was an uncomfortable call, made less so because Khalida had again called the ANSA with a bizarre message reflecting her newness to the task she was assigned to accomplish. The national security advisor questioned Frank severely about his judgment of Khalida.

Finally, after what seemed an age to Frank, the ANSA was satisfied, if not thrilled, by Frank's explanation and directed him to proceed to Islamabad while he worked through the State Department and CIA to try to pressure Pakistan's civilian leaders to reestablish control over their military.

CHAPTER THIRTY

***

JERUSALEM – ISRAELI NATIONAL SECURITY ADVISOR-II

It was after midnight when Frank returned to the King David Hotel. He went straight to his room and fell into bed and into a dreamless, fitful sleep. He awoke at seven a.m. feeling as if he had hardly slept. He called room service for breakfast, but halfway into his waffle, the phone rang. It was the Israeli NSA, personally.

"Frank, sorry to interrupt your morning, but there have been developments. Can you come over?"

"I'll be there straightaway, Mr. Member." He was dressed in ten minutes and waiting for a taxi.

When he reached the INSA's office, he was struck by the tension in the air. People wore faces of concern and hastened about the hallways. The INSA's personal assistant was grim. This time, there was no Nathan Pearlstein. He would be alone with the INSA. Immediately on entering the office, Frank knew something was terribly wrong.

"I'll get directly to the point, Frank. When we parted yesterday, we were talking about this group of senior military officers and their influence on Pakistani governance. We discussed their role in the military and the ISI. We have just now received some information on the status of the brigadier. He was a newly initiated member of the group, a brigadier in the Army. According to him, he was the only member of the group ever to have defected in its entire history. He found their current goal so horrible he could not abide it."

"Where is he? I must talk to him! This is incredibly important for the security of the subcontinent."

"Unfortunately, you may not. He was assassinated not one hour ago by a sniper at the airbase in Rawalpindi. I just got the report. Sadly, our man was murdered. His agent wired the information to me. Apparently, they found the Wyeth group and were in the process of developing escape plans when they were attacked by a member of this Broken Spark cell, a savage terrorist if there ever was one. I had, incidentally, sent a wire directly to Islamabad telling our man to make contact with Wyeth if he could. I assume that's okay."

"Of course! Thank you. What, then, was the current goal of this group that Brigadier Zardari found so appalling?"

"Nothing less than a nuclear first strike on India!"

"Whaaat?" Frank gasped. "You've got to be kidding!"

"I wish I were, Frank, but I'm not. It is set to take place in a matter of days, unless it has been changed because of the defection. And, the unfortunate reality is, we may not know what the target date is until after it has passed."

"But, Mr. Member, we cannot, we must not let this happen! Can you imagine? Can any of us imagine the immediate loss of life, the ultimate loss of life, the casualties from radiation poisoning? It would be the greatest conflagration of the modern world. Even the horrific wars of the 20th century would pale by comparison to this cataclysm.

"Surely these people know that a first nuclear strike against India would invite a rain of nuclear weapons equally as devastating. I cannot even comprehend the most awesome measure of destruction that would result from such a strike. Did this man know what targets were contemplated? The massive concentration of people in both India and Pakistan would guarantee the most awful spread of devastation. I cannot imagine it!

"Surely this group doesn't have the power to initiate such an attack. It's beyond my comprehension that a modern nation state would be willing to execute such a plan! It would ensure their self-destruction as well as the destruction of their target."

"Perhaps not! Of course I am in agreement with the concerns you express. The one factor which appears to unsettle the equation, at least in the minds of the group, is their diabolical calculus regarding the ability of the Indian government to retaliate. This is where the EMP cell Wyeth and Ms. Singer were searching out ties into the plans of the Pakistani military."

Frank noted the INSA had used Joan's name in conjunction with Wyeth and wondered how deeply Joan's intelligence connections ran to Jerusalem.

"We believe EMP technology, e-bombs, can render the retaliatory capability of India ineffective, or at least less effective, against the first strike."

"What do you mean, Mr. Member? I'm aware of certain technologies that could render computer control systems inoperable, but I don't know of any that have actually done so."

"Don't be coy, Frank. I know Wyeth has been pursuing Broken Spark for some time now. The raison d'être for that cell is to place and detonate e-bombs at Indian launch sites to prevent a retaliatory strike. If the Pakistanis can cripple India's ability to retaliate, it upsets the strategic balance on the subcontinent, which is now heavily tilted in India's favor. The tilt is not only expressed in nuclear terms. India has a far greater population, far greater natural resources, a much greater business establishment and business culture, a much stronger economy, and a more stable government.

"The most important factor, however, is that India is growing much faster from a much larger base. This disparity in growth will skew the military imbalance even further and will continue to do so until the balance becomes unsustainable in the future.

"The Pakistani military see this happening. They see the window of opportunity closing. If Pakistan is a poor cousin of India today, in ten years there will literally be no comparison. New generations of launch facilities make India's nuclear infrastructure every moment more secure. Opportunities which exist today for penetrating India's security may irrevocably disappear in the near future.

"All of this we know. What we don't know is how the military is calculating the odds. They know they cannot totally incapacitate India's launch system, so they have to calculate the level of casualties they will experience and whether it is acceptable. If India could launch even three missiles in retaliation, it could destroy Karachi, Rawalpindi-Islamabad and Peshawar. Against that loss, the Pakistani first strike of five or ten nuclear tipped missiles could destroy India's 'brain center', Bangalore, the manufacturing and educational center of Pune, the heart of government and military in Delhi, the shipping and population center of Kolkata and the population and tourism center of Mumbai. It would leave a cloud of nuclear poison covering that country for a decade. India's economic and military power would be destroyed for many years.

"The loss of 25 or 50,000,000 people would immediately be dismissed as unacceptable to you, and of course to us, since we only have 6,000,000 people. However, the subcontinent has almost a billion and a half people. On such a scale, the loss of 50-100,000,000 people is less problematic. As Stalin once famously said, the death of one person is a tragedy; the death of 1,000,000 is a statistic. So, the calculus might be acceptable. But that is based on our estimation of the rational calculations of the Pakistani military. Enter the group of senior military officers! Zealots have a different way of looking at things. If the whole world dies and one zealot remains alive, the result is worth the cost.

"You say, Frank, that there are checks and balances in the Pakistani government which would preclude a decision to launch nuclear weapons. And you assert that this group would not have the power to override the checks and balances already in place. Perhaps the most alarming part of Brigadier Zardari's incredible story was the description of the membership of the group. You know the decision structure in place in Pakistan to control the launch of nuclear weapons, so I will just summarize it for the purpose of demonstrating the power of the military group.

"The National Command Authority has responsibility for the final decision. The NCA has three committees reporting to it: the Launch, or Employment Committee, the Development Control Committee, and the Strategic Plans Division. The Launch Committee is the key committee. All of this is known. The composition of these committees is also known. However, it is not always clear who occupies the membership chairs in NCA. The NCA itself is comprised of the ministers of Finance, Interior and Defense; the chairman of the Joint Chiefs of Staff; the director general of the Strategic Plans Division; and the commanders of the Army, Air Force and Navy, the president and the prime minister, a total of ten. The president has the final vote. The military has absolute control over six of the votes, and probably Interior for seven. In the face of the dominance of the military, the president, in the event he/she is a civilian, is unlikely to be successful in offering a contra vote. In any case, the military could execute a military coup, as it has done at least three times in the past, and then realize absolute domination on the committee.

"What is truly alarming, according to Zardari, is that the group is comprised of military officers occupying every one of the key positions the military has on the Launch Committee. There is little doubt the military controls the decision to launch a nuclear strike."

"This is indeed a grave situation, Mr. Member. Leaving aside the numbers of killed, maimed and injured, one can almost understand the urgency that possesses the Pakistani military. Of course, one cannot leave aside the killed, maimed and injured. What causes the Pakistani military, which is comprised of decent, honorable men, to override the moral implications of a nuclear strike?"

"You're asking a profound question which I may not be able to answer, nor any man. Why does a group of men become so obsessed with an idea that it overrides their basic humanity and impels them to commit acts which are fundamentally contrary to their basic nature? I don't know. Unfortunately, there are instances in history where such is the case. Certainly, one can cite the ideology of the Nazis, which compelled them to commit acts of atrocity which were outside of the culture of their entire history. In this particular case, there is a history which reflects an ideological claim to an ancient philosophy that places one group of military officers outside of and beyond the culture and values of current Pakistan."

Frank looked aghast. "Mr. Member, this is appalling! This is similar to Hitler's rantings in Mein Kampf. What makes this worse is that this group has control of nuclear weapons. How many nuclear bombs does Pakistan have? I seem to recollect that their inventory is less than a hundred. Can their Shaheen missile reach Israel?"

"First, Frank, your own government has estimated their inventory at about sixty. Since it would only take about two nuclear bombs to destroy my country, sixty seems to be an ample number. Second, it is approximately 3500 km from Islamabad to Jerusalem. The Shaheen-II Medium Range Ballistic Missile has a maximum range of 3500 km, so it would be a long shot for that particular MRBM to reach us.

"They do of course have other delivery vehicles. You have given them F-15s and F-16s, and they have some older Mirage-IIIs and Chinese A-5s that have been modified to carry nuclear weapons. We don't worry about a few aircraft carrying nuclear weapons, even if they have been modified with extra tanks in order to get here. Their pilots are no match for our pilots, and we would intercept them over Jordan or Iraq well before they had a chance to unload. Pakistan has had a Guari-III under development since 1999. It is a three-stage liquid-fueled missile with a range of over 3000 km and can be launched from a mobile launching platform.

"More worrisome, however, they have had a new Shaheen-III under development for some time. It is a three-stage solid-fueled IRBM with a range of up to 4500 km. Since it is solid fueled, it could be prepared for launch in hours. We believe it is operational. That could give us a problem. It would certainly be able to strike anywhere in India. We do not know how many of these missiles they have."

CHAPTER THIRTY-ONE

***

RAWALPINDI

We were huddled near the steam boiler in the central heating plant. We had been there for almost fourteen hours. It was very cramped, but whenever we tried to leave the boiler room, we encountered Army patrols. None had sensed we were just below their feet. So far, we were uninjured, but we needed water and food, and the intense heat was wearing. We had to deflect our pursuers' attention and then put some daylight between us. I had a plan to do that, but what happened next both helped and hindered the execution of that plan. It was 1:30 in the afternoon.

The slightest sound of a carefully planted footstep announced that we had a visitor. I raised the Colt 45 to eye level, right arm extended, left hand tapping the butt of the 45. I dropped my hands in order to flick my head around the corner and back. I saw a young Pakistani lieutenant with his own 45 extended. As I prepared to engage him, a soft voice said, "Anderson Wyeth, I'm with Israeli Intelligence." I was shocked, relieved, and alarmed all at the same time.

"How am I to know this isn't a trick?"

"Your employer is Frank Pierce. He left the office of Israel's NSA less than two hours ago. My control received a message from our NSA about an hour ago directing us to expend every effort to contact you. My deep cover is with the Pakistani Army. I was aware that you were brought to this barracks. When I heard the commotion made by the Army, I suspected you had tried to escape. I asked my control for instructions, he told me the story, and after it was apparent the Army lost you, I suspected this was the only place you could have escaped to. Does that satisfy you?"

I looked at Joan and al-Tabari. They both nodded. "Yes, that satisfies me." We stepped out from behind the boiler and I shook his hand.

"How were you able to get into the Pakistani Army?"

"I am a Pakistani citizen, of Jewish ethnicity. There are only a few hundred of us left in Pakistan. I wanted to do my duty to be a good Pakistani and so joined the Army. However, the open hostility and anti-Semitism of the Pakistani people as well as the explicit government hostility toward Israel and Jews made me open to recruitment. When I was approached by an agent of the Mossad, himself under very deep cover in Islamabad, I agreed."

"Well, we are very glad to meet you. Can you help us get out of this place?"

"Yes, I can, but we must wait a few minutes until my control arrives. He will have a Pakistani brigadier with him who can help us through the security checkpoints, that is if he himself is not being hunted by the military." The agent removed an electronic device from his pocket and punched a button three times, then returned it to his pocket.

"It's a very simple device to tell my control I have found you, and we are currently safe. It transmits at a very high frequency in short bursts, making it impossible to lock onto by anyone attempting to track it. He should be here within half an hour."

"How does he get on a military base?"

"He has the brigadier with him, and even if he didn't, he's extraordinarily good at talking his way past security checkpoints. He may even be wearing a uniform."

Waiting was excruciating. There was little to talk about except my half-cooked plan of escape. We didn't want to talk about personal things in a three-way, or four-way conversation. I casually asked the agent if he knew what the mobilization was all about, and he said he got an inkling when he talked to his control, but the sparse details were so bizarre he didn't want to repeat them. I asked him if he had heard of any developments involving EMP technology. He said he and his control had talked about some developments in the ISI. Apparently they had been developing a cadre of physicists who could be used to exploit the technology, but he didn't have anything concrete.

Three times we heard the boots of a search team clump across the floor over our heads, but it apparently never occurred to them that we might be in the basement. Al-Tabari fared the best under the pressure. He seemed to turn inward in a cross between Zen and Sufi meditation. He closed his eyes and seemed transported to another place. Joan and I competed for faring the worst. Every time the footsteps crossed the floor overhead, we squeezed each other's hand in an almost death grip until the noise receded. The agent was alert but cool.

Finally, a quiet voice whispered something in Urdu, to which the agent replied in Urdu. Two figures abruptly appeared around the corner of the steam boiler. One was obviously the brigadier and the other could have passed for another Pakistani but was an Israeli. The space was getting crowded with five of us plus one dead body congregated there. The heat from the steam boiler was intense and we had to avoid getting near it at all costs, as parts of it were fiery hot to the touch. There was no time for introductions.

The Israeli said, "We have to get out of here fast. I thought it was a good time and place to meet, but we picked up a tail on the way out of Islamabad. I thought we shook him, but I'm afraid not."

Just then we heard the scrape of a shoe against the floor and before we had time to react, Ibrahim rounded the corner with a silenced 45 in his hand. His face was twisted with a grimace that might have resembled a smile, but it made him look like one of the gargoyles on Notre Dame Cathedral. I started to raise my 45 and a shot rang out, sounding like a cannon in the confined space despite the silencer. My fingers went numb as my Colt 45 twisted out of my hand with a clanging vibration. I started to move toward Ibrahim, and he raised his gun for another shot, just as the Israeli smashed into him from the side, slamming him against the steam boiler. Ibrahim let out a scream of agony and dropped his gun as the left side of his face connected with the red-hot steel of the boiler, but with an iron will, he turned toward the Israeli and in the same motion pulled a knife from his tunic.

The Israeli was off balance as he slid away from Ibrahim's body and was unable to react. In the split second it took for the Israeli to right himself, Ibrahim had plunged the knife into his left chest up to the hilt. As he slowly slid off the knife, I leapt forward, and with

Ibrahim off balance, I grabbed his head with both of my hands and in a rage crashed it against the sharp edge of the boiler where the top section was bolted to the bottom section. I hit him against the boiler again and again until no sound escaped his lips and his body sank to the floor like a rag doll. The young Mossad agent had cradled his control's head against his knees and was trying to staunch the flow of blood. But life ebbed away as fast as the gush of blood.

Al-Tabari had emerged from his meditation and stood witnessing the carnage as two men died in less than a minute. Joan's face was white with horror, and she held her hand to her mouth to keep from screaming. Brigadier Zardari stoically viewed the scene, realizing intuitively that he was the cause.

"How can we get out of here, Brigadier?" I demanded. He tore his eyes from the two dead bodies and slowly turned to me.

"We came onto the base in an Army jeep. We were not challenged at that time. They must be holding my defection quite confidential at this point in order to avoid embarrassment."

"Are we safe here for another ten minutes?"

"We are not safe anywhere, but you have lasted here for some time. It might be good for another ten minutes."

"Come with me, Brigadier! Al-Tabari, bring the body of the Pakistani soldier, please! Both of you follow me!" I said, picking up Ibrahim's body. I told Joan and the Mossad agent to wait there for our return.

The three of us climbed the staircase leading out of the basement, and when we reached the first floor, the exit door was just next to the staircase exit. Ibrahim's body was surprisingly light, as if the soul that had recently fled took all of the substance with it. We unceremoniously dumped the bodies into the back of the jeep, but al-Tabari sat in the back and prayed for the souls of the dead Muslims. The brigadier sat in the front with me. It took all of my restraint, but I did manage a moderate speed as we headed in the direction of the control tower, visible not far away.

The brigadier gave me instructions on where and when to turn and we quickly reached the tie-down area for private executive jets. The Falcon that brought Ibrahim from Paris was sitting in the parking area. It was one chance in 1,000,000, but I drove the jeep to a spot just aft of the cabin door. I jumped on to the jeep's hood and shoved on the door. It moved! In their haste, the pilots must have forgotten to lock it. I grabbed the edge of the door and hauled myself up and into the plane. It took a few seconds to find the red button that lowered the folding staircase. I descended and grabbed Ibrahim's body once again. With al-Tabari immediately behind me shouldering the dead Pakistani soldier, we went up the stairs and turned left into the cockpit. I told al-Tabari to belt the Pakistani soldier's body into the co-pilot's seat and to leave the plane and drive the jeep away to a safe spot.

Two air traffic controllers watched the unfolding events with sharp interest. They had not yet been advised to watch for three escapees, and they had no expectation that anyone would be so brazen as to steal a private jet before their very eyes. They did advise the military that there was unusual activity on the tarmac in front of them, but that it could be the pilots returning after being away from the plane all day, and that the two bodies were either unconscious or asleep.

The air traffic controllers eyed the airplane, but only one pair of eyes was watching the jeep as it was driven away by the defecting brigadier with al-Tabari in the passenger seat.

I sat in the pilot's chair, drawing on the observations I had made on every flight I had ever flown sitting in the right seat, I scanned the controls, found the ignition switch and engaged the left turbine. I started my taxi on one engine before engaging the second. I hadn't bothered to put on the headset because I didn't want to hear or talk to the tower. I taxied to the beginning of a runway headed to the southeast. Fortunately, not many military aircraft were using the airport at this time of day.

I turned the nose of the plane in the direction of the runway, then stopped and set the brakes. I jumped out of the seat and stuffed Ibrahim's lifeless body into it. I belted the safety harness and, reaching between the two dead bodies, shoved the throttles to the firewall. The Pratt & Whitney engines screamed as the RPMs exceeded the recommended power settings for takeoff. I released the brakes, making sure the nose continued to be pointed down the runway, and headed for the exit. When I estimated the plane had reached approximately 30 knots, I gritted my teeth and jumped.

I scarcely had time to tuck my knees in before my feet hit the concrete runway. I had my hands clasped over my head, hoping to protect against a cracked skull. I rolled for what seemed like forever, but mercifully I rolled off of the runway and onto the grass. I was conscious of innumerable scratches and scrapes and a throbbing in my left arm which indicated either a break or a severe strain. I looked up just in time to see the Falcon veer to the left, right into a long red refueling truck. The explosion and resulting fire were nothing short of spectacular. Columns of flame and smoke leapt a hundred feet into the air. The red lights and sirens of the emergency vehicles started immediately. By the time they positively identified the bodies, I hoped we would be a considerable distance away from Rawalpindi.

CHAPTER THIRTY-TWO

✳✳✳

LAHORE

I stood up and felt a serious scrape on my right knee, which caused me to limp and inhibited my movement. However, I was able to make it to a vacant area at the side of the runway approximately an eighth of a mile from the spot where I had boarded the plane. With all attention focused on the burning plane and tanker, no one was interested in me, except al-Tabari, who drove the jeep up to my side. The brigadier was slumped in the passenger seat.

"What happened?" I asked.

"I believe it was a sniper, Anderson. We were just sitting waiting to come for you when Brigadier Zardari slumped forward against the wheel. I heard nothing. It's devastating. I could only move him into the passenger seat."

Noticing my limp, al-Tabari asked if I was injured. I said not seriously. The pain in my arm was abating somewhat and I was able to help move Zardari's body into the back seat of the jeep.

Then al-Tabari said, "You drive. I don't have much experience with cars of any kind, even less ones with a manual shift. I normally walk or take public transport."

"We need to get out of here while they're focusing on the burning Falcon, plus, if that sniper is still around, I don't want to wait for him to decide he has two new targets. Our window of opportunity will close fast after they find only two bodies in the Falcon."

I drove back to the heating plant as fast as I could without attracting undue attention. Joan and the Mossad agent were waiting for us at the entry. The agent had carried the body of the Israeli up the stairs with him.

When I looked at him questioningly, he said, "I will take his body. We have a makeshift synagogue in Islamabad, and I will ensure he has a proper Jewish burial. I will also advise Jerusalem so that his family can be notified."

"How will you get off the base?" I asked.

"I am still in uniform, and I have acquired another jeep. The Army is quite casual about controlling their inventory of these things. I will simply disguise the body and drive out the exit."

"Do you have any suggestions about how we get off the base?"

"Yes, I do. You will follow me. At the exit gate, I will tell them you are three foreign diplomats meeting with the base commander, whom you must prop up so that in their haste it will not be evident he is dead. I will tell them you are under my care. You know, getting off of a military base is always much easier than getting on. If we move fast, the men at the gate will not have been instructed to watch for us."

Al-Tabari jumped from the jeep and climbed in back. "I will sit with the brigadier's body and say prayers for his soul. Perhaps if we get free of this place, we can dig a decent grave for him. I don't see how we can possibly contact his family. But we can't just dump the body without proper care."

Our little two-jeep caravan headed for the base gate with the Pakistani soldier in the lead. At the gate he had an animated conversation with the guard, at times gesticulating wildly. Twice the guard looked back at our jeep, but in resignation finally waved both vehicles through. We drove as one for about a mile then the agent pointed us to National Highway No. Five to Lahore and we parted company.

I knew we had to get out of the military jeep, and I scanned the parked cars for a candidate for theft. The ideal car would be simple, nondescript and amenable to hotwiring. After half a mile of scanning, I spotted an old Fiat, a really basic model. I *should be able to hotwire that,* I thought.

As I slowed down, Joan asked, "What are you doing?"

"We have to get out of this jeep. It's too obvious! I'm trying to find a vehicle I can heist, and I think I have."

"How do you know how to steal a car?"

"Many years in a partially misspent youth. While others were partying, I learned what makes a car work. Under the right circumstances, I can take any car for a ride, and I think this is one of those circumstances."

I told Joan to take the jeep to the end of the street while I worked on the Fiat. I was in luck. The Fiat didn't have a locking steering wheel, so it was a simple matter of detaching the ignition wires and hotwiring them together. It was old but seemed reliable. One turn of the starter motor and the engine caught. I sat up in the seat and pulled out of the parking spot, flashing the headlights as I did so. Joan drove the jeep to the now vacant parking spot and parked in it. It was not the perfect solution, but the jeep wasn't terribly obvious.

The Fiat didn't have a full tank of gas, but it had enough to get us to the motorway from Islamabad to Lahore, where there would assuredly be petrol stations. Fifteen minutes later, we were on the motorway with a full tank of gas and a six-hour drive to Lahore. If we made Lahore, it was less than a one-hour drive east from Lahore to Amritsar in India.

We were able to cruise at fifty miles an hour. Anything above that and the Fiat began to vibrate and shake and steering became difficult. We didn't see anyone following us, but we knew that that could change at any moment. Finding the jeep might be relatively easy, finding the Fiat it replaced would not be. It hadn't appeared that anyone had seen the switch.

After three hours behind the wheel, I was exhausted, not only from lack of sleep, but the exhaustion that comes after a drop from a high level of adrenaline. Joan and al-Tabari had fallen asleep shortly after leaving Rawalpindi.

We still had the brigadier, and I felt we should bury him on Pakistani soil if at all possible. About 150 miles from Lahore, we found a rural road leading away from the motorway and I took it. I came to a stop near an irrigated field and roused al-Tabari. It was getting toward dusk, but our search for sticks to dig a shallow grave was rewarded. Al-Tabari loosened the earth with one stick while I scraped the loosened earth out with my hands. We finally had a combination of a shallow grave and enough earth to cover the brigadier's body. I returned to the car while al-Tabari prayed over the makeshift grave.

I asked Joan to drive for two hours while I got some sleep, which got us very close to Lahore. We needed more petrol as well as directions, both of which we obtained at a service stop. We not only got petrol and directions, we were given an amateur tour guide's facts about Lahore and Amritsar. First, there was no way to bypass Lahore. National Highway No. Five, which we were on, went right into the central part of Lahore, where it connected with number 70, which in turn connected with National Highway No. One going toward Amritsar.

We were also told that the Wagah border crossing was known as the 'Berlin Wall' of Asia. The road was blocked by a heavy iron gate and security procedures were thorough, manned by burly and surly border guards. The Fiat would be shredded if we tried to crash the gate, and even if by some miracle we got through the Pakistani guards, the Indian Border Security Force was apparently equally demanding.

Security procedures on both sides were more severe because of the history of Lahore and Amritsar. Prior to Partition, the cities were mirror images of each other, with Lahore populated 50% by Hindus and Sikhs and Amritsar populated 50% by Muslims. The wounds of communal violence and population relocation during that time were still deeply felt.

"Anderson, it is time to get some official help. We have gone further than we had any reason to expect we could, but we need Frank's help." It was al-Tabari speaking softly from the back seat.

"But how can I contact Frank now that Khalida had poisoned his mind against me?"

"The only possibility is through the American national security advisor," Al-Tabari said.

Joan interjected. "I agree with al-Tabari. There must be an American Consulate in Lahore."

I turned to the Pakistani attendant and asked him if there was a US Consulate, and he affirmed that there was. He made a quick trip to talk with his manager and then consulted a phonebook. Finally, he wrote the address out on a piece of paper: 50, Empress Road, telephone number 042-636-5530-9.

By this time, we were all totally exhausted. The Consulate would not be open until morning, and no hotel would accept us without passports, credit cards or cash. We had none of these. I borrowed the use of the phone from the service attendant and called the Consulate. There was a recording on the answering machine, in English and Urdu, announcing the opening hours. At the end of the message, there was a message for emergencies only, and it gave a telephone number.

I called the number and reached a Marine guard. I carefully explained our circumstances and the nature of my relationship to Frank and the ANSA. I said it was urgent that I reach the chief consular officer. The Marine guard told me to come to the Consulate and he would call the chief. By midnight, I had given the chief consular officer all of the details of our experiences since Casablanca. He had to go through the chain of command, but since it was mid-afternoon in Washington, he was able to reach the deputy secretary for Pakistani affairs at the State Department.

Fortunately, she was very alert and was able to get an audience with the secretary of state. From there, it went to the ANSA, who called Frank and asked for an explanation. Frank was still smarting from his last conversation with the ANSA, and after a lot of soul-searching, he realized that Anderson, Joan and al-Tabari were in a critical position, possessing critical information and in need of assistance.

The national security advisor, with the assistance of the secretary of state arranged for air transport from Lahore to New Delhi. All of this took the better part of three hours. The chief consular officer drove us to Lahore Airport where a US military aircraft sat on the tarmac with its turboprops idling. We were bundled on the aircraft and immediately collapsed into a fitful sleep. The US Air Force C-130, which had been on standby for disaster relief, took off for Delhi. It was a relatively short flight, but we slept the sleep of the dead, and before we knew it, we were landing.

We were met at the airport by the US ambassador to India. His information was sketchy, and he displayed a natural skepticism, but he knew it was of the utmost importance. On the way to the US Embassy, we related the entire story of our abduction and escape. The ambassador was still skeptical, but in an effort to be helpful he took us directly to a hotel in Delhi and checked us in, out of courtesy to the ANSA. We arranged to meet with the ambassador an hour later. The three of us wanted desperately to shower and get some sleep, but we knew we had to reach the Indian minister of Defense without delay. I asked Joan and al-Tabari to meet me in the lobby half an hour later.

When we met, Joan said, "What do we do now, Anderson? I'm asleep on my feet. It's eight o'clock in the morning and for all we know Pakistani launch vehicles are already preparing their missiles."

"I don't know, Joan. There isn't enough time to go through proper government channels to get the message to the Indian defense officials. The Ambassador was so skeptical I don't think it would be worth the delay to meet with him. The only thing I know to do is to go to the Ministry of Defense itself and try to make contact with someone who will listen to us."

"That seems like a long shot to me, but we have to do something," Joan agreed.

"Anderson, I think I have done as much as I can being with you," Al-Tabari said. "I have some close friends in the Muslim community in Delhi. I will contact them and see if there is any way I can engage their assistance."

I put out my arms and gave al-Tabari an embrace. "Al-Tabari, please do what you can. We are in desperate circumstances. One of the things we must know is whether Broken Spark has been able to corrupt the software of the Indian Defense Command. If you find out anything, please contact me through the hotel."

"I will, Anderson."

Al-Tabari controlled his emotions with an iron fist, but I could see tears welling up in the corners of his eyes.

Despite his religious disinclination, he gave Joan a hug and said, "May God be with you."

CHAPTER THIRTY-THREE
***
ISLAMABAD

In Islamabad, the Senior Military Officers Group had been meeting in the Ministry of Defense since early morning. All morning, the eleven officers debated the nature of the crisis and the policy options they needed to consider. After they broke for lunch, they invited the president, the prime minister and the ministers of Interior and Finance to join them.

With all members present, the group constituted the National Command Authority. Significantly, the chairman of the Joint Chiefs of Staff chaired the meeting. He was seemingly deferential to the president and the prime minister, but there was no question in the mind of any person in the group who was in charge. By the time the afternoon session commenced, they had reviewed all of the options and had concluded that the defection of Brigadier Zardari had triggered the need for action.

The chairman opened the meeting by what he called reviewing the obvious. "Our best estimates of the Indian nuclear delivery capability would suggest that in a first strike they could launch eighteen to twenty-four nuclear weapons on the AGNI-II intermediate range ballistic missile platform. The AGNI-II has a range of 3300 km with a payload of 1000 kg and a range of 4450 km with a payload of 700 kg. That would deliver warheads of 15 to 250 kt anywhere in our country. The AGNI-II is launched on a mobile rail launcher, which makes it a difficult to destroy in anticipation of a first strike.

"Moreover, the Indians are developing the AGNI-III, which will have greater range and/or be launched from submarines. This missile has already been tested. Although several flaws were found in the first tests, we can only assume that they have now been corrected and are in an operational capacity. In addition, in less than three years, India will have the Indian Regional Navigation Satellite System (IRNSS), which is a group of seven satellites for navigational purposes which will make their missile navigation incredibly accurate.

"In short, in a first strike mode, India has the capacity to turn our country into rubble. Despite having a nuclear advantage at various times in the past two decades, we have never used it. As a result of our failure of will, India's natural population, economic and military advantages now threaten to overwhelm us. We must get down to the most elemental level in our conflict with India, and make no mistake about it, gentlemen, our enemy is India, it is not the Taliban or Al-Qaeda, who share our Islamic religion and our hatred of India and India's principal military supplier, Israel.

"To repeat, at its most elemental level, the issue is whether we continue to spend enormous sums of our resources, which we do not have, on building our nuclear arsenal, which we are afraid to use, and will be even more afraid to use in the future, as India's weapons get more and more sophisticated. I ask you the question, what happens when they have anti-missile missiles, ABM's, as good as the Americans? It will render our entire nuclear arsenal useless.

"So! Do we continue increasingly to be a subservient puppet to India—to a country our forebears once ruled? In its most primitive sense, this is hand-to-hand combat. Possibly we cannot win, whatever 'win' means. But we can inflict maximum pain on our enemy. Look! The subcontinent has 1.6 billion people. How many people can it support? We must not shirk from the reality that the subcontinent might actually be better off with 100,000,000 fewer people, especially if they were Indians. Whoever initiates the first strike has a decided advantage. Undoubtedly, India's ability to survive a first strike and retaliate is considerable, and we would sustain enormous damage.

"However, we and the ISI have been working night and day on the preparation of devices which will alter that balance in a very significant way. For the past six months, we have been working with our Islamic brothers in India to insert electromagnetic pulse devices, e-bombs if you will, in strategic locations which will seriously debase their launch and control software, and their communications capabilities from Indian Defense Headquarters in Delhi to their launch platforms in the field. In the last two weeks, we have made Broken Spark, the name of this effort, operational.

"Broken Spark is an operation being implemented by our cell in Paris, which has now moved to India. This cell is made up of Pakistani physicists who have worked for the ISI in the field under deep cover for many years. Parenthetically, I might say the cell at one time included an Egyptian of, shall we say, unique abilities who provided security for the operation. While he was able to kill an Israeli spy, he was, unfortunately, killed by the American, Anderson Wyeth, who, we can only suppose, gleaned important information about our plans from Brigadier Zardari when he defected.

"Undoubtedly, he has communicated this information to his superiors in Washington. Thus, decision time is now. We must not lose the temporary advantage we have been able to engineer. If we do not act now, the Americans will insist on inserting their troops to secure our own weapons!

"I ask you, is that our destiny? We are descended from the Aryans. We date our civilization from over three millennia. The Americans are a polyglot culture barely two hundred years old. We must not accede to their dominance!

"For the last two weeks, operatives under the direction of Broken Spark principals have been active in India, inserting e-bombs in the Indian science and space research center in Bangalore, in the space launch facility in Sriharikota, in the nuclear missile launch facility in Balasore and in the Ministry of Defense in Delhi. Our latest information is that they have successfully completed the insertions.

"These e-bombs can be triggered remotely in each of these four locations, corrupting the software and electronic equipment that manages the Indian communication command and control systems, as well as the launch and control systems at their launch facilities. It is our intention to trigger all e-bombs simultaneously eight hours before our launch.

"It is the proposal of this body that we bring the various components of our nuclear arsenal together into launch readiness. That means our unassembled warheads will be assembled. We will bring the fissile core together with the non-nuclear explosives and we will bring the assembled warheads together with our missiles in their launch positions.

"In our theoretical and practical drills, we can accomplish this in twenty-four hours. Therefore, at T minus eight, we will issue the order to detonate the e-bombs. At T minus twelve, we will evacuate all essential personnel from Islamabad. At T minus twenty-four we must make the decision to proceed. T minus twenty-four, gentlemen, is now! We have already squandered too many opportunities when we had temporary advantage. The advantage we have created by the insertion of e-bombs gives us a window of opportunity which will close very soon. Any questions?"

The president and the prime minister, as well as the minister of Finance, were too shocked to marshal a cogent response. They had been given a fait accompli, and they knew it! They were outvoted, outmaneuvered and outwitted. The president knew that to dissent from the obvious decision would only insure a military coup. They stared straight ahead and made no comment.

After a brief pause, General Rashid, who had been in the Kashmir retreat, said, "General, you identified only four targets in India. I believe we have enough material for five e-bombs."

"That is correct, General. The fifth e-bomb, and the subsequent targeting of one Shaheen-III is saved for the running dog of India, Israel! This meeting is adjourned!"

CHAPTER THIRTY-FOUR

✳✳✳

DELHI

Joan and I were alone on the streets of Delhi. We were dirty, exhausted and totally stressed out.

"Anderson, what are we dealing with here? Have we lost our perspective? Are we imagining something that isn't really happening?"

"No, Joan, this is not our imagination. It isn't hard; in fact, it is impossible not to imagine multiple atomic clouds erupting across the surface of the Indian subcontinent. The cost in human life will be stunning. I'm afraid the world has been living with nuclear weapons under the assumption that their use would be contained by the great powers, but the spread of the technology to developing countries with bitter territorial disputes has guaranteed their use in some context of time and place.

"Every target city in India, according to what Brigadier Zardari told the Mossad agent, has ten or more million people and there were, at least, four cities targeted. Of the total of 40,000,000, perhaps half would be killed or maimed. Hospitals would be overrun. The casualties would exceed in an instant all of the European casualties of World War II for the entire length of the war. It's urgent that we inform the right people here in Delhi who might be able to do something in defense of the country.

"But I'm at a loss. We can't march into government offices and expect to be received as intelligent, rational people."

Joan and I simultaneously thought of Sunil, but Sunil had not given us a card or a telephone number. Sanjay had offered help from the government in New Delhi, but all we knew about Sanjay was that he was with the Indian ambassador's office to the UN. Sunil was probably at this moment in New York. But, we reasoned, the Indian ambassador to the UN was probably a part of the Indian foreign minister's office.

With little hope, Joan and I approached a traffic policeman and asked him directions to the Ministry of External Affairs. He surprised us by pointing us down Vijay Chowk Road, told us to turn left and inquire within. We hailed one of the ubiquitous scooter rickshaws and asked for the ministry. We were delivered to the front of the ministry, but our credentials for being able to talk with anyone in authority were really slim. We got as far as the first security check. We argued as strenuously as we could, dropping Sunil's name every fifth word it seemed, but to no avail. We were resigned to failure.

At the final, "There is no Sunil Dandekar listed," we turned away just in time to hear a well-dressed man address us. "Excuse me, I was not trying to eavesdrop, but are you looking for Sunil Dandekar?"

"Yes, yes, do you know him?" I blurted out eagerly.

"I do, as a matter of fact. He is back for consultations from his assignment to the UN. He normally doesn't come to this building, but rather debriefs in another part of the government, but I think you're in luck. He was here yesterday and I think I recall him saying he would be back briefly today. He is not actually debriefing in my office. That's why the guard does not have a record of him. How can I help you?"

"It's urgent we talk to him. We met him in New York, not a week ago. I'm quite sure he'll remember us. My name is Anderson Wyeth and this is Ms. Singer-Taylor."

"Let me ring him!" And with that, he asked a security guard for his phone. When someone answered, probably an assistant, he recounted our story and our names, and said, "Yes, they are Americans." There was silence as the party on the other hand apparently consulted with a third party.

Then, our helpful intervener turned to me and said, "Sunil would like to speak with either Anderson or Ms. Singer-Taylor.

I reached for the phone and said, "Sunil, thank God!"

"What are you doing here?"

"We've got to talk to you, Sunil. It is extremely urgent. We have information on a Senior Military Officers Group in Pakistan who are contemplating military action."

"I'll be right down."

Within minutes, he stood on the other side of the security gate. As soon as he recognized us, he came out of the secured area and shook hands.

"Let's go to the park where we can talk privately."

When we were seated on a couple of benches under a banyan tree, Sunil looked from one to the other of us and raised his eyebrows quizzically. "Well, you got my attention. What do you have on the Pakistanis?"

"We have the entire story from a defecting Pakistani brigadier," I said.

Joan interjected hurriedly, "We obviously don't know what information you have or are aware of. However, thanks to several people in Islamabad, we were able to learn of the extreme and barbarous plans contemplated by the Pakistani military. Since India is the focus of the attack, it is urgent that we be given the opportunity to place the information in the hands of your PM, defense minister and senior military officials without delay. Finding you was a godsend."

"What does this plan entail?"

Joan and I started to speak at the same time, then looked at each other.

I motioned for her to continue.

"Sunil, there is a group of senior Pakistani Army officers, including ISI senior officers, who have apparently made the decision to launch a nuclear attack on India, possibly a simultaneous attack on Israel as well. They are fully aware of the horrific effects of a retaliatory strike, especially from India, but also from Israel. What they have done is to develop electromagnetic pulse e-bombs to disrupt, corrupt and interfere with your launch and control procedures. If these e-bombs are successful, it would render your retaliatory capability ineffective."

Sunil's eyes opened wide and the color drained from his face. He pulled out his cell phone and speed-dialed a number. When the call was answered, Sunil said crisply, "Code Red. Meet me in the PM's office. Notify defense and military chiefs. Include the head of the ISRO. There is no time to waste. All defense units must be placed on immediate red alert. I will be at the PM's office in ten minutes."

Sunil turned back to me and the sudden tension in his face betrayed the pressure he felt. "I would like you to accompany me to the first part of the meeting, as there will be obvious questions about the validity of your information. After that has been established you can expect to be excused as the discussion will be taken up by confidential military matters."

CHAPTER THIRTY-FIVE

***

DELHI

Joan and I did attend the meeting of the highest level of the Indian military, intelligence and other governmental officials. We were grilled about our involvement with Indian intelligence, about our relationship with Brigadier Zardari, even about our relationship with Israeli intelligence and their operations in Islamabad. After they had squeezed us dry, we were politely excused.

As we left the building, I could almost hear the wheels of Indian National Defense spring into action. I knew that missiles were rising on their launch pads, on their mobile rail launchers, and on the flatbed semi-trucks. The tension in the air was palpable. This was a nation getting ready to go to war, the greatest, the most awful and destructive war mankind had ever seen. When the US dropped atomic bombs on Hiroshima and Nagasaki, it was a one-way trip. There was no nuclear retaliation. In this case, there would be an exchange of nuclear tipped missiles. The threat was to destroy more than the destruction inflicted on the first recipient unless the terrorists were effective in destroying, or impairing, India's retaliatory capability, the threat would work.

As we walked the streets of Delhi, it was apparent that the news had been leaked to the press and people were individually spreading the word to friends, family and acquaintances. There was an evident increase in the pace of activity, a pace which was already frenetic. You could see it in their faces. This was a people preparing for the worst. They knew they would be the primary targets of a first strike. Would they die? Would they be horribly burned? Would they develop cancer? These questions were written on the faces of every man woman and child, written in indelible ink, scurrying about the streets. No other people have had to confront the possibility of nuclear war known in advance. The people of Hiroshima and Nagasaki didn't know until the bombs exploded in their midst. The people of Delhi knew that the bombs were coming.

Joan and I returned to our hotel, with the awful knowledge that, at any moment, a nuclear explosion would destroy our world. We had done what we could. We were among those who possessed the terrible knowledge that two nuclear powers stood irrevocably ready to launch. The Pakistani first strike was at this moment on the launch pad. The Indian retaliatory strike, ever in readiness, was at this moment being raised from launch pads all over northern India. All it took now was one person, one general, to say, "Launch!"

We had no idea how much time we had. As we entered the hotel, it was with incredible relief that I saw Frank standing there.

"Frank!"

"Anderson, Joan!" We embraced. Frank was unrestrained in his joy at seeing us. "Thank God you're alive and okay! Let's get out of here! My plane is ready at the airport. We have no time to waste. The US has done everything to restrain Pakistan. India can do nothing but what they are already prepared to do. That is, launch a retaliatory strike if the first strike is launched. There is nothing more we can do. Let's just hope and pray that we have time to get to the airport and get aloft before the exchange occurs."

We turned and walked with Frank from the hotel. We were exhausted, we hadn't paid our hotel bill, but all of this disappeared in the urgency of departure. Frank had a hired car waiting at the curb. We literally jumped in and collapsed against the backs of the seats. The tension in our lives had reached such a point that any release unwound us like a weakened rubber band.

"Can the United States do nothing?" I asked. "Have we talked to the presidents and prime ministers of both countries?"

"Sadly, the military in Pakistan is in command. They have control over their nuclear weapons and they are not listening to the president of the United States, or to any other chief executive of any of the Western countries. They apparently believe that destiny has called upon them to assert the temporary nuclear superiority of Pakistan. Approximately seven hours ago, they detonated e-bombs in the Ministry of Defense of India, in its launch facilities, and in space research facilities in Bangalore. The Ministry of Defense is desperately trying to communicate with its distributed launch facilities on mobile rail cars and on trucks. The AGNI-II is an effective missile launch platform, but it would be better for the Indians right now if the AGNI-III were fully operational, since it can be launched from submarines, which would be a totally secure platform. Sadly, that's not the case. I don't know what else can be done. We must escape this holocaust if we can."

While Frank didn't know the details, apparently the operation rolled out essentially as the terrorists planned. Seven hours earlier, Taufig and the two Moroccans managed to insert themselves into the Ministry of Defense. The Moroccans, Amal and Khalid, had been left in Islamabad after guarding Joan, al-Tabari and myself on the flight to Islamabad. They were then infiltrated into India by sympathetic Muslim Indians who crossed the border with Pakistan on a daily basis for business purposes.

They simply walked into the South Block of the Secretariat Building, and while Taufig was detained by security, the Moroccans visited the restroom. While there, they plugged two e-bombs into outlet plugs above the sinks. As Taufig was turned away by security, the three exited independently. After exiting, they detonated the e-bombs by wireless devices synced to the correct frequencies. Within minutes, the electrical grid failed in the entire South Block, including the Defense Ministry, the Prime Minister's Office and the Foreign Ministry. The buildings went dark, computers ground to a stop, their motherboards irretrievably corrupted, and telephones died in the hands of their users.

At the same time, in Balasore, Shahid, working with an Indian of Muslim birth and faith, was able to enter the launch and control facilities of the giant launch platforms near Balasore. He could have missed everything, but luck was with him. He entered the main launch control building and was able to insert an e-bomb into the electrical grid before a security guard challenged him. He resisted and was shot through the heart, but the launch and control software was irretrievably corrupted.

Salman, motivated by his hatred of Israel and Judaism, chose Israel as his target. He flew from Paris to Damascus, then went by truck through Lebanon to the Mediterranean. He set out with three operatives on a black rubber raft, completely covered in a black wetsuits, hoping to make landfall on a deserted stretch of beach just north of Tel Aviv and south of Netanya, avoiding the heavily guarded northern border of Israel and Lebanon.

His goal was the Israeli Ministry of Defense compound in HaKirya, Tel Aviv, where he hoped to rupture the brain center of Israeli defense with an e-bomb strategically connected to the electrical grid serving the ministry and the IDF.

Unfortunately for Salman, his assessment of Israeli defenses was clouded by his strong emotions. He and his operatives were picked up by special Israeli defense forces before they had penetrated one mile from their landing site on the beach.

Ahmed was assigned the Sriharikota Space Launch facility near Chennai. Far from the government in New Delhi, security was not as tight at the launch platform. Ahmed and an Indian-born Muslim operative were able to penetrate the heart of Sriharikota, the command center for launch operations, connect an e-bomb into the electrical grid and safely exit the facility. The e-bomb was detonated remotely and its magnetic pulse shredded the launch and control systems, melting the motherboards in computers and destroying the software.

Ironically, it was Taufig, the gentlest of all the terrorists, I was told, who had the most devastating effect on India's retaliatory capability. Without communications from the central command in Delhi, the commanders 'on the ground', those whose fingers were on the nuclear button, were paralyzed, their reactions stilled by indecision.

"Frank! We cannot leave al-Tabari! He's here in Delhi."

"There's nothing we can do, Anderson. There are tens of millions of people here. We can't possibly find him."

I slumped against the back of the seat, totally emotionally destroyed. My loyal companion meant so much to me that I could not face his death, but I had exhausted my resources, body and soul.

Frank's hired car moved agonizingly slowly through the crowded streets of a people already knowing that death awaited them momentarily. Finally, we arrived at the Delhi airport. The hired car drove directly to Frank's Gulfstream 550. Joan and I dragged ourselves out and ascended the folding staircase. Within minutes, the

Gulfstream was aloft, and we were rocketing away from the impending inferno.

All of Khalida's scheming came to naught. Al-Tabari, Joan and I ended up not being pawns in her elaborate chess game. But the Broken Spark operation worked as designed. India's high-tech leadership was crippled by the e-bombs. Launch and control procedures at launch sites were thrown into total disarray and communications from headquarters in Delhi were scrambled beyond comprehension. Field commanders prepared their nuclear-tipped missiles for launch, but absent clear communication from the prime minister's office and from the Ministry of Defense, they were unwilling to take the last fateful step, leaving India defenseless and unable to retaliate.